QUINTON'S DESIRE

A Novel

by

Cassandra J. Sperry

ISBN 978-0615892139

In loving memory of

Jeremy

Without whom this book wouldn't have been conceived.

QUINTON'S DESIRE

PROLOGUE

Andrea unlocked the door to her parents' home. It was late and she was tired. Another fight with Tony. That's all they seemed to do lately... fight. It was always the same fight.

Andrea had let her mind wander to Quinton Masterson... again. She'd seen him last Christmas when both families had celebrated together in Atlanta.

"You're thinking about him again." Tony accused.

"No... I'm not thinking about him again." Andrea lied.

"You don't lie very well, Andie." Tony told her.

"What do you want, Tony?" Andrea asked.

"I want you to promise you won't see him again and that you'll seriously consider taking our relationship to the next level." Tony demanded.

"I don't see Quinton, we don't have a relationship. I've told you I will not sleep with you." Andrea said.

She turned her back on Tony, walking several feet away from him.

She'd met Quinton the first Christmas Kyle and Abby, her twin sister, had been married four and a half years ago.

Despite her feelings for Tony she'd developed feelings for Quinton as well. Of course, Tony was making it easy for her to distance herself from him.

"Everyone knows we're getting married and I didn't say anything about you having a relationship with Masterson." Tony said.

"Apparently everyone except me knows we're getting married. I'm not going to sleep with you because we'll get married one day." Andrea said.

"Don't you love me?" Tony asked.

"It's not a matter of whether I love you or not. I'm not sleeping with you." She told him.

"Are you seeing Masterson?" Tony asked.

"Drop it, Tony. I told you I don't have a relationship with Quinton. I'm not sleeping with you." Andrea said.

"Maybe we should see other people."

"If that's what you want."

"Andie, you know I love you, why are you making this difficult?"

"I'm not making it difficult. You've expressed the desire to see other people, go, do what you think is best."

Tony walked away then and she didn't expect to hear from him again.

Well that suited her just fine. She didn't need to complicate her life by sleeping with him. She was free to date whomever she chose.

A picture of Quinton popped into her head. Shaking her head, Andrea tried to dispel the picture.

Andrea thought about the night they met. She should have known then Quinton was going to be trouble.

"I'm Quinton Masterson and you are?" He said holding out his hand.

Openly curious, he looked her over.

At twenty-four Andrea Phillips was a five foot seven picture of curvaceous femininity. Her close-set large emerald eyes, upturned nose and full mouth sat on a heart shaped face. Her straight blonde hair had gold and white streaks, falling past her waist.

"Andie... Andrea Phillips, Abby's twin sister." Andrea said taking his hand.

Sparks of electricity shot through her. Curious, but less obvious she looked at him.

At thirty-two Quinton was six feet two inches, with a powerful chest which fell into a washboard stomach down to lean hips. His distinct face held hazel eyes, a Grecian nose and sensual mouth. Untamed sand colored hair curled over his forehead.

"Are you the oldest?" Quinton asked.

"No, Eric is…" Andrea began.

"No, are you the oldest twin?" Quinton said.

"No, Abby beat me by seven minutes." She answered.

"The baby?"

"Excuse me."

"The youngest of the family, right?"

"Yes, please excuse me I need to freshen up, long flight."

Andrea escaped Quinton then.

"I have Tony… Anthony back home. I don't need to play the field." She told herself.

Andrea snapped back to the present.

Why was she remembering the first Christmas she'd spent with Quinton? She made it sound like they were a couple instead of virtual strangers.

Falling back to the night they met, Andrea thought how she had wanted Quinton; she couldn't help the feel of attraction that pulled her toward him.

She'd hidden in the dining room until Kyle and Abby had arrived home.

When Abby found her there she hadn't been able to pull herself together.

"Andie, are you okay?" She asked.

Andrea turned haunted emerald eyes toward Abby.

Abby went to her sister, kneeling before her chair. "Andrea what is it? Tell me, please. You're scaring me." Abby beseeched.

"You tried to tell me, but I didn't understand. I can't go out there, Abby. I just can't." Andrea wailed softly.

"Andie, I don't understand. What did I tell you? Have I hurt you in some way?" Abby asked.

Not for anything in the world would she hurt Andrea.

"He's different than Kyle yet they're so alike. I can't explain it. He's Kyle's brother. He makes me feel..." Andrea trailed off.

"Quinton, what has he done? Damn it, Andrea, talk to me."

Abby stood up, grabbing her by the shoulders, shaking her.

"If he's done something we'll talk to Kyle. He'll be able to straighten him out." Abby had said.

Andrea came back to herself again. Realizing Abby was still holding onto her she said, "Forgive me Abby. I don't know what got into me. I'm fine now."

Abby released her. The haunted look was gone; it was replaced by sadness, reservation.

Ever since Andrea wasn't able to free herself from the attraction that pulled her toward Quinton.

She wondered what it would feel like to have his strong hands mold her body to his, to have him kiss her until she couldn't think anymore.

Andrea came back to the present.

The one kiss they'd shared had sent electricity shocking through her. She wanted him to kiss her again.

He flirted with her when their respective families celebrated Christmas together.

Theirs had been a shadowy courtship, just lurking in the air awaiting its time. All during that time Andrea had felt hunted.

Andrea knew she wanted more from Quinton but couldn't bring herself to tell anyone, not even Abby.

She couldn't say why she was afraid of letting a man get close. Abby had been the same way with Kyle.

She hadn't understood it at the time, but now she did, so had let Tony walk out of her life instead of sleeping with him.

CHAPTER ONE

Andrea was in Atlanta visiting her sister Abby. She'd come after the break up with Tony, her longtime boyfriend.

"When did you say Kyle would be going out of town?" Andrea asked again.

"Do you have short term memory loss, Andie? I've told you half a dozen times I don't know. We're not sure he'll have to go out of town." Abby said exasperated.

"No, I do not have short term memory loss." Andrea snapped.

"Why are you so jumpy? Are you expecting Quinton to show up unannounced?" Abby asked.

"No!" Andrea said too quickly.

Abby laughed.

"I suppose if I believe that you have swamp land to sell me." She said.

Andrea threw her sister a deadly look.

"I don't care one way or another whether he stops by or not."

"Andie, you never were a very good liar. Quinton scares you."

"He does not scare me."

Abby raised an eyebrow at her sister. "So then, why do you pace from the moment you get up until you go to bed?"

"Nerves, you are eight and a half months pregnant. I don't think it was a good idea for me to be your coach."

"You suggested it. Why are you having second thoughts now?"

"I don't know. I'm nervous because I don't know what to expect."

"Quinton has nothing to do with this?"

"Abby, why does this have to be about Quinton? I haven't seen or talked to him since Christmas."

"That's it; you're upset because he hasn't contacted you."

"I am not. I have Tony, remember."

"Variety is the spice of life, besides you told me Tony and you decided to see other people."

When Andrea didn't comment Abby grasped onto a thought.

"When Quinton and you are anywhere near one another electricity crackles in the air." She said.

"You're imagining things." Andrea retorted.

"Okay, you're going to have to handle your feelings for him sooner or later." Abby told her.

"I don't have feelings for him." Andrea grumbled.

"Swamp land." Abby muttered.

Andrea turned toward the window ignoring her sister.

Abby was right. Quinton did scare her and she did have feelings for him.

"Aunt Andie will you play a game with us?" Kayla asked.

Kayla brought Andrea out of her musings.

"Yes, Kay Rae. What would you like to play?" Andrea said.

"We can play a game on the computer." Kayla suggested.

"Not Cake Shop, that's a girl's game." Kerry refused.

"It is not." Kayla argued.

"Yes, it is." Kerry insisted.

"What would you like to play Kerr Bear?" Andrea asked.

"Gazzoline, it's a boy's game." He said.

"We can play both." Andrea told them.

"Mama said we're supposed to play together." Kayla said.

"You will, first we'll play your game." Andrea said.

Kerry groaned.

"Then we'll play Kerry's game." Andrea told them.

Kayla smiled sticking her tongue out at her twin brother.

"You're such a baby." Kerry grumbled.

"I am not." Kayla responded."

"Are too." Kerry said.

"Kerr Bear, what did your mother say about calling names?" Andrea asked.

"We aren't supposed to call others names because it hurts their feelings." Kerry said.

"What are you supposed to say to your sister?" Andrea said.

"I'm sorry, Kay Rae." Kerry mumbled.

Kayla smiled then walked over and hugged her brother.

"It's okay, K.T. I know you didn't mean it." She said confidently.

Andrea smiled; she knew when they used their nicknames for each other things were fine between them.

"Okay, so how do we play Cake Shop?" She asked.

Kayla took Andrea's hand leading her to the home office.

Settling in front of the computer, she clicked on the screen to bring up her game.

Andrea watched fascinated as her niece quickly and efficiently put together the orders for customers who came on the screen.

After several minutes of playing Kayla closed her game slid out of the chair behind the desk to let Kerry begin his game.

"Watch this Aunt Andie." Kerry said.

Andrea watched as her four year old nephew pumped gas, brought his customers merchandise from inside the station and took money to put in the till.

Absorbed in watching her niece and nephew play games on the computer she forgot her worries.

"Kerry, Kayla lunchtime." Abby said walking into the room.

Startled Andrea looked at her sister.

"Is it lunchtime already?" She asked.

Abby laughed.

"Yes, you've been in here for two hours." She said.

Andrea hadn't once thought about Quinton or Tony while she'd been absorbed in watching her nephew and niece skillfully navigate through their games.

"Time flies when you're having fun." She said.

Kayla and Kerry walked ahead to the dining room.

"Aren't children amazing?" Abby asked.

Andrea looked at her. "Amazing?" She repeated.

"They have a way of drawing you into their world and making you forget your problems." Abby told her.

"Yeah, I guess they do." Andrea admitted.

She pulled a chair out and sat next to Kerry at the table.

"Do you like my game Aunt Andie?" He asked.

"Yes, it was interesting to watch. You have very good hand, eye coordination." Andrea told him.

"What about my game, Aunt Andie?" Kayla asked.

"Watching you make cakes, cotton candy, and ice cream and serve beverages made me hungry." Andrea said.

~ 4 ~

Kayla and Kerry smiled and began eating their lunch.

"Amazing." Andrea reiterated.

She ate her lunch without being aware of what she ate. Once again thinking about the problems the two men in her life presented.

Not that Quinton was in her life, at least not yet. Tony had walked out of her life because she wouldn't sleep with him.

At twenty-eight she was a virgin because she hadn't been interested in anyone that way. At least not until Quinton had walked into her life.

It wasn't like he'd tried, which irritated her.

The one and only date they'd had, over four years ago he hadn't exactly been a gentlemen; she had noticed he'd warned their server away from her when he'd shown an interest in her.

Quinton hadn't pursued her either. Why? What was wrong with her?

Why was she concerned that Quinton hadn't made any advances toward her?

He made her want him just by being himself. She answered herself.

"Andie, what's wrong?" Abby asked.

Andrea came out of her musings.

"What?" She asked.

"You look upset." Abby told her.

"No, I was thinking." Andrea said.

"I'll bet I know who you were thinking about." Abby said.

"Don't start that again, Abby." Andrea warned.

"Just an observation."

"Yeah, well… you're wrong."

"Did I mention you're a rotten liar?"

~ 5 ~

"Only every other sentence."

Abby smiled. "When are you going to admit you have feelings for him?"

"Shut up, Abby. You don't know what you're talking about.

"Actually, I do. I was in the same position at one time. Look how well it's worked out for me."

"We're different, Abby. Quinton scares the he... scares me."

Abby rolled her eyes. "Gee, I have no idea what that feels like, Andie."

"Mama I'm done eating can I be excused?" Kerry asked.

"Me too." Kayla chimed in.

"May I be excused?" Abby corrected.

"May we be excused?" Kerry said.

"Yes, go wash up and get ready for rest time." Abby told them.

"Mama we don't want to rest." Kayla said.

"Yeah, we're not tired." Kerry added.

"You know after lunch it's rest time." Abby reminded them.

"Aunt Andie are you going to rest?" Kayla asked.

Andrea looked at Abby for direction.

"Yes, I'm a little tired." She agreed at Abby's nod.

"Will we have to rest when the baby comes?" Kerry asked.

"Yes, the baby is going to need a lot of attention." Abby told them again.

"When is the baby coming to live with us?" Kayla asked.

"Dr. Cooper says in about two weeks." Abby said.

"Aunt Andie when are you going to have a baby?" Kayla asked.

"Not anytime soon." Andrea said.

"Don't you like babies?" Kerry asked.

"Of course, I love babies." Andrea said.

"Why aren't you going to have a baby?" Kayla asked.

"I don't have anyone to have a baby with." Andrea said.

Abby coughed.

Andrea threw her a warning look.

"Uncle Quinton likes babies. Maybe he'll give you one." Kerry stated.

Abby laughed outright.

"Out of the mouths of babes." She stated.

"I'm going to my room to lie down." Andrea announced.

"Rest well, Andie." Abby said.

Andrea snorted.

Like that was going to happen.

She walked to her room, closed the door, climbed into bed and pulled the blankets up to her chin.

Quickly falling asleep she began to dream.

Quinton was kissing and caressing her.

She moaned in her sleep.

When she touched him he felt hot.

Andrea kissed him back wishing he would let himself go.

He stopped.

"Quinton?" She questioned.

He looked at her questions in his eyes.

"What's wrong? Why did you stop?" She asked.

"Tell me you don't want this, Little One. Tell me to stop." He forced out.

"What? I don't understand." She said.

"You're hesitating. You want me to stop, say it." He demanded.

"I… can't." She admitted.

"Are you saying you want me to make love to you?" He asked harshly.

Andrea looked into his eyes pleading with him not to make her say it.

"Say it, Little One, tell me you want me to make love to you."

"Quinton, please… Don't make this difficult."

"Difficult? It's nearly impossible for me to stop. Say the words, Little One."

Andrea drew in a deep breath and let it out.

"I want you to make love to me."

Quinton pulled her to him molding her body to his. Kissing her he thrust his tongue into her eager mouth.

Pulling her mouth from his she took a ragged breath and said, "Quinton I'm a vir… I've never…"

"I know Little One, I'll be gentle." He assured her.

Andrea suddenly woke up.

A dream, she'd been dreaming.

There was a light knock on her door.

"Come in." She said, her voice husky.

Abby opened the door, sticking her head in.

"Are you okay? I heard you cry out." She said.

That must be what woke her.

"I was dreaming." Andrea said.

Abby stepped into the room closing the door behind her going to sit on the bed.

"Do you want to talk about it?" She asked.

"There's nothing to talk about. I had a dream, that's all." Andrea said.

"You don't want to talk about it." Abby guessed.

"Uh huh. How do you get over the fear?" Andrea asked.

"You don't. Take one step at a time and trust it'll all work out." Abby told her.

"The fear never goes away?" Andrea questioned.

"Fear isn't something you get over, you work through it."

"How did you...?"

"Kyle threatened to divorce me."

"He did?"

"Yes, that was enough to make me admit my love for him."

"How did you keep from telling him?"

"I convinced myself the love was one-sided."

"How long did you... When did you...?"

"A year and a half, on our first wedding anniversary."

Andrea shook her head in confusion.

"You have to open yourself up, Andie. Otherwise you'll never know." Abby advised.

"I'm afraid he doesn't think of me that way." Andrea confessed.

"Yeah and I still think you have swamp land for sale." Abby said standing.

She went to the door, opened it, walked out and quietly closed it behind her.

How can I open myself up when I'm not sure he has feelings for me? Andrea thought.

She threw the blankets off, swung her legs over the side of the bed, stood up and went into the bathroom to freshen up.

Going into the kitchen she saw Agnes standing at the stove.

"Can I help?" Andrea asked.

"No, there's not much to do. Mrs. Masterson suggested something light for the evening meal." Agnes said.

"Where is Mrs. Masterson?" Andrea queried.

"Outside with the children." Agnes told her.

"Thank you." Andrea said and walked out.

She went in search of her sister; finding Abby and the children in the flower garden.

"Hey what are you doing Kay Rae?" She asked.

"Looking at bugs, want to see." Kayla said.

Andrea shuddered. "No thanks, I'll pass." She said.

"There are a lot of bees making honey." Kerry told her.

"I'll take your word for it." Andrea told him.

"Kyle called while you were asleep." Abby began.

"And?" Andrea questioned.

"He invited Quinton to supper tonight." Abby finished.

"Playing matchmaker?" Andrea asked.

"No, just thought Quinton would like a home-cooked meal." Abby said candidly unable to keep a straight face.

"Tabitha!" Andrea said under her breath.

"Don't blame me. I don't control what Kyle does or who he invites to supper." Abby said.

Unaware of her aunt's anger Kayla innocently asked, "Aunt Andie are you going to ask Uncle Quinton to give you a baby?"

Andrea's cheeks flamed bright red. "Certainly not." She said as politely as she could manage.

She looked helplessly at her sister to stop Kayla's questioning.

Abby shook her head letting her know she was on her own.

"Thanks a lot." Andrea muttered.

"Why aren't you going to ask Uncle Quinton to give you a baby?" Kayla asked.

"That would be rude." Andrea told her.

Kerry added his two cents. "Mama will have three children, Aunt Andie won't have any. We'll ask Uncle Quinton for her."

Andrea's cheeks grew red again. "That will not be necessary." She stammered.

"Kerry, Kayla go in the house and tell Aggie it's time for your snack." Abby said.

"Okay." They said in unison.

"Wash up before you eat." Abby reminded them.

"We will, Mama." Kayla promised.

Alone with her sister, Andrea said, "I'd rather you didn't make remarks about Quinton in front of Kerry and Kayla. They're beginning to get ideas."

"They're bright children, they catch on quickly." Abby said.

"Well they're catching onto something they shouldn't be." Andrea mused.

"You haven't thought about having a baby with Quinton?" Abby asked.

"Of course not. What would make you think I had?" Andrea responded.

"Nothing really. I was just wondering." Abby confessed.

"Well thanks for the idea, now I will wonder."

Abby laughed.

"My pleasure."

Andrea scowled at her.

"Not everyone is like you and Kyle."

"No, but it's going to be interesting to see how you handle Quinton." Abby said.

"I won't be handling Quinton. In fact I won't go near him." Andrea said.

"Fat chance. I'll make a bet with you." Abby offered.

"A bet?" Andrea questioned.

"I'll bet by the end of the night Quinton kisses you. If I win you have to tell me how you really feel about him."

"If I win?"

"On the off chance that you do I won't say another word about Quinton and you as a couple."

"What about Kayla and Kerry?"

"I'll talk to them."

"You've got yourself a bet."

Sometime later Kyle came home from work with Quinton following behind.

"Hi Darling, how was your day?" Abby asked Kyle.

Kyle kissed her in greeting. Pulling away he said, "Rough, we're still working out the rough patches in the new business contract."

"Do you know if you'll have to go out of town?" Abby asked.

"No, we'll be discussing that in a few days." Kyle told her.

"Hello, Andrea how are you?" Quinton said.

"I'm well thank you Quinton and yourself." Andrea said.

"I'm well." Quinton told her.

His eyes told her more than his words.

She wanted to look away but couldn't drag her gaze away from his.

He took a step toward her, she backed up a step.

Quinton smiled letting her know he knew what affect he was having on her.

Her temper flared. How dare he presume to believe he knew what she was thinking?

Cautiously she turned in the direction of the living room. One misstep and he'd be laughing at her.

She didn't care how damn sexy he was he didn't have to flaunt it.

Andrea balled her hands into fists and made a noise in her throat.

Quinton looked at her.

"Something wrong, Little One?" He asked amused.

"No." She said sharply.

She stopped turning to look at him.

He was so close she just had to reach out to touch him.

Remembering her bet with Abby, she turned back heading for the chair in the corner of the living room.

Quinton chuckled.

Abby let her go, she had told Agnes to sit Quinton and Andrea next to one another at supper.

"Are you enjoying your visit to Atlanta, Andrea?" Quinton asked

"Yes, it's a lovely city." Andrea said.

"I'd be glad to take you on a tour." Quinton offered.

"Thank you but I wouldn't want to take you away from work." Andrea answered.

"Let him take you on a tour Andie. He needs to take time off." Kyle said.

Quinton threw him a deadly look.

Abby smiled at her husband. "Darling, Quinton is old enough to know whether he needs time off or not." She said.

Kyle picked up on Abby's train of thought. "Yes, dear." He said smiling.

"Kyle." Quinton warned.

Andrea looked at Abby who showed no sign that she was plotting anything.

Agnes came in to announce that supper was ready.

Abby stood up. "I'll get Kerry and Kayla." She said.

"We agreed I'd care for our children in the evenings." Kyle reminded her.

"We'll share the duties tonight." Abby said.

Kyle smiled, he knew exactly what his wife was doing.

He followed Abby to find their children.

"That's my cue to escort you into dinner, Little One." Quinton stated.

"I know my way to the dining room." Andrea told him.

"Very well." Quinton said.

Andrea began the walk across the living room.

Quinton made no move to leave. He fell into step with her when she came next to him.

Putting his hand on the small of her back, Quinton felt Andrea shudder.

This was going to be fun.

When she tried to move away from his guiding hand he put his arm around her waist pulling her toward him.

Andrea gasped when their bodies made contact.

"Relax my sweet, you'll enjoy it more." Quinton said.

"I do not want to enjoy it." She said sharply.

"Liar, you want to know how our bodies will fit together." He whispered near her ear.

Andrea stopped the cry that was aching to be released at the close contact with his body.

"We have all night to be lovers." Quinton breathed.

Andrea turned to him, losing her balance, she clutched at his arm to keep her balance.

"Finally, you've come to your senses." He said.

He bent his head toward her.

~ 14 ~

"No, please no." She whispered.

Quinton kissed her, holding her against him as though he were going to make love to her.

Her mouth opened to his, refusing to obey her command not to respond.

His mouth trailed hot kisses down the long column of her neck.

She held him to her aching for him. Her breathing was ragged in his ear.

"Quinton we can't..." She stammered.

He forced himself to look into her eyes.

They told him she didn't want him to stop, but this was not the time or place to pursue their desire.

"You will be mine." He told her.

"No." She whispered.

Quinton held her to him as their aching bodies cooled from the heat of their desire.

Walking into the dining room Andrea was surprised to see Kyle, Abby and their children at the table eating.

They must have walked through the back entrance to the dining room.

Abby looked up as Andrea sat down. She made no apology.

Andrea guessed Abby knew her courtship with Quinton would inevitably progress quickly.

She must also know she couldn't help her decide what to do or give her the advice Andrea was hoping for.

Andrea joined in the conversation while they ate. She listened to Quinton and Kyle describe in detail the new business contract they had acquired.

Outwardly she showed no signs of her inner turmoil; her body still hummed from Quinton's lovemaking.

When everyone was through eating Abby dismissed Agnes for the evening.

Andrea helped Abby clean up from supper.

"The bet is off." Abby said.

"What?" Andrea asked.

"It was a stupid thing to do. Your relationship with Quinton is none of my business. I'm sorry didn't think about your feelings." Abby told her.

Andrea sighed. "That's one less thing to worry about. Can I talk to you?" She said.

"Andie, you know you can talk to me about anything." Abby told her.

"How do you get through the awkwardness?" Andrea asked.

"Don't think about it. Let Quinton guide you." Abby advised.

While they cleaned up Andrea and Abby discussed what needed to be done before the baby arrived.

Andrea steered clear of any subject she felt she couldn't talk to her sister about.

She knew there were just some things she couldn't talk to Abby about. She'd have to experience them first hand.

When they were through clearing up Andrea stayed in the kitchen to make fresh coffee. She forced herself to go to the living room after she was through.

"I made fresh coffee." She announced walking in.

Abby looked up from the blanket she was making and smiled. "Thanks, Andie." She said.

Andrea smiled. "No problem. Your blanket is coming along nicely." She said.

"Uncle Quinton do you like babies?" Kerry asked climbing onto Quinton's lap.

Pulling Kerry higher up onto his lap, Quinton said, "Yes, K.T."

Andrea groaned.

Quinton looked at her a question in his eyes.

She ignored him.

He turned his attention back to Kerry.

Kayla joined her brother on their uncle's lap.

"Aunt Andie wants a baby too." She said.

"She does? What can I do to help?" Quinton asked amused.

"Kayla, Kerry." Andrea hissed.

"She can't ask you because that's rude so we're asking for her." Kerry told him.

Quinton looked to Andrea again silently questioning her.

She kept her expression impassive.

"Do you want a baby, Aunt Andie?" Quinton asked all trace of amusement gone.

"We are not discussing this." Andrea snapped.

"She doesn't have anyone to have a baby with like mama." Kerry said.

"Kerry, Kayla bed time." Andrea ordered.

"But we're not tired." Kayla complained yawning.

"Move it, now." Andrea commanded.

At the tone in her voice Kerry and Kayla hugged Quinton then climbed off his lap.

Going to their parents they hugged and kissed them good night.

"We're ready, Aunt Andie." Kayla said.

"I'll be back after I put them to bed." Andrea said.

Walking up the stairs with her niece and nephew Andrea kept her temper under control.

The children went to their own rooms.

"Brush your teeth, wash your face and hands." Andrea reminded them.

Kayla and Kerry nodded then sullenly did as they were told.

"I'm ready to be tucked in, Aunt Andie." Kayla said.

Andrea went into her niece's room. Kayla was sitting in the middle of her bed looking like she was going to cry.

"Did we do something wrong, Aunt Andie?" She asked.

"No, Kay Rae. Don't worry I'll make it all right." Andrea promised.

Kayla stood up throwing her arms around Andrea's neck hugging her tightly.

"I love you, Aunt Andie." She said.

"I love you more, Kay Rae." Andrea said.

She tucked Kayla into bed and kissed her forehead, "Good night, sweetie, sleep well."

"You too, Aunt Andie." Kayla said.

Andrea walked to the door, shut off the light and closed the door slightly.

Going to Kerry's room she wondered what she should say to him.

"Aunt Andie are you going to tuck me in?" He asked.

"Coming, Kerr Bear." Andrea answered.

She stopped in his doorway, Kerry sat on the edge of his bed with his hands folded in his lap.

"Something wrong, Kerr Bear?" Andrea asked.

"Am I going to be punished?" He asked.

"No." Andrea assured him.

Kerry climbed off his bed running straight to Andrea wrapping his arms around her.

"I love you, Aunt Andie." He said.

"Not as much as I love you." Andrea giggled.

Kerry hugged her tighter; he took her hand pulling her to his bed so she could tuck him in.

"Good night, Kerr Bear, sleep well." Andrea told him.

"You too, Aunt Andie." Kerry repeated Kayla's words.

Andrea tucked the blankets around Kerry, kissed his forehead then headed to the door.

She shut off the light, stepped out of the room and partially closed the door.

In the hallway she stood listening to the sounds of the house.

With her nephew and niece tucked into bed the house had a strange feel to it.

Andrea forced herself to go into the kitchen to get the coffee to serve.

Putting a smile on her face, she took it into the living room.

"Coffee." She announced.

Kyle and Abby were arguing over the couch.

"No, I want it over here." Abby said.

"We've had it there twice, Querida. Are you sure that's where you want it?" Kyle said.

"Yes, Kyle." Abby snapped.

Andrea laughed.

"Anything I can do to help?" She asked.

"No, I have everything under control." Abby said confidently.

"Would you like coffee, Quinton?" Andrea asked.

Quinton stood up, walked to where Andrea was, took the tray from her and put it on the coffee table.

Taking her hand he headed toward the door. "We need to talk." He told her.

Andrea tried to pull free of him.

Quinton put his arm around her waist, tugging her outside.

Once outside, in a low hiss Andrea said, "Let go of me."

Quinton pulled her closer bringing his mouth within inches of hers.

"Did you ask Kerry and Kayla to talk to me?" He asked harshly.

"No. I would not put myself in that humiliating position." She stated clearly.

"Humiliating? You think me fathering your child would be humiliating?" He questioned.

"Quinton, please let go of me." She begged.

"Answer the question, Little One." He ordered.

When she didn't immediately answer he pulled her closer.

She struggled in his arms. Her breathing became ragged at the proximity of their bodies.

Quinton kissed her then.

Andrea went completely still feeling his arousal push against her abdomen.

"Quinton…please." She said in a whispered cry for release.

"Not tonight, Little One, but soon. Soon I'll make you mine." He said and released her.

Andrea stumbled back against the porch railing.

Her eyes were a dark emerald color. "When hell freezes over." She said.

Quinton took a step toward her.

Andrea instinctively tried to step back but there was nowhere for her to go.

"Stay away from me." She snapped.

Quinton cupped her cheek in his hand, slowly lowered his head and kissed her again.

Andrea commanded her arms to stay at her sides, they defiantly clutched at him.

His mouth trailed hot kisses down her neck. Her breathing became uneven.

"Now tell me you don't want me to be your lover." He demanded.

Andrea moaned into his mouth greedily demanding more.

"You're making this difficult, Little One. Tell me no, to stop, anything that will stop this ache from building." He ordered.

Andrea drew in an uneven breath. "I... can't." She confessed.

"Andrea, Kyle and me are going to bed, we'll see you in the morning." Abby said.

Andrea felt like someone had thrown cold water on her.

"Good night, sleep well." Andrea said huskily.

She listened to Kyle and Abby walk through the house to the stairs.

Quinton stepped back. Pulling his hand from her cheek he was still close enough he could reach out to pull her into his arms and continue his lovemaking.

"I'll bid you good night as well, Little One." He said.

"Good night." Andrea said wistfully.

Quinton cupped her cheek in his hand again.

Andrea closed her eyes at the intimate contact.

"I'll see you tomorrow." He promised.

Andrea just nodded and kept her eyes closed, she didn't want to watch him leave her.

She listened as he walked to his truck, stepped in and drove off.

Sinking down onto the porch floor she let the tears fall. They were tears of joy, pain and sorrow.

During the time of her shadowy courtship with Quinton, Andrea had fallen in love with him.

She had to get away but she couldn't go home. Abby was depending on her to be here when the baby came.

How could she have been so foolish? Why Quinton, the one man who scared her? Why couldn't it have been safe, reliable, dependable Tony?

Andrea answered her own question. Tony couldn't stir her desire the way Quinton did.

Quinton made her want to explore unknown parts of herself. Tony wasn't capable of that.

Andrea opened her eyes, slowly stood up and headed to bed.

CHAPTER TWO

The following morning she slept late.

She found Abby in the living room.

"Why didn't you wake me?" Andrea asked.

"I thought you could use the rest." Abby told her.

"Where are Kayla and Kerry?" Andrea questioned.

"Agnes took them to the park. It's just you and me until lunchtime." Abby said.

She looked at Andrea.

Suddenly Andrea felt years younger than Abby.

"Quinton didn't stay the night?" Abby asked.

"Of course not. Why do you think he would?" Andrea replied tensely.

"No reason, just wondering." Abby said smiling.

"I know that look, Abby. Why would you think Quinton would stay the night?" Andrea asked tensely.

"I'm not blind, Andie. I can see what's going on." Abby told her.

"There's nothing going on." Andrea snapped.

"Okay, if you say so."

"I'm going to get coffee."

Andrea was furious. Angrily she walked to the kitchen.

When she reached it she took a cup out of the cupboard.

Pouring coffee into it she gave serious thought to letting herself get involved with Quinton. She also thought about what she'd do now that she didn't have a job.

Ian, her former boss had sold the flower shop so he could retire. Andrea hadn't seen eye-to-eye with the new owner so had accepted the generous compensation package to end her employment.

Afterward on one of her regular calls to Abby she'd told her about losing her job.

Abby had told her that Kyle and Quinton were trying to get a new contract and Kyle may not be here when she gave birth to their third child.

That's when Andrea had offered to be Abby's birthing coach when she gave birth.

She hadn't thought by coming to Atlanta and ending her relationship with Tony she'd be jumping from the frying pan into the fire.

Taking a sip of her coffee Andrea started back to the living room.

The phone rang.

Andrea automatically reached for the receiver to answer it.

"Masterson residence." She said.

"Andrea?" Kyle asked.

"Yes Kyle." Andrea answered.

"Have you seen Quinton today?" Kyle questioned.

"Kyle, you and Abby have to stop assuming there is a relationship between Quinton and me." Andrea snapped.

"Quinton didn't come to work today and no one has heard from him." Kyle said without apology.

Andrea's heart sank into her stomach. She was silent for several minutes.

When she was finally able to speak it was barely above a whisper. "When was the last time anyone heard from him?"

"Last night... when you and he disappeared onto the porch."

"We did not disappear."

"What happened between you last night?"

"Nothing."

~ 24 ~

"Andrea, no one has heard from or seen Quinton since last night. What happened?"

"Kyle, I told you nothing."

Not that she hadn't wanted it to. She thought.

"Would you mind going over to his house to check on him?"

"I don't know where he lives."

"Abby can give you directions. Thanks Andrea, I appreciate your help."

Kyle hung up.

Andrea hung up.

Putting her coffee down, she walked into the living room.

"Who was on the phone?" Abby asked.

"Kyle. Quinton didn't show up for work this morning. No one has heard from or seen him since last night." Andrea told her.

"Since you and he disappeared onto the porch." Abby said.

"Why do you and Kyle say we disappeared?" Andrea asked irritably.

"You left without telling anyone." Abby told her.

"I'm not a child, Abby. I'm not accountable to anyone for my whereabouts." Andrea said angrily.

"What did Kyle want?"

"He wants me to go to Quinton's and check on him."

"My keys are hanging up in the hallway by the door."

"Abby, I don't know where Quinton lives or how to get there."

Abby went to get paper and a pen from the office.

Andrea followed her.

"What are you doing?"

"Writing down the directions to Quinton's house."

"What makes you think I'll go?"

"You're concerned about Quinton."

Abby began writing down directions to Quinton's.

Andrea took the paper from Abby when she finished writing down the directions, stopping in the hallway to get Abby's keys.

Walking out to Abby's car Andrea refused to think about what she was doing or why she was doing it.

Twice she looked at the directions Abby had given her, committing them to memory.

As she drove she was careful to think only of Quinton's wellbeing.

When she pulled into his driveway his truck was parked there.

Amazingly Andrea was calm when she walked towards the house.

When she arrived at the door she didn't bother knocking. Turning the knob she was surprised to find the door unlocked.

Cautiously Andrea opened the door listening for signs that something was wrong.

Walking through the house nothing looked out of place or amiss.

Following her instincts, she found the stairs leading to the second floor.

Climbing the stairs Andrea began to tremble. What would she find? Was Quinton hurt, dead, missing?

Walking around the upper floor there were no signs that Quinton had been there.

Her trembling became worse when she didn't find Quinton. She came to what she believed to be his bedroom.

The bed hadn't been slept in; no indication that he had even been in the room in the last twenty-four hours.

Agitated, Andrea headed back toward the stairs. Descending them, she decided to look through the rest of the house.

Not expecting to find answers, she looked around the house for any sign that Quinton had been there.

The air conditioner was humming in her consciousness, she rubbed her arms creating friction to warm herself.

Finding Quinton's home office Andrea went in.

Her temper flared. She slammed the door closed after finding Quinton laying on the couch asleep an empty Scotch bottle sitting on the floor next to him.

Quinton was instantly awake.

"What the hell." He said.

Looking toward the direction the noise had come from he saw Andrea.

"What are you doing here?" He asked.

"Looking for you." She said angrily.

"Come to warm my bed?" He questioned.

Andrea's face became red. "No, I did not." She enunciated clearly.

"Why are you here?"

"Kyle called. He's worried about you. When you didn't show up for work this morning he called me."

"As you can see I'm safe and sound."

"And drunk."

"Not anymore. Go home, Little One. I don't need a nursemaid."

"I didn't offer…"

Quinton slowly stood up, watching Andrea as he walked toward her.

Andrea backed herself against the door as he made his way to her.

Smiling, Quinton hastened his pace stopping a few feet from her.

"I'm in no condition to take you up on your offer."

"I'm not offering…"

Quinton took a step toward her.

Andrea defiantly stood her ground.

He let his amusement show in his eyes.

She shot him a dark emerald glare.

"Go home, Little One. Tell Kyle I'm fine." Quinton commanded.

"Tell him yourself." Andrea told him defiantly.

"I suggest you take my advice, otherwise you'll be joining me in the shower as well as my bed." Quinton told her.

A spark of interest lit in Andrea's eyes. She quickly squelched it.

She turned around looking for the door knob. Finding it, she turned the handle to leave.

Quinton was quickly behind her. Pulling her against him, he said, "You're wondering when."

"When?" Andrea managed to squeak out.

"When I'll take you to my bed and make you mine." Quinton told her.

"No… I'm not." Andrea lied.

"Liar."

"Quinton please…"

Andrea closed her eyes gathering the strength to walk away.

Quinton released her. "Go home, Little One."

Andrea opened her eyes, hesitantly she said, "I'm going."

Quinton stepped back so she could open the door.

Pulling, Andrea easily opened the door. Without a backward glance she walked out.

Driving to Abby's she couldn't deny the feelings that ran through her when she was near Quinton.

Andrea walked into the house.

"Did you find Quinton?" Abby asked.

"Yes." Andrea answered.

"How is he?" Abby questioned.

"He's fine." Andrea snapped.

"Uh oh, what did he do?" Abby said.

"Nothing." Andrea said sharply.

"Do you want to talk about it?"

"No, call Kyle and tell him Quinton is fine."

Andrea walked through the house, up the stairs to her room.

How was she going to get through the next few weeks until Abby had the baby? She couldn't avoid Quinton, Abby would get suspicious at best.

Pacing her room, Andrea tried to convince herself she wasn't in love with Quinton.

"I am not in love with him. We're acquaintances, that's all." She told herself.

"You're not very good liar, Andie." She said aloud.

She refused to let herself think about Quinton making love to her.

Going back downstairs Andrea went to the kitchen to pour herself a fresh cup of coffee.

Walking into the living room she said, "May I borrow your car to go visit Aunt Millie?"

"Of course. Will you be home for lunch?" Abby said smiling.

"I don't know. I'll call if I won't be here." Andrea answered wondering why Abby was smiling.

"Okay." Abby agreed smirking.

"What are you up to Abby?" Andrea demanded.

"Nothing." Abby said.

"Uh huh, I don't believe you."

"You're paranoid, Andie."

"I don't think so. I'll see you later.

Putting her coffee cup down Andrea walked out to go to Aunt Millie's.

Arriving at Millie's she found her waiting.

"Tabitha called, she said you need my help." Millie said.

"Don't you start too, Aunt Millie. I came to visit nothing more." Andrea said.

Looking skyward, Millie asked "Why are my nieces so difficult?"

"What are you doing, Aunt Millie?" Andrea asked.

"Asking for divine help." Millie replied.

"Why?" Andrea questioned.

"I'm going to need it." Millie responded.

Millie motioned for Andrea to go into the house.

After they were settled in the living room drinking tea, Millie said, "Now what can I help you with, Andrea?"

"Nothing, I told you I came to visit." Andrea repeated.

"Young lady I'm not unaware of your problem. I'll do what I can; now talk to me." Millie told her.

"Aunt Millie there's nothing to talk about." Andrea said.

"Andrea Renay Phillips, don't play games with me." Millie said.

"Aunt Millie…"

"Is it Kyle's brother?"

"Quinton? What makes you think it has anything to do with him?"

Andrea's mouth dropped open.

Millie laughed.

"You've admitted it involves Quinton, now what can I do to help?"

"I didn't admit…"

Millie gave Andrea a subduing look.

Caught in her aunt's trap Andrea sighed.

"Okay, Aunt Millie, yes it's Quinton." Andrea admitted.

"What's going on?"

"Nothing."

"You're not lovers?"

"No."

"You're in love with him."

"Yes, but he scares me."

"Scares you how?"

"The feelings I have when I'm near him."

"How's your relationship with Tony?"

"We've decided to see other people."

"May I ask why?"

"I wouldn't sleep with him."

"You'd sleep with Quinton if he asked."

Andrea refused to answer.

Seeing the stubborn set to her niece's jaw Millie readied for battle.

"Difficult." Millie said.

"I am not difficult." Andrea said annoyed.

She stood up and began pacing the room.

Millie let her pace and sort out her feelings.

After several minutes of pacing Andrea stopped and asked, "Why not Tony? Why did it have to be Quinton that stirred my desire?"

Andrea looked at Millie for the answers.

"Only you can answer that Andrea. If I had to give you an answer I'd say you know Tony too well. Quinton intrigues you." Millie said.

"You're not helping, Aunt Millie. I've never met anyone like Quinton before. He stirs my desire which pulls me to him; he also scares me which makes me want to run as far away from him as I can get." Andrea admitted.

Millie laughed.

Andrea looked at her in consternation.

After several minutes of silence Andrea said "My heart aches when I think of him and it beats uncontrollably when I see him."

"That's how love is." Millie told her.

"Aunt Millie I don't want to be in love with Quinton. It's too hard he'll break my heart." Andrea told her.

"How do you know he'll break your heart?" Millie asked.

"You've seen him. He couldn't settle down with me and be happy." Andrea answered.

"You're not going to give him a chance; you're just going to let him go?" Millie asked.

"He's not mine to let go."

"That settles it then."

"Aunt Millie what are you plotting?"

"Nothing. You've said you're not going to pursue a relationship."

"I didn't say I wasn't going to pursue a relationship…"

Millie laughed.

"Andrea, you are your father's daughter." She said.

Andrea scowled at her aunt. She knew she'd been tricked but she couldn't fault Aunt Millie.

She began pacing again.

"What's going on in that pretty head of yours?" Millie asked.

"I'm thinking how to avoid Quinton... and not fall into whatever trap you're setting for me." Andrea admitted.

Millie stood. "I do not set traps, my dear niece; I merely create situations that are mutually beneficial to the parties involved." Millie corrected.

"Okay, have it your way. I have to avoid the situation you're trying to create for Quinton and me." Andrea conceded.

"Good luck." Millie said.

Andrea looked at her watch. "I have to get back to Abby's. Agnes should be back with Kerry and Kayla." She said.

She walked over kissed her aunt on the cheek, gave her a hug and asked, "You honestly believe in instant attraction don't you?"

"If I didn't I'd be a poor judge of character." Millie responded.

"Why didn't you ever get married Aunt Millie?"

"I'll tell you one day, Andrea. It may ease your heart to know why I believe you shouldn't dismiss instant attraction and love at first sight."

"Thanks Aunt Millie."

Andrea hugged Millie again then walked out to Abby's car, stepped in and began the drive back to her sister's.

She thought about what Aunt Millie had said about instant attraction, love at first sight.

She'd certainly had instant attraction to Quinton when they'd met, but love at first sight? How was that possible? Didn't you have to know something about a person?

When Andrea pulled into the driveway at Abby's she saw Quinton's truck. Her heart began to pound wildly.

After putting the car in park and turning off the engine she tried to calm herself. Her pulse accelerated to the point she thought she'd faint.

Unable to force herself to get out of the car, she sat talking to herself trying to convince herself Quinton's visit had nothing to do with her.

Unsuccessful, she undid her seatbelt, opened the door, stepped out and began walking toward the house.

When she came to the hood of the car she stopped, holding on because suddenly she felt faint and weak at the knees.

Quinton sat on the porch swing looking intently at her.

Seeing her struggling to get to the house he quickly went to help her.

"Are you all right?" He asked, putting his arm around her waist.

Andrea tried to speak but no words came out when she opened her mouth.

He helped her to the porch, lowering her to the swing.

Sitting next to her he rubbed her back, pulling her close.

"Little One talk to me." Quinton begged.

The ringing in her ears had stopped, her pulse stopped racing and her heartbeat slowed.

"What are you doing here?" She asked finding her voice.

"I came to apologize for my behavior this morning and to thank you for coming to check on me." He said.

"Thank you for the apology; the thanks isn't necessary. I wouldn't have known to check on you if Kyle hadn't called." Andrea said.

"You did take the time to drive over to check on me, I appreciate that." Quinton said.

"Leave it, Quinton. It's not a big deal." Andrea said irritably.

Not detecting her irritability, Quinton asked "May I take you out to supper to further thank you?"

"I don't want or need your thanks Quinton, leave me alone." Andrea snapped.

She stood up and walked around him into the house. Once inside she encountered her sister.

Seeing the look on Andrea's face Abby asked "What did Quinton do to make you mad?"

"What makes you think it has anything to do with Quinton?" Andrea retorted.

"He came looking for you and said he wasn't leaving until he talked to you." Abby said.

"Quinton has a way of getting under my skin." Andrea said.

Abby was aware that Quinton was probably still outside waiting.

"Would you like me to talk to him?" She asked.

"No, I can take care of myself." Andrea said.

She went back onto the porch to talk to Quinton.

He stood up when she stepped onto the porch.

"Forgive my rudeness earlier. I'm a little anxious with the new baby coming, not knowing what to expect. I'm also a little disoriented from losing my job. I don't know what I'm going to do now." Andrea said.

"Let me take you out to supper." Quinton said.

"You don't have to…" Andrea mumbled.

~ 35 ~

"I know, I want to. You need to get out of the house for a few hours." Quinton told her.

"That may not be a good idea." Andrea said.

"Why don't you trust me?" He asked.

"It's not you I don't trust."

Intrigued, Quinton stepped closer smiling.

"You don't trust yourself."

Andrea walked to the other side of the porch. Turning to him she refused to answer.

Kyle pulled into the driveway just then saving Andrea from having to explain why she didn't think she and Quinton should go out.

Kyle walked onto the porch.

"Am I interrupting?" He asked.

"No." Andrea said sharply.

"Yes." Quinton said.

Without comment Kyle walked into the house.

"I'll pick you up at six o'clock for supper." Quinton said.

"I haven't agreed to go out with you." Andrea argued.

"You'll be ready." Quinton said confidently.

He walked to her, pulled her close then kissed her until her body shook with desire for him.

When she would have given in he cut the kiss off.

"I'll see you at six." He said then walked off.

Andrea didn't know how long she stood there while her heated body cooled from Quinton's desirous pursuit but when her mind was finally clear she went into the dining room.

"Where's Quinton?" Abby asked.

"He left." Andrea said blushing.

"You didn't invite him to stay for lunch?" Abby said.

"It didn't occur to me. My mind was elsewhere." Andrea admitted.

Kyle chuckled.

Andrea threw him a warning look.

"Aunt Andie?" Kerry asked.

"Yes Kerr Bear." Andrea answered.

"Is Uncle Quinton going to give you a baby?" Kerry asked.

"I don't know, I didn't ask." Andrea told him honestly.

Surprised by her own desirous admission she looked at her sister who looked at her questioningly.

"Don't you want a baby, Aunt Andie?" Kayla asked.

"Yes Kay Rae, I want a baby." Andrea told her.

More than anyone can imagine. She said to herself.

"Kayla, Kerry finish your lunch, rest time." Abby said irritably.

Kerry and Kayla knew better than to argue with their mama.

"Yes, Mama." They said in unison.

"Querida are you all right?" Kyle asked.

"I'm fine, Kyle just a little tired." Abby said.

She quickly moved out of her chair.

"Querida?" Kyle questioned.

"I don't think you'll be going back to the office this afternoon." Abby told him.

It was evident that her water had broken.

"Agnes." Kyle called.

Agnes came rushing into the dining room at the tone of Kyle's voice.

"Yes, Mr. Masterson." She said.

"I'll be taking Mrs. Masterson to the hospital. Miss Phillips will be going with us; you'll have charge of Kayla and Kerry." Kyle told her.

"Yes, Mr. Masterson." Agnes said.

Kyle stood up and walked over to Abby.

"I'll get her bag." Andrea said her voice surprisingly calm.

"Thanks, Andie." Abby said.

"Mama?" Kayla asked anxiously.

Abby looked at her daughter, "Yes, Kayla." She said.

"When will you be home?" Kayla asked.

"Come here, Kayla and Kerry." Abby said.

Kerry and Kayla obediently went to their mother.

Abby pulled them into her arms hugging both of her children tightly.

Andrea's heart ached. She wanted to experience what Abby now had but wasn't at all sure she'd ever be a mother.

She was afraid she'd always be the adoring, spoiling, childless aunt.

Looking away from the scene in front of her Andrea wiped the tears from her eyes.

Leaving the dining room she went to get the bag Abby had packed for the hospital.

When she went back to the front of the house Agnes was comforting Kayla and Kerry.

"It's all right children, your mama will be home before you know it and you'll have a baby brother or sister to help take care of." Agnes said.

"What if the baby doesn't like us?" Kerry asked.

"Babies like everyone; they love everyone but we have to remember they need a lot of attention and love." Agnes told him.

"We can help mama, we're good helpers." Kayla promised.

"Good for you, now go wait for your mama and daddy to come back." Agnes urged.

"Okay." Kerry said.

Kayla and Kerry hugged Agnes tightly.

Seeing their aunt, they took her by the hand to lead her into the foyer to wait for their parents to come downstairs after Abby changed out of her wet clothes.

Finally Kyle and Abby appeared.

"Ready?" Kyle asked.

"As ready as I'll ever be." Andrea said.

"Let's go." Kyle said.

"Oh, I forgot something. I'll be right behind you." Andrea said.

"Alright." Kyle said.

Andrea walked into the kitchen.

"Agnes." She said.

"Yes, Miss Phillips." Agnes said.

"Will you please call Mr. Masterson and tell him I won't be having supper with him tonight and explain why?" Andrea asked.

"Yes, ma'am, shall I reschedule for you." Agnes asked.

"No, I'll do that myself." Andrea told her.

"Yes ma'am." Agnes said.

"Thanks." Andrea said hugging her then going to catch up with Kyle and Abby.

When she climbed into the backseat Kyle asked, "Ready?"

"Yes." Andrea answered.

The trip to the hospital was short.

When they arrived Kyle went in to get a wheelchair for Abby.

Andrea stepped out of the backseat bringing Abby's bag with her.

Going to Abby's door and opening it she asked, "Do you want me to help you get out?"

"No, I'll wait for Kyle to come back." Abby said.

"What's it like?" Andrea asked curiously.

"I'm not sure I can adequately describe the feeling but I can tell you it is worth it; although it doesn't feel like it right now." Abby said.

Andrea nodded, stepping back as Kyle came back to the van with the wheelchair he'd gone to get.

He helped Abby out of the van and into the wheelchair.

Andrea stood by watching. She put her hand on her stomach imagining what it would be like if she were pregnant, heavy with... Quinton's child.

Her heart ached with longing for the chance to carry a child inside her of the man she loved.

Coming back to the present she followed Kyle and Abby to the emergency section of the hospital.

"How far apart are the contractions, Mrs. Masterson?" Nurse Tavia asked.

"About five minutes." Abby responded.

"You've been in labor all day and didn't say anything." Andrea said.

"I wasn't sure it was real. I am two weeks early." Abby said.

"You were two weeks early with Kerry and Kayla." Kyle reminded her.

"I thought this time would be different, it is a single birth." Abby told him.

"Querida." Kyle reprimanded.

"I'm sorry, Kyle. I should have told you this morning." Abby apologized.

Pain shot through Abby. She gasped as the pain went through her.

"This baby is not going to wait." Abby managed to say.

Quickly Kyle and Andrea were put into hospital gowns and Abby was prepped to give birth to her third child.

Barely an hour after arriving at the hospital Abby gave birth to a healthy son, who had Abby's dark hair and Kyle's eyes.

After having cleaned him up and tending to the newborn's birthing needs Nurse Tavia brought her newborn son to her.

Andrea's eyes welled up with tears at the miracle of birth she'd just witnessed. She went to her sister's side to look at her newborn nephew.

"He's beautiful, Abby." Andrea said.

"Thank you, Andrea. Meet your nephew Ethan Samuel." Abby said.

"Nice to meet you, Ethan Samuel." Andrea said.

Ethan let out a loud cry letting his mother know he was hungry.

Kyle was at Abby's other side as he had been the entire time Abby had been in labor and giving birth.

"How are you feeling, Querida?" He asked.

"Happy and exhausted, what about you?" Abby asked.

"I'm happy and grateful I didn't have to deliver our new son." Kyle told her.

Abby laughed. "Well the nursery is complete." She said.

"I told you we'd be ready for Ethan when he arrived." Kyle reminded her.

"Ethan? Where did that come from?" Andrea asked.

"It's my late grandfather's name." Kyle told her.

"Mrs. Masterson we'll need to take the baby to the nursery then we'll take you to your room." Nurse Tavia said.

"Okay, thank you." Abby said.

Andrea turned to Kyle. "What do we do now?" She asked.

"Call our parents and family to let them know Abby had the baby then we can go to the cafeteria for some much needed coffee." Kyle told her.

Andrea nodded.

Before the nurses took Ethan off to the nursery and ushered Kyle and Andrea out they kissed Abby then left to make their phone calls and meet in the cafeteria.

Andrea walked out of the room straight into Quinton.

"Hello, Little One. How's Abby?" He asked.

"Happily exhausted. We have a healthy, newborn nephew." Andrea told him.

"Thank God. When can I see them?" Quinton said.

"The baby was just taken to the nursery and they'll be taking Abby to her room soon. Kyle is going to call your parents. I have to call my parents and family." Andrea told him.

"You look like you're about ready to faint." Quinton said.

He put his arm around her leading her to a waiting room to sit down.

Andrea wondered what was wrong with her; twice in one day she'd gone weak at the knees at the sight of Quinton.

Drawing on her inner strength she pulled away from him.

"I'm fine, excuse me. I have to call my parents." She said.

Andrea stood and walked away from Quinton, one of the hardest things she'd ever done.

She pulled her cell phone out of her bag and turned it on.

Dialing her parents' number she again drifted back into the image of being pregnant with Quinton's son.

Judy, her mother answered the phone.

"Hello." She said.

"Hi, Mama, I'm calling to tell you Abby had the baby. You have a healthy new grandson." Andrea told her.

"That's a blessing. How's Abby?" Judy said.

"Happily exhausted. She'll be in her room soon." Andrea told her.

"What's wrong, Andrea?" Judy asked.

"Nothing." Andrea lied.

"I know you better than that young lady, what's going on?"

"It's nothing, Mama. It will pass."

"Your time will come child, be patient."

"I have been patient, Mama. I don't know how much more patient I can be. I want a baby of my own."

Quinton came around the corner to hear Andrea talking on the phone.

That was the answer, give her a baby of her own. How could he give her a baby and make her admit she wanted him in her life.

An idea came to him. He walked off to begin planning his future with Andrea.

Unaware that Quinton had overheard her Andrea said, "I'm twenty-eight Mama and I don't exactly have a line of men waiting to ask me out."

Judy smiled. No just one and Millie had already set plans in motion to get her niece to take Quinton as her lover.

Aloud she said, "Don't think about it so much; it will occur naturally without you being aware it's happening."

"How can you be so sure, Mama?" Andrea asked.

"You'll have to trust me, Andrea." Judy told her.

"Alright." Andrea agreed.

"I'll let you go so I can call your father, grandfather and brother. They've been waiting to hear about the baby. I love you, call if you need me." Judy said.

"I love you too, I will." Andrea said.

She hung up, called Millie, and then went to see if Abby had been put in her room yet. The nurse gave her Abby's room number.

Walking to Abby's room Andrea tried not to think of being pregnant with Quinton's son.

Unsuccessful, she pushed it to the back of her mind when she walked into her sister's room.

"How are you feeling?" Andrea asked.

"Exhausted and happy." Abby answered.

"Where's Kyle?" Andrea said.

"He went to ask if I could have a mocha caramel latte." Abby told her.

"Mocha caramel latte?" Andrea questioned.

"Yeah, I've been having weird cravings like that since I became pregnant with Ethan." Abby said.

Andrea turned away from her sister's too observant gaze, hiding the tears that were never far from the surface lately.

"I'm afraid I'll never know the joy of being pregnant and giving birth." Andrea said.

"Why do you say that Andie?" Abby queried.

"I was with Tony as long as you've been with Kyle; we broke off our relationship..." Andrea trailed off.

"One relationship ending doesn't mean doom for future relationships. What's really going on Andie, you're not usually pessimistic." Abby said.

"Nothing's going on. I'm feeling lost after leaving the flower shop." Andrea half lied.

"Have you thought about what you're going to do?" Abby asked.

"I did complete two years of college right after high school. I've thought about going back." Andrea told her.

"Are you going to stay in Atlanta or go home to Shelby?" Abby asked.

"There's nothing here for me, but there's nothing for me in Shelby anymore either."

"Andie, you have family in both Atlanta and Shelby. You're welcome to stay with us; as far as not having anything here there is someone who'd be glad you're here."

"Abby, I'm not basing my decision to stay on Quinton."

Abby smiled. "I could have meant your niece and nephews, your family."

"Yeah, right."

Kyle walked into the room.

"What's going on?" He asked feeling the tension.

"Your wife thinks she's being subtle about her hints and suggestions with relationship advice." Andrea told him.

"My wife? Apparently you don't like her advice." Kyle said chuckling.

Andrea snorted.

"Didn't you get Abby's mocha caramel latte?" She asked.

"I ran into Quinton while I was trying to find Dr. Cooper." Kyle said.

Andrea groaned.

"Not you too." She mumbled.

"Face it, Andie. You're going to get advice from everyone." Abby told her.

"Great, unsolicited advice, just what I need." Andrea muttered.

Abby laughed saying "That's what family does."

"I'm going to the cafeteria." Andrea said.

On the way she ran into Quinton.

Already in a bad mood, she snapped "Following me?"

He always seemed to light a passionate fire in her which pleased him.

Not caring why, Quinton said, "No, just happen to be going to the same place at the same time."

He put his hand on her waist. When she tried to pull away he held her a little tighter.

Not wanting to make a scene Andrea didn't struggle with him.

He's just being a gentleman. She told herself.

Yeah and if you believe that I have a story to tell you about the tooth fairy. She retorted.

Andrea went to get coffee then walked to one of the tables in the dining area.

Quinton followed.

"Why are you following me?" She asked angrily.

"I've already told you, I'm not following you. We happen to be going to the same place at the same time." Quinton answered.

"It feels like you're following me." Andrea argued.

"Don't you like my companionship?" Quinton asked.

"We both know it isn't companionship you're offering." Andrea said.

Quinton smiled.

"Which is why you don't trust yourself with me?" He stated.

"Don't you have something you'd rather be doing?"

Quinton raised a quizzical eyebrow at her.

"Or should be doing."

"No, I'm where I want to be, doing what I want."

"Following me and…"

"And what Little One? Making you want me, think things you shouldn't or believe you shouldn't."

"Quinton please stop."

"I've never been one to be subtle; I want you Little One. I will not let your shyness stop me from having you."

"Shyness? No one has ever accused me of being shy."

"You seem to develop it around me. You will be by my side soon… and in my bed."

Quinton walked away.

Andrea's mouth dropped open.

Realizing her mouth was hanging open she closed it.

Her mind was blank. She had no response to Quinton's statement; apparently he hadn't expected one he was sure she'd comply with his wishes.

Andrea groaned, she wasn't altogether certain he wasn't right.

Standing, she promised herself she'd do her best to avoid Aunt Millie's trap and her best to avoid Quinton in the future.

CHAPTER THREE

When Andrea and Kyle walked into the house that evening she wanted nothing more than to scoop her niece and nephew into her arms and let them drain her worries away with their childish chatter.

She knew that wasn't going to happen because Kyle needed to talk to them about their newborn brother.

Instead she headed to the bathroom connected to her room. Closing the door she ran a warm bath adding bubbles.

When the tub was half full she discarded her clothes, climbed into the bath tub and sank into the warm water to let the warmth seep into her muscles to relax her.

As she relaxed in the warm water and bubbles she imagined what it would be like to be in Quinton's arms.

He'd told her she'd be by his side and in his bed soon. What had he meant by soon?

Why did he excite her to the point she let all rational thought fly out of her head.

Normally she guarded against letting herself fall for the domineering type. What was different about Quinton?

She'd let her control slip, why? What was it about Quinton that made her want to share unknown parts of herself with him?

Her attraction to him was scary but strangely exciting. She couldn't wait to discover what he had planned.

Andrea began draining the water from the tub then climbed out. She wrapped a towel around her head then pulled her robe on.

Walking into her bedroom she stopped mid-step.

"What are you doing in my room?" She asked.

"Waiting for you." Quinton answered.

"Why?" Andrea questioned.

"We have a date tonight." He said.

"I asked Agnes to call and cancel it." She said.

"She tried, I told her I'd speak to you."

"I'm not ready for a date."

Quinton walked over to her, put his hands on her waist pulling her to him.

"You're ready." He said.

Lowering his head he kissed her.

Andrea tried to remain unresponsive to the kiss, her body melted into his as though they'd been together for years.

Quinton trailed kisses down her neck, moving her robe aside to get to the valley between her breasts.

She held him to her as her body reacted to his touch.

"Quinton please I want…"

"Tonight you shall have what you want." He whispered in her ear.

Andrea shivered.

Forcing polite coolness, she said "I have to get dressed."

"Wear something loose and comfortable. Don't forget to pack an overnight bag." Quinton said.

"You're awfully sure of yourself." Andrea snapped.

Quinton was still holding her.

"I'm sure of what I want and I'm sure of what you want even if you aren't willing to or won't admit it." He said.

"Get out of here." She said.

Quinton kissed her again. This time he left no doubt about how "their date" would end. Sensuously caressing her cheek he left.

Andrea took a moment to compose herself before pulling the towel from her head.

Taking her robe off, she took it into the bathroom to hang up, then searched through her clothes to find the appropriate clothing to wear for her date with Quinton.

Grabbing a V-neck coral tunic blouse, matching peasant skirt, coral sandals and matching bra and panties Andrea went into the adjoining bathroom to dress.

Emerging several minutes later she was surprisingly calm.

When she went to pack her bag for her overnight stay at Quinton's she became nervous.

Should she pack pajamas? She didn't have anything remotely resembling sexy or that could be mistaken for sexy.

What did it matter when he discovered she was a twenty-eight year old virgin he'd be turned off anyway.

Quinton would wonder what was wrong with her that she'd made it to twenty-eight and was still a virgin.

Refusing to let herself think about what she was doing, Andrea packed her overnight bag with enough for two nights.

Afterward she went down to meet Quinton in the living room.

Shyly handing him her bag she went to find Kyle.

Finding him in the office with Kayla and Kerry she lightly knocked on the door.

Kyle looked up smiling, "Yes, Andie." He said.

"I have a date with Quinton, unless you need me to stay with Kerry and Kayla." Andrea said.

Kyle continued smiling. "No we were just getting ready to leave for the hospital, Kayla and Kerry want to see Abby and meet Ethan." He said.

"I have my cell phone if you need me." Andrea told him.

"We'll be fine. Have a good time." Kyle said.

"I will, thanks." Andrea said.

She walked back to Quinton.

"Ready?" He asked.

Andrea looked into his eyes for any sign that this evening was only meant as a conquest for him, finding none she said, "Ready."

He took her by the hand leading her out to his truck. Helping her in he kissed her and put her bag behind the seat.

While they drove to his house Quinton held her hand giving it a reassuring squeeze letting her know she was in good hands.

Pulling into his driveway Quinton put the truck into park, let go of Andrea's hand, stepped out of the truck and walked around to her side.

Opening the door he took her hand to help her out letting her body slide down the length of his.

Andrea moaned erotically.

"Quinton…" She said.

He put his finger against her lips.

"Not now." He said.

Resisting the urge to hold her to him, Quinton took her bag from behind the seat then led her to the house.

Unlocking the door and opening it he indicated she should enter first.

Andrea walked into the house. She had the opportunity to observe her surroundings this time.

The foyer was decorated in silver and blue, walking through the rest of the house she found the color scheme the same.

Quinton led her to the dining room after dropping her bag by the stairs.

He held out a chair out for her.

"Supper is served, Miss Phillips." He said.

Smiling, Andrea sat down.

"Thank you, Mr. Masterson." She said.

Smiling, he bowed.

"Although I can cook I asked Katie to make supper for us tonight." He said.

"It looks delicious." Andrea said.

On the table there was fried chicken, oven roasted potatoes, glazed carrots and a Beautiful Summer Salad.

Quinton took Andrea's plate to fill with food.

He placed a piece of chicken, a spoonful of potatoes and glazed carrots and used tongs to put salad on her plate.

Placing the plate in front of her he looked lovingly into her eyes.

"Thank you." Andrea said shyly.

Quinton nodded then began filling his own plate.

Several minutes ticked by as they ate silently.

"How are your parents?" Quinton asked.

"Well, they've been waiting to hear news of their newest grandchild. How are your parents?" Andrea answered.

"Well, also waiting to hear news of their newest grandchild; in the meantime wondering when I'm getting married and going to provide them with grandchildren." Quinton told her.

Andrea smiled. "My family is a little more subtle, but they're wondering the same about me." She stated.

"You mentioned earlier today you've lost your job." He said.

"Yes, my boss sold the flower shop and I didn't get along well with the new owner. She offered me a

~ 53 ~

compensation package to end my employment. I accepted and came to Atlanta to help Abby." She told him.

"Have you decided what you're going to do?" He asked.

"I talked to Abby today. I've decided to finish college, get my degree." Andrea answered.

"Is there anything I can do to help?" He queried.

"No, I need to decide if I'm going to stay in Atlanta or go home." She said.

I'll have to convince you to stay in Atlanta. Quinton said silently.

Aloud he said "If I can help in any way you'll let me know?"

"Yes, Quinton."

While they'd talked they'd eaten.

Andrea looked at her plate, it was empty. She wiped her hands as best she could on her napkin.

Looking at Quinton she asked "Powder room?"

"Down the hall, second door on the left." He said.

Standing Andrea said, "Excuse me, I'll be right back."

Quinton stood, "No need to rush, we have all the time we need, Little One." He told her.

Andrea nodded and headed to the bathroom to wash her hands and prepare for the night ahead.

Going back to Quinton she tried her best to relax and calm her nerves.

Sitting in her chair she smiled at him.

Quinton excused himself heading in the direction of the bathroom.

Several minutes later he came back with a package whistling "Tonight's The Night."

"Ready for dessert?" He asked.

Andrea nodded.

Quinton took her hand, helped her stand then led her into the home office.

When they arrived the room was lit by electric candles and a roaring fire.

"A fire in July?" Andrea questioned.

"Ambiance." Quinton stated.

Andrea shivered in the warm room.

Quinton pulled her close.

"Relax, Little One we have all the time we need." He repeated.

"Quinton..." She stammered.

He kissed her.

Andrea couldn't hold back her want of him. She held him to her as he trailed kisses down her neck leading him to the hollow between her ample breasts.

"Quinton please I need..."

He stopped her with a kiss so hungry all thought left her.

His hands left a hot trail when they caressed her love starved body.

Andrea was forced to cling to him as if she were drowning and he were a life raft.

When his hand slid between her thighs she gasped, urging him to love her.

Abruptly he stopped.

Stricken cold by the abrupt end to their lovemaking Andrea pulled away from him.

Quinton pulled her to him.

"I promised you dessert." He reminded her.

"I don't need..." She started.

"You'll love what I have planned." He promised.

Leading her to a small table, Quinton pulled out a chair to seat her.

After she was seated he stuck his finger in the fondue pot filled with melted chocolate.

Letting the contents drip from his finger he put it to Andrea's lips urging her to take it into her mouth.

Hesitantly Andrea took the offered sweet from Quinton's finger. Instinctively she sucked at his finger until the chocolate was gone.

Quinton returned his finger to the fondue pot repeating the process with the chocolate.

Again he offered the sweet to Andrea; a little bolder this time she took his finger trailing it down the hollow between her breasts.

Enjoying her game, Quinton obediently followed his finger with his tongue licking the chocolate as he followed the trail.

Andrea's breathing became labored as his tongue left a wet, warm trail on her skin.

Quinton took a strawberry from a dish on the table dipping it in the chocolate he let it drip into the pot then held it over the hollow of Andrea's breasts.

When the warm chocolate came into contact with her skin Andrea moaned closing her eyes at the sensuality.

"Open your mouth, Little One." Quinton demanded.

Andrea's sensual lips parted for him.

Quinton put the chocolate laced strawberry against her mouth; obediently she took a bite.

Quinton bit into the other side. They ate their own halves until their lips met.

He took her mouth with his.

Not content to feed her just one strawberry, Quinton proceeded to continue the game with the strawberries.

Andrea shook with desire for him.

When they'd eaten the last strawberry Quinton molded her to him so he could feel her aching body next to his.

Rubbing her back in a soothing manner he said "This is the last chance to tell me to stop."

"Stop…"

Quinton stiffened.

"I can no more tell you to stop than I can stop breathing." Andrea confessed.

Quinton lifted the tunic over her head, revealing the silky bra underneath.

He dipped his head between her heaving breasts, kissing as she clutched at him.

"Quinton, please I need you." She said.

Pulling his head up, Quinton took her hand leading her to the area in front of the fireplace.

Kneeling, he pulled her down with him, cradling her against him he kissed her moist, sweet lips.

Looking at her he said, "Now and forever you're mine."

Andrea nodded.

Releasing the catch on her bra Quinton slid the straps down her shoulders capturing one hardened nipple in his mouth when her breasts were exposed to him.

Andrea held him to her as his mouth aroused her aching breast leading his mouth to her other aching breast when she couldn't stand the ache any longer.

She pushed him away just enough to release the buttons on his shirt. When his bare chest was exposed she put her hands on it feeling the strength and warmth.

"Touch me, Little One, tell me you want me." He demanded.

Andrea caressed his chest arousing him to the point he ached to have his way with her if she'd been more experienced.

He knew he had to be gentle and tender as this would be her first time; he wanted her to ache for more as the night wore on.

Capturing her mouth with his he kissed her gently and tenderly until her eagerness and hunger demanded he satisfy the ache deep inside her.

Discarding their clothing Quinton and Andrea twined their bodies together as they kissed and caressed each other.

When he knew she was ready for him Quinton quickly covered himself, went back to Andrea and gently eased himself into her aching body.

Andrea tensed at the welcome invasion. Quinton held back as she accepted him inside her.

Unable to wait any longer she pushed her hips forward to meet him.

Gasping at the instant of pain Andrea let him guide her into womanhood.

During their lovemaking she whispered words of love and when her release came Andrea's "I love you" echoed from the walls.

While she lay in the circle of his arms Quinton felt Andrea shudder.

"What's wrong, Little One?" He asked.

"I didn't know." She said her voice quivering.

"Lovemaking is beautiful with the right person and emotions." He assured her.

"I know, thank you." Andrea said hovering over him.

Kissing him she teased him with her tongue until he forced her onto her back.

"Now my sweet, you show me what to do." He said.

Andrea kissed him letting her tongue trace the outline of his mouth. She darted her tongue into his mouth teasing him.

Quinton held himself tightly in control as Andrea seduced and teased him.

When she circled his nipple with her tongue he almost lost control. Her mouth made a trail across his chest to the other nipple driving Quinton mad with desire.

"Little One…" He warned.

Giggling she said "Not yet."

Pushing his chest she laid him on his back.

Following him, she lowered herself onto him.

"Little One we need protection." He told her.

Andrea kissed him then said "I'm on the pill."

Moaning into her mouth, he rolled over pinning her beneath him then made love to her.

Andrea reveled in his lovemaking crying out in sweet ecstasy as her release neared.

"Quinton!" She cried.

"Let it happen, Little One." He told her as his own release was near.

Quinton clasped their hands together raising them above Andrea's head.

She used the pressure of their clasped hands to intensify their climax.

When it happened Andrea's release forced "I love you" from her.

Quinton knew he hadn't misunderstood the forced words, he also knew she was unaware she'd said them.

His own climax brought tears of joy at the words but the tears were also ones of sorrow; he knew she wouldn't remember them.

Prolonging their lovemaking so she wouldn't see his tears he showed Andrea his love hoping she'd see he wanted to spend his life with her.

While she lay within the circle of his arms her eyes hesitantly met his.

"Why?" Quinton asked after they finished making love.

"I wanted you to be the first." She said shyly.

"You're alright, no regrets?" He asked.

"Yes I'm fine, no regrets." She said then kissed him.

Quinton pulled away.

"Why me?" He asked.

"Because I love you." She said silently.

Aloud she told him "You've intrigued me from the moment we met."

Quinton stiffened.

"What about your boyfriend?" He asked.

"Anthony? We're no longer dating. We decided to see other people." Andrea said.

"So I was handy." Quinton said angrily.

"No, Quinton please…" Andrea begged.

"Get dressed, I'm taking you home." He said standing to find his clothes.

"Quinton I don't want…"

He looked at her, the look told her there wasn't going to be an argument.

She ducked her head, hiding her expression from him fighting back the tears that threatened to fall.

Quickly she gathered her clothes then rushed to the bathroom down the hall and closed the door.

Once alone she let the tears fall. How could she have let this happen?

She'd known Quinton would break her heart; what she hadn't known was how much it would hurt.

Quinton pulled his clothes on. He thought over the evening. How could he have misinterpreted her signals? All the signs told him she loved him.

What had gone wrong? Why wouldn't she say it? When he made love to her it was clear that she loved him; she said it in the shelter of his arms but outside the shelter of their lovemaking she couldn't admit it.

He'd find a way to make her admit it one way or another; Kyle had told him the one person who could help him.

Andrea washed her face with soap and water to erase the telltale signs she'd been crying. Sorting through her clothes she quickly dressed then reluctantly went back to Quinton.

"I'm ready." She said with false strength.

Quinton looked at her. She gave nothing away by word or action as to how she felt.

Walking to her he tried to draw her into his arms, she pulled away as if he'd burned her.

Andrea walked toward the door, Quinton had no choice but to follow.

She walked out to his truck without a backward glance.

He grabbed her overnight bag then met her at the truck.

Quinton turned Andrea to face him, "We have to talk about this." He told her.

"What's there to talk about? We had a date and fulfilled our families' wishes." Andrea shot at him.

"Fulfilled our families' wishes?" He questioned.

"Yes, we went out on the required date; I don't think the sex was part of their plan." She said.

"Sex?" He said angrily, shaking her.

"Let go of me." She snapped.

Tossing her bag aside, Quinton pulled her to him kissing her.

Andrea tried to pull away but her desire to be in his arms was stronger than her desire to get away from him.

When he finished kissing her she couldn't stand on her own, she had to cling to him for support.

"Now tell me it was sex." He demanded.

"Quinton please don't..." She begged.

"Say it." He ordered.

"It wasn't" She admitted.

"You have until your birthday to plan our wedding. That's when we're getting married." He told her.

"We're not getting married." Andrea denied.

"The subject is not open to discussion, Little One. You have until your birthday." Quinton stated.

He opened the truck door helped her in, picked up her bag, set it behind her seat, closed the door then walked around to the driver's side and climbed in.

On the drive to Kyle and Abby's Andrea opened her mouth to argue with Quinton about their wedding day but found she'd lost the ability to speak.

She couldn't recall ever having lost the ability to speak in her life.

Quinton chuckled at her inability to argue with him. He knew he had to enjoy it now because it would be the one and only opportunity he'd get.

Andrea threw him a dark look. He'd pay for this, she wasn't sure how, but he'd pay.

When he pulled into the driveway Andrea couldn't move fast enough to get out of the truck.

Quinton put his hand on her arm. "Don't let your anger get the best of you, Little One put it to constructive use." He advised.

Andrea opened the door lowering herself out of the truck seat.

Quinton was quicker, meeting her on the passenger side of the truck.

Taking her bag from behind the seat he took her hand then closed the door.

Andrea tried to pull her hand away from him.

"Let go of me." She repeated.

Tiring of her repeated efforts to push him away he tossed the bag on the ground and pinned her against the truck.

"You will be my wife, sleep in my bed and give birth to my children make no mistake about it Little One." He told her.

Quinton kissed her effectively stopping her from struggling by seducing her to the point all she wanted was his lovemaking to continue.

Wrapping her arms around his neck Andrea drew closer to him.

Quinton pulled away.

"Quinton no please…" She begged.

"We have to go inside unless you want me to make love to you out here." He said.

Andrea blushed.

He went over to pick up her bag, went back to her, took her hand then led her into the house.

Walking through the house to the stairs neither of them saw Kyle standing in the doorway to the office.

He smiled.

Once in Andrea's room Quinton put her bag down, pulled her into his arms and began his slow seduction of her again.

She didn't want him to take his time, she wanted him to make love to her now.

"Quinton, please the ache is building." She told him.

"Slow, Little One." He said.

Quinton caressed her breast through her top, touching it gently, lovingly.

Andrea cried out.

She let her hands wander down his chest to his manhood lingering just above before she unclasped his jeans to discard his clothes.

When their clothing was finally out of the way Andrea took him in her hands stroking until his release came.

"Andrea." Quinton called out.

They hadn't made it past the closed door. Quinton leaned against the door as his breathing went from climactic release to normal.

Without losing contact with her, Quinton urged Andrea toward the bed.

Once there he gently pushed her onto it.

He loved her with his hands and mouth without allowing her release.

"Quinton…"

He kissed her abdomen, then continue lower hovering above her womanhood.

Andrea couldn't object, the ache was too much for her.

He brought her to release.

"Quinton… I love you." Andrea cried out.

Her admission made him more determined to prove to her that he loved her and that they belonged together.

CHAPTER FOUR

The following morning Quinton was awakened by quarreling outside Andrea's bedroom.

"Anthony you can't just go into Andrea's room." Kyle said.

"I have to tell her I made a mistake. I love her and can't let her go." Anthony said.

"She's moved on, Tony." Kyle told him.

"Moved on? It's him isn't it, your brother." Anthony snarled.

"Do yourself a favor and go back to Shelby forget Andie." Kyle advised.

"I'm not giving her up without a fight. I'm not going home without her." Anthony told him.

Quinton climbed out of bed, leaving Andrea to sleep.

Putting on his clothes he went out to confront Anthony.

"Andrea's made her choice Caldoni. We're getting married in two and a half months." Quinton said.

Anthony turned on him.

"What are you doing in Andrea's room?" He questioned.

"It should be obvious." Quinton said.

"I don't believe you. Andrea isn't that kind of girl." Anthony said.

"Take Kyle's advice and go home. I'll tell Andrea you were here." Quinton said.

"I'm not leaving until I talk to Andrea." Anthony demanded.

Andrea came out of the bedroom just then, walking to Quinton's side she wrapped her arms around him.

"What's going on?" She asked sleepily.

"I came to take you home." Anthony said.

"I'm not going to Shelby. I'm staying in Atlanta, going back to school and marrying Quinton." Andrea told him.

She'd surprised herself with the instant decision she'd made.

"You can't be serious. After all we've meant to each other. You can't just throw that away." Anthony said.

"Go home, Tony. Forget me." Andrea said.

Anthony took Andrea's hand to lead her away.

"Talk to me, Andrea." He demanded.

"I'm not going anywhere with you Tony; there's nothing to talk about." She said pulling her hand away.

"I'll go but this isn't over. I'm staying at The Regency, call me later." Tony said.

He leaned over to kiss Andrea's cheek.

She pulled away.

Tony looked at her angrily, looked at Quinton then walked away.

Andrea walked back to Quinton leaning against him.

"Are you all right?" He asked.

"He won't give up. When he wants something he doesn't stop until he gets it." Andrea said.

"You're mine, he won't get you." Quinton said.

"I'm not an object, Quinton." Andrea said.

"We probably should move the wedding date up since Caldoni came to take you to Shelby." Quinton said.

"We're not moving the wedding up because Tony came to Atlanta." Andrea insisted.

"I hate to interrupt but when did you decide to get married?" Kyle asked.

"Last night." Quinton answered.

Standing next to Quinton Andrea wondered why she'd agreed to marry him so easily.

She loved him but it wasn't like her to just agree to something like this.

Removing her arm from around his waist she walked away from him into her room.

Quinton followed closing the door.

"Something wrong, Little One?" He questioned.

"Why are we getting married, Quinton?" She asked.

He couldn't tell her it was because they loved each other. She wouldn't admit it in the cold light of day.

"We both want a child." He stated without emotion.

He may as well have slapped her across the face as cold as his statement was.

"To create a child is our reason for getting married?" Andrea asked.

"Yes." Quinton stated.

Andrea refused to let his cold statement hurt her.

"We don't have to be married to create a child." She argued.

The look Quinton gave her told her that was not an option.

Andrea shivered in the warm room.

"I can go without making love to you until our wedding, Miss Phillips." Quinton stated clearly.

"Hell, he'd waited four years to make love to her what was two and a half months?" He thought to himself.

Andrea shivered again.

The thought of Quinton not making love to her for two and a half months left her cold.

She would not make the mistake of letting him know what affect his statement had on her.

Quinton knew the affect his statement had on her. The shiver that ran through her told him all he needed to know.

He wanted to go to her, pull her into his arms and make love to her but wanted her to know he was serious about being abstinent if necessary.

Andrea wondered why it was so hard for her to tell Quinton she loved him.

She opened her mouth to say the words, they stuck in her throat.

Staring at Quinton she tried again… nothing.

What was wrong with her? She never had this much trouble communicating with people.

Andrea remembered her conversation with Abby. " He scares me."

Why did Quinton scare her? He'd never done anything to make her fear him.

"Little One are you all right?" Quinton asked..

Andrea didn't seem to hear.

He walked over put his hands on her arms.

Andrea jumped.

"What?" She asked.

"Are you all right?" He repeated.

"Yes, fine, I was lost in thought." She said.

"Something you want to share?" He asked.

"Uh, no. A puzzle I'm trying to solve." She said.

"I'm good with puzzles." Quinton stated.

"Unfortunately only I can solve this one." Andrea said.

Unable to resist Quinton kissed her.

Andrea let herself get lost in the kiss.

Quinton pulled away saying, "You are very addicting, Little One."

Andrea smiled.

"Does that mean you'll be breaking your threat of abstinence?" She questioned.

"Don't tempt me, my sweet. You'll find yourself in more hot water than you ever imagined." Quinton threatened.

Andrea snuggled closer to get his reaction.

Quinton growled.

Taking her mouth with his, he showed her what her closeness did to him.

Andrea lay in the circle of Quinton's arms.

"Quinton?" She said.

"Yes, Little One."

"I like it when you don't abstain." She told him.

Chuckling, Quinton wrapped his arms more firmly around her.

"I'll have to learn to be strong around you. You're much too tempting Little One." He told her.

" Am I?" She asked.

Quinton swatted her on the bottom.

" You know very well you are." He reprimanded.

Andrea jumped. Anthony had never told her let alone showed her that she was tempting.

She lowered her eyes, not meeting his.

" No, I don't." She said quietly.

Startled, Quinton took his hand, lifted her chin forcing her to look at him.

"Caldoni never told you?" He asked.

"No." She confessed.

Quinton swore under his breath.

Climbing out of bed he said, "How can you be in a relationship with someone for four years and not tell them how tempting they are?"

Andrea shrank back onto the bed away from Quinton's tirade.

He came back to the bed gathered Andrea up, pulled her out of the bed and urge her into the bathroom to take a shower.

She smiled at the way he took charge and the way he made her feel wanted and… loved.

She decided not to think about that last part; she'd just go along with Quinton, take a shower and go visit Abby and Ethan in the hospital.

While taking their shower Quinton had a very different idea on how to take a shower. Not the least of which was making love… twice.

By the time they emerged Andrea was shivering because the water had turned cold.

Quinton wrapped a towel around her, then pulled her toward him and kissed her.

"So much for my vow of abstinence." He said.

"You could always start now." Andrea told him.

"When I am around you I seem to lose control of myself." He told her.

"Want me to go home?" She teased.

"I'd just follow you and we'd create that baby without the benefit of marriage." He threatened.

Andrea grew warm at the thought of Quinton following her to Shelby and them creating a baby together.

She kissed him thinking how much she loved him and wanted to become pregnant with his child.

She'd content herself with the fact they'd be married in two and a half months then they could create a baby of their own.

"We need to get dressed to go to hospital to visit Abby and Ethan." Quinton said.

"I know, I'll be ready in twenty minutes." Andrea replied.

She gathered her clothing and bath essentials then went into the bathroom. When she emerged twenty minutes later Quinton was dressed and waiting for her.

Unable to resist, he walked over put his hands on her waist, pulled her to him and kissed her long and sensuously.

After he stopped he took her hand, together they walked downstairs to meet Kyle, Kerry and Kayla.

"Good morning, Aunt Andie and Uncle Quinton." Kayla said cheerily.

"Good morning, Kay Rae." Quinton said ruffling her hair.

"Who was that man that said he was taking you home?" Kerry asked disapprovingly.

Andrea had the grace to blush.

"An old friend of Aunt Andie's. Don't worry K.T. he won't be taking her home." Quinton told him.

"I don't like him." Kerry stated.

"Me either." Kayla chimed in.

Quinton laughed saying, "Out of the mouths of babes."

Andrea threw him a "not in front of the children" look.

He was instantly chastised but still amused.

She threw her hands in the air as if to say "trying to control you is pointless."

Quinton smiled and winked at her.

The gesture made her love him all the more. No matter what she couldn't stay angry with him for long.

"We're just getting ready to go to hospital to visit Abby and Ethan." Kyle said.

"We'll be right behind you." Quinton said.

Kyle took Kayla and Kerry then left for the hospital.

Quinton took Andrea by the hand and lead her to the loveseat.

Knowing he had to choose his words carefully he thought before he spoke.

Going down on one knee in front of her he stated seriously, "As you are aware Andrea I've become fond of you over these last four and a half years nothing would give me greater pleasure than you consenting to be my wife. Will you marry me?"

Tears welled in Andrea's eyes, she was sure that was as close to a declaration of love as she was going to get from Quinton.

"Yes." She said quietly.

Quinton arched an eyebrow at her.

"Yes." She stated louder and clearly.

Quinton smiled then kissed her.

"We'll get your ring after we visit Abby and Ethan." He told her.

"Quinton I don't need…" Andrea stammered.

Quinton put his finger against her lips.

"All Masterson brides wear their favorite gem as their engagement ring." He told her.

Andrea nodded.

"Emerald." She said.

"I know." Quinton said smiling.

"How did you…" Andrea began.

'It's my job to know." He replied.

"Tony doesn't know." Andrea stated.

"I'm not Caldoni, I took the time to learn."

"Why?"

"I wanted to know"

"Why did you want to know?"

"I'm interested."

Andrea blushed.

"We should go to the hospital." She said.

Quinton stood up, helped her stand then led her out to his truck.

When they walked into Abby's hospital room hand in hand Abby smiled.

"Good afternoon." She greeted.

"Good afternoon." Andrea said then kissed her cheek.

Quinton leaned over to kiss her cheek. "How's my favorite sister-in-law?" He asked.

Smiling, Abby said, "I'm your only sister-in-law."

"We have some news we'd like to share." Quinton said.

Abby tried to pretend she didn't know what Quinton was about to say.

"Last night Andrea agreed to marry me in two and a half months." He began.

Abby opened her mouth.

Quinton held up a hand.

"I officially proposed this afternoon, and she officially accepted." He finished.

"Congratulations, when is the wedding?" Abby asked.

Quinton started to answer but Andrea jabbed him in the ribs with her elbow telling him this was her news too.

He leaned over to kiss her. "Sorry." He apologized.

Andrea smiled, kissing him back.

"Two months." She replied.

"Atlanta or Shelby?" Abby queried.

Not wanting another jab in the ribs Quinton looked at Andrea.

"Atlanta." She said.

"Are you sure?" I don't want you to feel pressured." Quinton said.

"I'm sure. Atlanta is our home." Andrea responded.

Quinton smiled inwardly, she'd said Atlanta was their home.

"Do I get to hold my nephew?" Andrea asked.

Kyle stood up, walked to her handing his newborn son to her.

Andrea took her new nephew in her arms, cradling him to her.

Soon she'd have her own baby to cradle in her arms, she hoped.

Quinton watched Andrea hold Ethan, he saw the longing in her eyes to have her own baby.

First the wedding then they'd work on creating their own child. He didn't have a preference of boy or girl as long as it was healthy he'd be happy with the child God blessed them with.

A thought occurred to him. Twins ran in Andrea's family they may just have twins as well. He'd welcome a multiple birth as well as a singular one. Any child would be welcome and loved.

Quinton watched Andrea hold and cuddle Ethan imagining her showering their child with love and affection.

"Quinton are you alright?" Andrea asked.

He snapped out of his thoughts.

"Yes, I was thinking." He said.

"Care to share your thoughts, Little Brother?" Kyle asked.

"No." Quinton replied.

Kyle chuckled.

Quinton threw him a don't go there look.

"Quinton?" Andrea questioned.

He smiled at her. "I'm fine, Little One." He assured her.

Andrea gave him a hesitant smile.

"Do you want to hold Ethan?" She asked.

He walked over took Ethan from her and cuddled him to his chest.

Andrea imagined him cuddling their son in his arms; that led her to imagine Quinton making love to her to create their son.

She grew red and warm at the thought of Quinton making love to her over the course of the night.

"Andrea, are you okay?" Abby asked concerned.

Andrea looked at her. "Yes, fine why?" She said.

"You turned red all of a sudden." Abby answered.

"It's warm in here." Andrea replied.

"Andrea." Abby said.

"Tabitha." Andrea warned.

Abby knew when Andrea used her given name not to push any further so she let the subject drop.

Ethan began fussing, Abby began to unbutton her night gown.

Quinton took that as their cue to leave.

"I'm taking Andrea shopping for her engagement ring. We'll be back later." He said.

"Thanks for coming up. See you later." Abby said.

Andrea walked over to Abby, kissed her on the cheek then stood waiting for Quinton to bring Ethan to Abby.

After giving the baby to his mother Quinton kissed Abby's cheek.

"Congratulations you have a beautiful son." He said.

"Thank you, we think so, it's nice to have another unbiased opinion." Abby said.

Quinton smiled.

Taking Andrea's hand he walked out with her.

He felt Andrea's hand shaking.

"Are you all right, Little One?" He asked.

"I'm a little nervous." She admitted.

Unsure of how she'd react to a public display of affection Quinton resisted the urge to fold her in his arms to assure her everything was going to be fine.

He did however squeeze her hand in reassurance.

She smiled.

The smile told him more than he needed to know. He'd made the right decision in proposing.

Walking with their hands clasped they made their way to Quinton's truck.

Quinton wanted to get Andrea's pulse pounding. He knew just how to do it.

He helped her into the passenger side then went around to the driver's side and climbed in buckling his seatbelt, starting the truck.

Leaving the hospital Quinton's foot found the accelerator. He wound through the streets crazily.

Andrea put her hand on the dashboard clutching at it for safety.

What was Quinton doing, thinking? The way he was driving he was going to get them killed.

"Quinton." Andrea gasped.

He smiled, slowing the truck.

She'd said his name the same way she did when he made love to her. He knew it wouldn't be followed by the barely audible "I love you."

"Something wrong Little One?" He asked amused.

"Are you trying to get us killed?" Andrea asked angrily.

The smile left Quinton's face. He hadn't meant to scare her only excite her, bring out her adventurous side.

"No, I was trying to bring you a little excitement." Quinton stated.

"By scaring me out of my wits. Quinton, please refrain from trying to excite me in the future." Andrea snapped.

"I can't promise I won't try to excite you in the future, Little One." He said.

Andrea blushed.

That brought a smile back to Quinton's face.

"Concentrate on your driving." She told him.

He picked up her hand, kissing the back.

"Yes, my dear." He agreed.

Andrea slowly drew her hand back toward herself.

Her pulse was pounding; he had excited her. Images of them unleashing their desire for one another danced in her head.

The redness crept back into her face.

Quinton looked over just in time to see the color rush into her face for a second time.

His smile widened. There was a way to get her to think about him.

Quickly and safely they arrived at his jewelers to pick out Andrea's engagement ring.

Quinton leaned over to kiss her.

Her hungry response made him eager to take her up on the offer coming from her tightly controlled emotions.

It took all of Andrea's self-control not to beg Quinton to make love to her. She ached for him as a woman too long parted from the man she loved.

Quinton could feel the tight control she kept on herself. He willed her to let go.

Andrea fought her emotions she couldn't give in; not here, not now, not in public. She was adventurous but not that adventurous.

She fell back against the seat.

Quinton chuckled.

"You do have a limit, interesting." He said still chuckling.

Andrea threw him a puzzled look.

"I was wondering how adventurous you are." He said.

Andrea sobered. Putting her hand on his chest she pushed him away from her.

Quinton took her hand, brought her fingers to his lips, individually kissing each one.

Andrea gasped. "Quinton."

He let his warm tongue slide along her hand to her wrist. There he swirled it around.

Andrea cried out.

"Oh, please." She begged.

He put his mouth next to her ear.

"Here, now?" He asked huskily.

"Yes." Andrea said.

Quinton chuckled.

"We'll get arrested." He told her.

Someone may as well have thrown a pitcher of cold water on her.

"Oh, Lord what was I thinking?" Andrea asked.

"Obviously thought wasn't part of the equation." Quinton said.

Andrea tried to pull her hand free.

Quinton held onto it.

"May I have my hand back please?" She asked.

Reluctantly Quinton released her trembling hand.

Andrea pulled her hand to her chest holding it to herself as if it would protect her from her wanton desires.

"Shall we go get your ring?" Quinton questioned.

Andrea gave a slight nod of her head.

"My question requires more than a mere nod of your head, Little One." He scolded.

"Yes." Andrea agreed clearly.

Quinton smiled, slid back to his side of the truck, opened the door then stepped out.

Walking around to the passenger side, he opened the door extending his hand to help Andrea out.

He let her slide down the length of his body.

"Quinton, you're making it very difficult for me to behave myself." Andrea reprimanded.

"That's the point, Little One." He stated.

He captured her mouth with his.

Passersby whistled.

Andrea reluctantly pulled away.

"We cannot do this in public, we'll get arrested as you said." She said.

"I suggest we quickly find your ring so I can take you home." Quinton said.

"I am not going to quickly find a ring because you are unable to control your hormones." Andrea snapped.

She turned to climb back into the truck.

Quinton put his hands on her waist pulling her to him.

"I'm sorry, Little One. I didn't mean to sound unromantic. I want you all to myself." He apologized.

Andrea let herself be held next to Quinton as her heated body cooled.

"It's not easy for me you know." Andrea confessed.

"I'm glad to hear I'm not alone." Quinton said.

He turned her to face him.

"Let's go pick out the most beautiful ring we can find." Quinton said.

Andrea's eyes lit up.

He smiled, glad to have made her emerald eyes light up.

Together they walked hand in hand to the jewelers, walking by two giggling teenage girls.

Andrea's face turned red.

"Do you think they saw...?" She asked.

Quinton smiled. "I'm certain they did." He said.

Andrea's blush deepened.

Quinton leaned down to kiss her.

The teenagers giggled even harder.

"It's nice to see older people in love." One of the girls said.

"Older people?" Andrea thought. Is that how teenagers thought of them, older people.

Quinton noticed the change in Andrea. "They're teenagers, Little One. Don't let their comments bother you." He said.

Andrea wondered how the teenagers came to the conclusion that she and Quinton were in love. There was love on her part, but she doubted there was on Quinton's.

Walking into the jewelers they were greeted by a salesman.

"Good afternoon, folks, how may I help you?" He asked.

"We're looking for a very special engagement ring to match my fiancée's emerald eyes." Quinton stated.

"We have an excellent selection of emeralds, please come this way." The salesman said.

Quinton led Andrea to where the salesman directed them.

The salesman stopped in front of a display case full of emeralds.

Quinton looked at them. At first nothing caught his eye. He scrutinized each one to be sure he picked out the very best they had for Andrea.

Almost ready to give up, a sparkle caught his eye from the far corner of the display case. The ring was almost completely hidden from view.

Andrea saw the ring at the same time, she caught her breath.

It was a one carat, round emerald surrounded by a carat of diamonds in a silver setting.

"We'd like to see the ring in the corner please." Quinton said pointing to the ring.

The salesman hid his smile.

"Yes sir." He said.

Unlocking the display case he opened the door, withdrawing the ring.

Quinton took the ring held out to him inspecting it.

"Quinton, it's much too expensive." Andrea whispered.

"You're only engaged and married once, Andrea." Quinton reprimanded.

He took the ring from the box, then took Andrea's hand in his to slip it onto her finger.

Andrea instantly felt tied to him. The ring fit as though it had been made for her.

"We'll take it." Quinton said.

"You have excellent taste, sir." The salesman said.

"My fiancée will wear the ring." Quinton decided.

He followed the salesman to the counter to make the purchase forcing Andrea to trail behind.

She knew she was his for all time now. Nothing and no one could tear them apart.

CHAPTER FIVE

Silently Quinton and Andrea made their way back to his truck.

She felt the weight of the ring on her hand knowing it would always be a reminder of the love she had for him.

Quinton helped her into the truck purposely sliding his hand along her bottom giving it a little tap.

Andrea stiffened catching her breath. She knew it was for her comment about the ring being too expensive and he wasn't being cruel.

Smiling, she turned to give him a quick kiss and lost her footing.

Falling against him, she was caught in his strong arms.

"Careful, Little One." He said chuckling.

Andrea groaned, she always found a way to amuse him.

Gathering her dignity, she lifted herself into the seat.

Quinton watched her buckle herself in and closed the door.

He walked around to the driver's side, climbed in, buckled up and drove toward Kyle and Abby's house.

Andrea wondered if Quinton would stay the night with her. She was hopeful that he would.

She couldn't imagine not having him next to her in bed.

Odd, she didn't find it strange she'd already come to depend on Quinton lying next to her each night.

Quinton looked at Andrea, wondering what she was thinking.

She looked at him, gave him a shy smile then blushed a light pink.

Amused, Quinton smiled. By the blush that crept into her cheeks he knew what she was thinking.

"How have I amused you this time, Quinton?" Andrea asked.

"How do you know you've amused me?" Quinton questioned.

"By the way you're smiling." She answered.

"I could just be happy by the company I keep." He retorted.

"I know that smile, Quinton. It says I've amused you in some way." Andrea stated.

"I know what you're thinking." He said.

"You can't know. How?"

"You have a very expressive face, besides you blush."

Andrea groaned. Would she ever learn to keep her emotions hidden from him.

Did he know she was in love with him? How long would she be able to hide it from him?

Quinton called her name.

"Andrea." He repeated.

"Yes?" She said.

"Where did you go off to?" He asked.

"Nowhere." She lied.

"Has anyone ever told you you're a rotten liar?" Quinton questioned.

"Abby has told me a few times recently." She said.

"I don't want to be presumptuous but when is your next appointment to refill your birth control?"

"Around my birthday."

"If I may add my two cents, I'd like you to cancel the appointment and not refill it."

"Why?"

"I'd like to start our family right away."

"Based on the premise we're getting married to create a child."

Andrea sat closer to the door, again stung by the coldness of his words.

Quinton could feel her withdrawing from him. He couldn't pull her to him and make her feel the love he felt for her.

"It's not a business arrangement, Andrea." He snapped.

Lord he wished he knew why she was so afraid to let him know of her love.

Suddenly the thought hit Andrea. She was afraid to tell Quinton of her love because Abby had been betrayed by the two people she trusted most in the world.

Her heart ached. Being a twin sucked sometimes. She felt the same things Abby did and had the same fears.

Quinton pulled into the driveway.

After he stopped the truck and put it in park without waiting for him, Andrea unbuckled her seatbelt, opened the door and exited the truck.

She nearly ran into the house.

Quinton's longer stride enabled him to reach the door before her.

"You're not getting away that easily, Little One." He told her.

"Quinton, please." She begged.

He took her by the arm pulling her to the porch swing to sit down.

"What's wrong?" Quinton asked.

"Nothing, I just want to get inside." Andrea said.

"You're a rotten liar." He told her again.

Leaning over he kissed her.

Andrea relished in the kiss wishing it could go on forever.

Quinton controlled himself so he didn't take things too far.

She willed him to let go, take her in his arms and make love to her.

Kyle clearing his throat brought them out of their passionate mood.

"Sorry to interrupt, we do have neighbors." He said.

Andrea lowered her head in embarrassment but not before he saw the telltale signs of a blush on her cheeks.

A moment of silence passed before anyone spoke.

Quinton put his hand on Andrea's hip, pulling her to his side.

She didn't dare move away from him. Kyle would ask questions believing something was wrong.

"How are Abby and Ethan?" Andrea questioned.

"Well, the doctor will release them tomorrow." Kyle told her.

"Mama said we can help take care of Ethan." Kayla said excitedly.

"Having a newborn in the house will be exciting Kay Rae." Andrea told her.

"I'm not the only boy anymore." Kerry muttered.

"We've talked about this, Champ. You can teach Ethan many things when he's old enough. You're the big brother." Kyle reminded him.

"I don't want to teach him things. Why didn't you and mama have another girl?" Kerry complained.

"Kerry Tyler." Kyle reprimanded.

Kerry knew when his father used his full name he was not happy with his behavior.

"Why aren't you happy with your new brother Kerr Bear? Andrea asked.

"He takes too much of mama's attention. She'll love him more than she does me." Kerry told her.

Andrea hid a smile.

"Come here, Kerr Bear" She demanded.

Kerry scuffed his feet on the porch then went to sit next to Andrea.

"Mamas have so much love that no matter how many children they have the more love they have to give; their love just keeps growing." She told him.

Kerry looked at her in surprise. "Really?" He asked.

"Yes, that's how the Lord made mamas and daddies, they get extra love to give to all of their children." Andrea said.

Kerry threw his arms around Andrea's neck hugging her.

"I want to help take care of Ethan." He stated.

Andrea smiled looking at Kyle.

He mouthed, "thank you."

She gave a slight nod of her head.

"I get to help, he's my brother too." Kayla said.

"Yes, Kay Rae. You'll have to teach your brothers to be nice to girls, not to pull their hair, pinch them, hold doors open for them, pull out their chairs for them..." Andrea said.

Quinton gently patted her on the bottom reminding her to behave herself and not go too far in her etiquette lesson.

She smiled knowing Quinton was being playful. It made her love him all the more.

"Abby told me about your plans to go back to college." Kyle told her.

"I completed two years of college after high school. I dropped out because I didn't know what I wanted to do." Andrea responded.

"If I can help in any way let me know." Kyle said.

"If Andrea needs help I'll help her." Quinton said holding his temper.

He stood with his arm around Andrea, it forced her to stand with him.

Quinton urged Andrea inside. Leading her toward the stairs he walked to her room.

After he closed the door Andrea took a step away from him.

Quinton easily brought her back to his side, wrapping his arm around her and pinning her against the door.

He kissed her as though he'd never had the pleasure before.

The longer he kissed her the more Andrea's passion grew.

She moaned when he moved his mouth to include her neck in his kiss.

"Oh, Quinton please." She pleaded.

Suddenly he stopped.

Andrea felt a cold chill run through her body.

Helplessly she looked at him.

"Abstinence." He said to the question in her eyes.

"What?" She asked.

"I said abstinence." He repeated.

"Why?" Andrea asked.

"Let me do this, Little One. It's the one thing I can give you that's just for you." Quinton said.

"I don't need it, Quinton." Andrea stated.

He put his fingers on her lips to quiet her.

Andrea kissed his fingers.

"Little One." He scolded.

She smiled happy to know he wasn't as controlled as he pretended.

"All right I'll behave myself if you promise you won't use forced abstinence after we're married." Andrea said.

"Deal." He said then kissed her.

Before they were both carried away by the kiss Quinton broke it off.

Andrea smiled happy to know she could make him lose control of himself.

"I'll go see if Agnes needs help making supper." She said.

"Okay, I'm going to talk to Kyle." Quinton said.

They walked hand in hand downstairs.

"Hi, Agnes, can I help with supper?" Andrea asked cheerily.

"Yes, Miss Phillips. Will you make the salad please." Agnes said.

Andrea started on the salad.

They worked silently and quickly to put supper together for everyone.

Andrea went into the living room to call her family to supper.

"Supper is ready." She said.

"Thanks Andie." Kyle said.

He gathered Kerry and Kayla together taking them to the dining room.

Andrea waited for Quinton to join her.

When he stood next to her Quinton gathered her in his arms kissing her.

He stole her breath with a kiss that was supposed to be short but lasted several minutes.

"You are addicting, Little One. It's going to be a challenge to remain abstinent." Quinton told her.

Andrea blushed.

Hand in hand they walked into the dining room.

"What have you decided to study in college, Little One?" Quinton asked.

Andrea smiled. "Believe it or not I was inspired by K.M. Enterprises to check into Computer Science." She answered.

Quinton chuckled. "Keeping it in the family, wise choice." He said.

During the rest of the meal Quinton, Kyle and Andrea discussed her career choice and what classes she'd need to get her Bachelor's degree.

After supper Andrea helped Agnes clean up then went to get Kayla and Kerry ready for bed.

"Aunt Andie can we check the nursery to make sure we have everything ready for Ethan?" Kayla asked.

"Of course, Kay Rae." Andrea assured her.

Kerry and Kayla clasped her hands leading her to the nursery.

After checking the nursery they went downstairs to the living room.

"We checked the nursery, everything is ready for Ethan to come home." Kerry announced.

"I'm glad to hear that." Kyle said.

"Little One, I need to talk to you." Quinton said.

"All right." Andrea agreed.

Together they went to her room.

After walking inside Quinton closed the door behind him gesturing that Andrea should sit on the bed.

"We need to discuss wedding plans." He said.

"Yes, I know." Andrea said.

"Do you want to get married in Shelby or Atlanta?" Quinton asked.

Andrea looked puzzled. She thought it was understood they were getting married in Atlanta.

~ 90 ~

"Quinton, you know the answer." Andrea said irritably.

Quinton smiled inwardly.

"I didn't want to make any assumptions." He said.

"Have you forgotten that I told Abby we're getting married in Atlanta?" Andrea snapped.

She stood up and began pacing.

When Quinton started to go to her she gave him a look that stopped him.

Somehow he knew that look. It was meant to keep him at a distance.

Andrea opened her mouth to speak only to close it again when nothing came out.

Quinton chuckled, twice in one day he'd seen her speechless.

He'd known it was a rarity to make her speechless earlier that day, but to make her speechless twice was an oddity.

"Something on your mind, Little One?" He asked curiously.

'Yes." Andrea said tentatively.

He raised an eyebrow at her. "What's on your mind, Andrea?" Quinton questioned.

Surprised at his use of her given name, Andrea's heart sank into her stomach.

This was not going at all as she had planned.

She sighed. "We have to call off the wedding, Quinton." Andrea said.

"We are not calling off the wedding, Little One. You'll get used to the idea of being my wife." Quinton told her.

"Quinton what are we going to tell people? Why are we getting married?" Andrea questioned.

Quinton's face became a hardened, unreadable mask.

"Would it be so hard for people to believe we're in love?" He asked harshly.

Andrea stopped pacing at his harsh words; going to sit on her bed she pulled a pillow against her stomach to protect herself against his anger.

"If that's what you want people to believe I'll go along with it." Andrea said sadly.

Lord it wasn't what he wanted but until she admitted her love for him that's the best he was going to get.

"It's what I want." He said sternly.

Andrea scooted closer to the headboard.

Closing her eyes, silently she prayed, "Lord, please let him love me."

Andrea heard the door open then close.

Opening her eyes, she looked around the empty room, she let the tears that were so close to the surface fall.

How was she going to keep from telling the man she loved her feelings for him?

Quinton walked to the study where Kyle was talking to his children.

Knocking on the door he looked like a lost soul.

Kyle looked up a smile on his face; the smile quickly disappeared at the look on his brother's face.

"Kayla, Kerry go ask Aggie to give you your snack now please. I'm going to talk to Uncle Quinton." Kyle said.

"Okay, daddy." Kerry and Kayla said in unison, then left the room.

"What is it, Little Brother?" Kyle asked.

Quinton closed the study door, walked to the fireplace and stood there.

"Andrea." He said shortly.

"What about her?" Kyle said.

"Three little words... She can't say three little words." Quinton snapped.

"Have you tried saying them to her?" Kyle questioned.

"You know the curse and tradition, Kyle. The woman has to say them first or the marriage won't last." Quinton reminded him.

Kyle laughed. "You're going to let an old curse and tradition stand in the way of your future." He said.

Quinton gave him a deadly look. "Who said them first in your relationship, Kyle? You or Abby?" He questioned sarcastically.

The smile faded from Kyle's lips. "Abby did." He muttered.

"Who's afraid of the curse and breaking tradition, Big Brother?" Quinton asked triumphantly.

"The curse and tradition may have had something to do with it." Kyle admitted.

'You expect me to tempt fate, I don't think so." Quinton stated.

There was a light knock on the door.

"Come in." Kyle said.

Andrea opened the door poking her head in.

"I'm going to visit Aunt Millie." She said.

"Why?" Quinton asked.

"I need someone to talk to." Andrea stated shyly.

"You go on. I'll ask Agnes to keep supper warm for you." Kyle said.

"Thank you, Kyle. I'll see you later." Andrea said.

She walked out closing the door behind her.

"What did you do that for?" Quinton asked.

"Andrea and Abby trust Millie. Don't worry she'll talk Andie into coming back to you." Kyle said confidently.

"I wish I had your confidence." Quinton said.

"Trust me, Little Brother, I know Millie." Kyle told him.

Quinton nodded.

Andrea pulled into Millie's driveway. Sitting there she gathered her thoughts and took calming breaths to ease her tension.

Millie opened the front door. Seeing Andrea sitting in the car she folded her arms across her middle.

The look she gave Andrea told her to get out of the car and into the house.

Andrea obediently opened the door, stepped out of the car then walked up to the house.

"Something you want to talk about?" Millie questioned.

Andrea's eyes filled with tears.

"Yes." She said sadly.

"Quinton?" Millie asked.

Andrea nodded, afraid her voice would crack if she spoke.

"Come in, young lady." Millie ordered.

Andrea obediently went into the house, going into the parlor.

Millie went to the kitchen to make tea.

Several minutes later she took the tea into the parlor where Andrea paced.

"All right, Miss Andrea what can I help you with?" Millie asked.

Going to sit next to her aunt, Andrea burst into tears.

"Oh, Aunt Millie I don't know what to do." Andrea cried.

"What's happened?" Millie questioned.

"Quinton asked me to marry him." Andrea answered.

"I'm guessing you said yes." Millie replied.

"Yes." Andrea said.

"What's the problem?"

"I love him."

"Why is that a problem?"

"I don't think he returns my love."

Millie knew there was no sense in her trying to convince her niece Quinton loved her.

"Are you getting married in Atlanta or Shelby?" She asked.

"Atlanta." Andrea answered.

"Tabitha is going to be your matron of honor?" Millie queried.

"Of course." Andrea replied.

"Traditional or modern?"

"I don't know we haven't discussed it yet."

"Andrea, how do you expect to plan a wedding without discussing it with your fiancée?"

"He acts like it's a business arrangement rather than a marriage."

Millie laughed.

Andrea looked at her, raising her eyebrow.

"Sorry, child. Men can be so unromantic sometimes." Millie said.

"This is a bad idea. Nothing good will come of it." Andrea wailed.

"I think it's time I told you about my broken engagement." Millie stated.

"Aunt Millie you don't have to…" Andrea started.

"Andrea, I haven't spoken about Benjamin to anyone, except my mother, in a very long time." Millie said.

"If this brings up unhappy memories…"

"My time with Benjamin wasn't unhappy. The way he ended our relationship was hurtful."

"Aunt Millie please don't do this…"

"Andrea I don't want you to make a mistake because you're not thinking with your heart."

Andrea resigned herself to listening to Aunt Millie's romance with Benjamin.

"I was eighteen when I met Benjamin. He worked as a bartender in Daddy's pub. The one your daddy owns now."

Andrea nodded her head in acknowledgment.

"My first impression of him wasn't a good one. He was rough around the edges and somewhat crude."

Andrea laughed.

Millie smiled.

"As time went by he grew on me. He'd trap me in the store room and steal kisses without my father knowing it. It was all rather exciting I must say."

Andrea interrupted. "How old was he?"

"Twenty-six. He'd been on his own since he was sixteen."

Andrea took a sip of her now cooled tea.

Millie stood and began pacing.

Surprised, Andrea took notice of her aunt's nervous energy. Aunt Millie had always seemed unflappable. Talking about Benjamin must be harder for her than she'd anticipated.

As she paced, Millie began her story again.

"When daddy discovered Benjamin had taken a shine to me he warned him to be respectful of me and my virtue. Benjamin agreed as long as daddy didn't forbid me from seeing him."

"Granddaddy has always been stuffy and gruff?" Andrea asked.

"Yes, he always protected me. It broke his heart when I moved to Atlanta. I'm getting off the subject."

"After I graduated from high school Benjamin pursued me in earnest while supporting my dream of becoming a writer."

"You knew you wanted to be a writer while you were in high school?" Andrea questioned.

"Yes, my teachers said I had a gift for storytelling. I shared my vision with Benjamin. He seemed to believe I could make it as a writer with encouragement and support."

"For the next three years Benjamin and I courted then one day he proposed. I was as surprised as any young woman can be at that time, but my surprise was replaced by joy when he placed an engagement ring on my finger. I knew then he was serious, his intentions were clear."

"So what happened?" Andrea asked.

"I don't know. The day of the wedding he left me waiting at the church without any explanation. I haven't heard from him since. I came to Atlanta for my writing career and moved on with my life." Millie concluded.

Andrea wiped tears off her cheeks. "I'm so sorry Aunt Millie. That's why you helped Abby and why you're helping me." She stated.

Millie went to sit next to Andrea.

"Yes, I'll do what I can to avoid you getting a broken heart." She said.

Andrea hugged Millie.

"I'm going home to talk to Quinton." She said.

Millie smiled.

"If I can be of further help let me know. I'm always here for you." Millie promised.

"I know, I love you Aunt Millie." Andrea said then left.

Driving back to Abby's she felt lighthearted and in control of her feelings.

When she pulled into the driveway Quinton was sitting on the porch swing waiting for her.

When she walked up to him he stood, pulled her into his arms then kissed her.

Andrea hoped he was going to make love to her. Her hopes were dashed.

"Don't ever run off like that again." He said sternly.

"Quinton... please." She begged.

She couldn't ask him to make love to her; it would be the same as admitting her love to him.

"Please what, Little One?" Quinton questioned.

She couldn't ask him to make love to her but she could show him.

Kissing him she left no doubt in his mind what she wanted.

Holding her away from him he said, "Abstinence."

"No, Quinton please don't." She said.

"I promised I'd do this for you." He reminded her.

"I'm not a strong as you, I can't stand the waiting." Andrea cried.

"It's only for a short time, Little One."

"It will seem like an eternity."

To distract her Quinton changed the subject.

"We need to discuss the wedding."

"Small and simple."

"With my mother? Not a chance."

"Quinton I don't want a big fuss."

"You'll get as little fuss as my mother can get away with."

"This is our wedding. We should be planning it, not your mother."

Quinton looked sheepish.

"I um, asked for her help."

"You did what? Without consulting with me. Quinton how could you?"

Andrea pulled out of his arms.

"I'm sorry I was trying to take some of the stress off of you and mother loves to plan parties…"

"I can plan my own wedding. If I need help I know how to ask for help. Why are men so dense?"

"Not having grown up with sisters I'm unsure how to deal with these situations."

"So naturally you turn to your mother. Is this to be a marriage or a business arrangement, Quinton?"

Andrea's tone told him he'd crossed the line.

"I apologize, Little One. In the future I'll consider your feelings before I make any decisions. You damn well know this will not be a business arrangement, it will be a legitimate, real marriage."

"With you consulting your mother on everything from the linens to how many children we'll have." Andrea thought waspishly.

Aloud she said. "Apology accepted. Thank you for the promise to consider my feelings in the future."

Quinton nodded in acknowledgment. He searched his heart for an answer to her anguish as to whether their marriage was to be a business arrangement or a legitimate marriage.

He knew she loved him but getting her to admit it was going to be difficult.

Andrea interrupted his thoughts.

"Quinton are you listening to me?" She asked irritably.

"I'm sorry Little One. I was lost in thought." He admitted.

"We need to start planning our wedding. I'm not leaving the arrangements up to your mother. I will have a say in my own wedding." Andrea said.

Quinton smiled.

"Yes, dear." He said sheepishly.

Going into the house they headed to Kyle's home office.

Kyle was sitting at his desk.

Andrea knocked on his door.

Looking up, Kyle smiled.

"Quinton, Andrea what can I do for you?" He asked.

"I'd like a pad of paper and some pens. Quinton and I are going to start planning our wedding." Andrea told him.

Kyle's smile grew wider.

"Anything I can help with?"

"Not that I can think of but we'll let you know." Quinton said.

Kyle nodded opening a drawer, he withdrew a couple pads of paper and several pens. He held them out to Andrea.

She took them saying, "Thank you."

"You're welcome." He responded.

Quinton and Andrea left the office to go to her room.

After they walked into the room Quinton closed the door.

Andrea sat cross-legged on the bed. Beginning to write, she stopped when her mind went blank.

Looking up at Quinton, tears welled up in her eyes.

"What's wrong, Little One?" He asked.

"My mind went blank. I can't think of anything." Andrea said.

"Little One you're trying too hard." Quinton reprimanded.

"Quinton, it isn't that difficult. I just have to imagine what I want for our wedding. How hard can it be?" Andrea shot at him.

We're supposed to be working on this together, Little One. You're taking too much on yourself." He told her.

Going to her, Quinton sat behind her on the bed.

Massaging her shoulders he encouraged her to relax.

His action didn't invite images of a wedding, it invited more erotic images.

Andrea's shoulders slumped, rolling forward.

"That's better, relax Little One." Quinton said.

She knew he meant to soothe her but the images that danced in her head were anything but soothing.

Quinton kneaded her neck muscles.

Andrea's breathing quickened, her pulse pounded, her heart raced, her mind cried I love you.

Quinton wasn't making love to her but he might as well have been.

Andrea scrambled off the bed away from him; turning to look at him, his puzzled expression made her giggle.

"Just what is so damn funny?" He asked.

"The look on your face." Andrea told him.

"You act like a scalded cat when I touch you, then run away from me and laugh about it." He snapped.

"I'm not laughing. The look on your face is priceless." Andrea said.

Quick as a cat he was in front of her pulling her to him.

Andrea sobered up very quickly.

There was something dangerously alluring about Quinton. She liked the way he made here feel.

Quinton bent his head to kiss her.

Andrea welcomed his warm, moist mouth on hers.

"Quinton." She gasped when he let her up for air.

He kissed her cheek, moving to her jaw line then to her neck.

Andrea tried to pull away, he held her closer to his heated body.

She could feel his manhood press against her belly.

"Quinton, please this is torture." She cried..

"Abstinence Little One." He reminded her.

"Damn abstinence. I'm not a virgin." She snapped.

"Patience Little One." He told her.

"I'm all out of patience." She said.

Quinton looked into her eyes, he was mesmerizing. Just looking into his eyes had a calming effect on her.

"You promised no forced abstinence after the wedding." She reminded him.

"I'm a man of my word." He assured her.

"Uh, I think we better go get something to eat, occupy our minds with something else." Andrea stuttered.

Quinton smiled.

"As you wish Little One." He agreed.

Hand in hand they walked downstairs, told Kyle they were leaving then went to eat.

CHAPTER SIX

In the next few days Abby and Ethan came home from the hospital.

Andrea was occupied helping her sister recover from childbirth and helping care for her newborn nephew.

A week after Abby came home from the hospital the phone rang.

Andrea answered it.

"Masterson residence, this is Andrea." She said.

"Andrea it's Eric." He said.

"Hi, Big Brother. How are you?" Andrea answered.

"This isn't a social call, Little Sister. Granddaddy has had a stroke. You and Abby need to come home." Eric said bluntly.

Andrea dropped the phone. She quickly picked it up.

"Granddaddy had a stroke?" She asked dumbly.

"Yes, the doctor expects him to fully recover but advised us to gather at his bedside." Eric told her.

"Okay, I'll tell Abby and we'll be home as soon as we can. See you soon. I love you." Andrea said.

"Love you, too." Eric said.

Andrea put the phone in the cradle then went to look for Abby. She found her in the nursery.

Abby smiled at her when she walked in. The smile left her lips when she saw the look on Andrea's face.

"What's wrong, Andie?" Abby asked.

"Eric just called. Granddaddy had a stroke, we need to get home as soon as possible." Andrea told her.

"I'll tell Agnes we need help packing for Shelby." Abby said.

"I'll call Kyle from the home office phone and explain what's going on." Andrea stated.

She left to call Kyle at work.

"K.M. Enterprises, Atlanta Division." Sally, the receptionist answered.

"Kyle Masterson, please." Andrea requested.

"Whom shall I say is calling?" Sally asked.

"Andrea Phillips." She said.

"One moment please."

There was a click then Andrea was connected to another line.

"Kyle Masterson's office, may I help you?" Caroline said.

"I need to talk to Kyle this is a family emergency." Andrea snapped.

"Whom shall I say is calling?" Caroline questioned.

"Andrea Phillips." She said irritably.

"I'm sorry you were kept waiting, Miss Phillips. I'll put you right through." Caroline apologized.

There was a click then she was connected to Kyle.

"Masterson." Kyle said gruffly.

"Hi Kyle, it's Andie." She said.

"Andie, so good to hear a friendly voice for a change." Kyle said.

"Unfortunately this isn't a social or pleasant call. Granddaddy had a stroke we need to fly to Shelby as soon as possible." Andrea told him.

"Call Dirk, my personal pilot, to set up the flight. I'll be home as soon as I can bring Quint up to speed and turn the reins over to him until we know how granddaddy is." Kyle said.

"Thanks Kyle, you don't know how much we appreciate this; see you soon." Andrea said.

She hung up, looked up the number for Kyle's pilot then dialed the number.

The phone rang twice before it was picked up.

"Mastersons, Dirk speaking." He said.

'Hi Dirk, it's Andrea Phillips." She said.

"Miss Andrea, how are you?" He asked.

"I'm fine, I'm sorry I don't have time to chat. I need you to get Kyle's plane ready to fly us to Shelby as soon as possible; we have a family emergency." She told him.

'I'm sorry to hear that Miss Andrea. I'll have Mr. Kyle's gal ready in a couple of hours." Dirk promised.

"That will work out fine, thanks Dirk. Give my best to your family." Andrea said.

After hanging up she went in search of her sister.

Finding Abby in the nursery, she said, "Dirk will have Kyle's plane ready in a couple of hours. Kyle is handing the reins over to Quinton so we can be on our way when the plane is ready." Andrea told her.

"Agnes and I can handle things here, go get yourself packed. I know you're anxious to get going on your own packing." Abby said.

Andrea nodded then left to go to her room.

Packing she realized her hands were shaking. She sat down.

Putting her head in her hands she let herself cry. How long she sat there she didn't know but suddenly strong arms were picking her up and she was being cradled against a strong, familiar smelling chest.

Looking up she was blinded by tears. "He can't die, he's all we have left." Andrea wailed.

"He's not going to die, Little One." Quinton assured her.

Andrea put her hand on the back of Quinton's neck drawing his mouth to hers.

Kissing him she begged him to love her.

~ 105 ~

Quinton fought the urge to take what she was offering. He knew it was due to in part to the grief of her grandfather's stroke.

"Little One stop." He ordered.

"Oh, God don't please. I need you." She begged.

He could give her a release but not in the traditional way.

Standing he carried her to the bed gently laying her down he lay beside her.

Andrea moaned glad to know she would finally have the release she longed for.

Instead of removing her clothes Quinton kissed her and sensuously rubbed her back.

Andrea lay still as Quinton's hands kneaded her tense muscles.

Quinton felt her relax under his attentiveness. He gently kissed her moist lips.

Andrea hesitantly kissed him. She didn't want to push him away.

While he kissed her, Andrea snuggled closer to him.

Kissing, their passion slowly grew to consume them.

Quinton moaned into Andrea's mouth.

His hands wandered to the snap on her jeans, releasing it. He also lowered the zipper.

Andrea shuddered. "Quinton?" She whispered.

His response was to continue undressing her.

She reciprocated by pulling the sweater he'd worn to work over his head.

Getting carried away they're lovemaking was pushed to the edge of consummation.

Using his hands and mouth he made love to Andrea, taking her close to climax.

"Quinton!" She cried.

His response was to kiss her until all thought left her,

By instinct her hands found their way to his manhood. Taking him in her hands Andrea caressed him.

Quinton reciprocated, loving her to near completion. He took her onto his lap, bending his head he took a hardened nipple into his mouth.

Andrea moaned, then cried out as he suckled at her swollen breast.

Wriggling in his lap she straddled his hips.

Quinton's vow of abstinence was quickly fading as their loving got out of control.

He tried to pull away but couldn't force himself away from the only woman he'd ever love.

Damning the consequences, he allowed himself to bring the love of his life to climax with his hands.

Surprised, Andrea rode the waves of pleasure as Quinton loved her.

He pulled her into his arms, kissing her while her heated body cooled.

She touched him, giving him pleasure the same way he had her.

Quinton's body shuddered when his release came.

"Andrea!' He called.

She smiled, increasing his pleasure as she touched and kissed him.

His release complete, Quinton pinned Andrea to the bed kissing her.

Andrea arched her body up to meet his.

"As much as I'd like to stay in bed with you all day you have to pack for your flight." Quinton said.

Andrea groaned. "I know. I'm not looking forward to seeing granddaddy after his stroke. He's gruff enough when he's well, I can't imagine him after his stroke." She told him.

"He's a strong man, he will heal quickly." Quinton assured her.

"I hope you're right." Andrea said.

Quinton rolled off the bed onto the floor to his feet. Holding out his hand, he helped Andrea off the bed

Pulling her to him, he kissed her.

"We better get dressed before Abby comes looking for you." He said amused.

Andrea blushed then nodded.

Gathering their clothing they dressed then began packing Andrea's bags for her trip to Shelby.

When they were finished Quinton helped Andrea carry her bags downstairs.

Abby was putting down her own bags in the entryway when Quinton and Andrea approached.

"I'm ready." Andrea said.

"We're almost ready just waiting for Kyle to get home." Abby told her.

"Where are Kerry, Kayla and Ethan?" Andrea asked.

"Agnes is going to visit her sister while we're in Shelby. Kerry and Kayla are helping her pack, Ethan is asleep in the nursery." Abby said.

"I can imagine how much help Kayla and Kerry are being."

Abby smiled.

"Their idea of packing is to stuff as many toys into a suitcase as they can."

Andrea laughed.

Kyle walked into the foyer.

"There you are, Quint. I wondered where you'd gone." He said.

"I came by to see how Andrea is doing." Quinton answered.

"I'm guessing she's well." Kyle responded.

Quinton smiled in response.

"Quinton." Andrea admonished.

He went to her, put his arms around her then kissed her.

Andrea squealed in delight.

"I don't want to break you two apart but we have to go." Abby said.

"I have to pack." Kyle reminded her.

He headed to their bedroom with Abby sheepishly following.

"Will you miss me?" Andrea asked.

In answer Quinton pulled her closer.

Whispering in her ear, he said, "I'll miss you as a rose misses the summer sun in winter, as I miss the bird's song in the winter months, I'll long for your kiss as a man too long separated from his soul mate."

Andrea's eyes welled up with tears.

"Oh, Quinton." She cried hugging him.

He held her to him as the tears ran their course.

When her tears subsided Quinton lead Andrea out onto the porch to the swing.

They sat there to wait for Kyle and Abby to come downstairs.

Half an hour later Andrea heard them come down the stairs.

"Kyle and Abby are ready, I have to get ready to go." She said.

"I know. I'll be ready when you get back." Quinton told her.

"Ready?" Andrea asked.

"To become your husband." He told her.

Andrea smiled, tears in her eyes.

"I'm looking forward to our wedding day." She admitted.

Quinton walked Andrea into the house.

"Are you ready to go?" Andrea asked.

"Yes, we just have to get the children." Abby said.

Kyle and Abby went to get their children.

Quinton turned Andrea to look at him.

"Take care of yourself, Little One. Come back to me soon." He commanded.

"Yes." Andrea answered.

He kissed her.

Andrea relished in his kiss.

Kyle cleared his throat.

Andrea pulled away looking down in embarrassment.

"Sorry." Kyle said.

"Big Brother you have the worst timing." Quinton said chuckling.

"Aunt Andie we're going to ride in daddy's plane to go see great Granddaddy Phillips." Kayla said excitedly.

"Yes, Kay Rae. Have you missed your great granddaddy?" Andrea asked.

"Yes, he tells us stories." Kayla told her.

"Mama told us he's in the hospital. Will he be in the hospital when we get there?" Kerry said.

"Yes, Kerr Bear." Andrea told him.

"Speaking of the hospital, we better get to the hangar so we can get our flight to Shelby." Kyle said.

Everyone told Quinton good-bye and Andrea promised to keep him updated on her grandfather's condition.

On the plane ride to Shelby Andrea worried that her grandfather's condition was worse than she'd been told.

When they landed she drew a sigh of relief, glad the trip was over. The next several minutes were taken up by gathering luggage and getting the children ready for the ride to their Shelby home.

Eric had brought Kyle and Abby's van to the airport so it would be waiting for them when they arrived from Atlanta.

Andrea's nerves were frayed by the time they pulled into her parents' driveway.

When she walked into the house and saw her father her legs almost collapsed.

"Is granddaddy...? Andrea began.

"No, Wren I'm just worried sorry to frighten you." Andrew said.

"How is granddaddy?" Andrea asked.

"They're stabilizing him. It's going to be a long road." Andrew told her.

"Has he been sick?" Andrea questioned.

"He's been complaining of not feeling well but refused to see his doctor."

"Granddaddy has always been stubborn. When can we see him?" Abby said.

"Your mother is going to call when the doctor gives the okay for visitors. You know I'm not good when it comes to dealing with someone who's sick." Andrew said.

Andrea and Abby groaned at their father's lack of ability to deal with his father's illness.

"Kyle and I are going to go home to settle the children in. Call us when you hear anything." Abby said.

"Tabi, please don't go. I'd rather you stay here." Andrew beseeched.

Abby walked over to hug him.

"We'll only be a phone call away. It's been a busy day and long flight, daddy. The children are tired. We love you. Call me when mama calls." Abby said.

Andrew nodded.

Kerry and Kayla walked to their grandfather to hug and kiss him.

"It's going to be okay, granddaddy." Kayla and Kerry said together.

Andrew hugged his grandchildren tightly and held out his arms for Ethan.

Kyle obediently took Ethan to him.

Andrew cuddled him close uncharacteristically showing affection toward his newborn grandson.

Andrea and Abby were shocked, Andrew didn't show affection easily.

Andrew pulled Kerry and Kayla to him cuddling them too.

Andrea guessed his change in behavior was due to his father's stroke.

The phone rang.

Andrea was closest so anxiously answered it.

"Hello." She said.

"Andrea, it's Mama, put your daddy on the phone please." Judy said.

"Yes mama." Andrea obeyed. "Daddy it's mama."

Andrew held out his newborn grandson to Abby.

She walked to her father taking her son.

Andrew gave Kayla and Kerry one quick hug then took the phone Andrea held out to him.

'Hello." He said.

"Dr. Hastings wants the family to come to the hospital." Judy told him.

"Is daddy…?" Andrew couldn't finish the sentence.

"No, no. Dr. Hastings just wants the family here so papa knows we're here for him." Judy told him.

Andrew let out a sigh of relief.

"Alright, we're on our way." He said.

Disconnecting the call he looked to his family.

"Dr. Hastings wants us to go to the hospital so daddy knows we're there." Andrew told them.

"I'll take my car." Andrea said.

There was a knock at the door.

Kyle went to answer it.

"Hello, Kyle. Is Andrea here?" Tony said.

Andrea couldn't believe what she was hearing.

She walked to the door.

"Tony, what are you doing here?" Andrea asked.

"I heard about your grandfather and came to see if you needed anything." Tony told her.

"Thanks, but no Tony. We're just leaving for the hospital." Andrea informed him.

"Excellent, I'll go with you." Tony stated.

"Tony, we don't need you..." She began.

"Wren, there's no need to be rude." Andrew told her.

Looking at her father in confusion, she relented.

"Fine, you can join us, Tony." Andrea said reluctantly.

Tony smiled smugly then kissed her cheek.

Andrea had a knot in the pit of her stomach. She had a feeling Tony was up to no good, only time would tell what it was.

"What the hell did you do that for?" She spat.

"Can't an old friend show affection?" Tony asked smiling.

"I suppose." Andrea answered suspiciously.

"Daddy, why is that man kissing Aunt Andie?" Kayla asked.

"He's an old friend. Friends do that sometimes." Kyle explained disapprovingly.

"Uncle Quinton will be mad." Kerry stated.

"That's why we can't tell Uncle Quinton." Kyle told him.

Kayla and Kerry gave their father a look that told him they didn't like that idea at all.

Kyle chuckled.

"What's so amusing, Darling?" Abby asked.

"Our children don't approved of Tony getting chummy with Andie." Kyle told her.

"I don't either." Abby whispered.

"Alright, we're ready to go. Kyle you take your family to the hospital. Eric will ride with me and Tony will drive Wren in her car." Andrew stated.

Andrea bristled at her father pairing her with Tony but didn't object.

Gathering outside everyone climbed into their respective cars then headed to the hospital.

Upon arriving at the hospital Andrew lead his family to his father's room.

Checking in at the nurses' desk he introduced everyone so the nurses would know who would be visiting Samuel during his convalescence.

"The children aren't allowed in Mr. Samuel's room." Twyla said.

"They can't go in for a few minutes?" Andrea asked.

"No, they're too young." Twyla responded.

"I want to see great granddaddy." Kayla whined.

"Kayla." Abby scolded.

"We'll alternate visiting granddaddy and keeping Kerry and Kayla occupied, and caring for Ethan." Andrea said.

"Good plan. You and I will take the first shift with the children." Tony said.

Andrea gave him a disdainful look.

"Wren and Tony take the children to the main lobby, someone will be down to relieve you in fifteen minutes." Andrew said.

"Yes, daddy." Andrea agreed.

She and Tony took the children to the main waiting room of the hospital.

"How are you, Andrea?" Tony asked.

"I'm fine, Tony." I'm engaged to Quinton." Andrea said abruptly.

"Engaged doesn't mean married." Tony said offhandedly.

"What does that mean?" Andrea snapped.

Tony only smiled in answer.

She groaned inwardly, that wasn't a good sign. He was up to something.

Tony engaged Kayla and Kerry in a game of eye spy.

Reluctantly they joined in the game all the while watching their suspicious aunt for any signs they could stop.

Kyle and Abby came to take over so Andrea and Tony could go up to the Intensive Care Unit to see Samuel. When Andrea saw all of the machines connected to her grandfather she became lightheaded, nearly fainting.

Tony was there to hold her up.

"You alright, Andie." He asked.

"Uh, yes just a little lightheaded for a moment." She responded.

He led her to a nearby chair, helping her to sit down.

"Are you okay, Wren?" Andrew asked solicitously.

"Yes, daddy. All the machines are making me a little nauseous." Andrea told him.

"They're to help sustain daddy's life while he recovers." Andrew told her.

"I know, I wasn't prepared so it was a shock." Andrea said.

"Daddy has made a noticeable improvement in the three days he's been here." Andrew said.

"Andrew, let's not get ahead of ourselves." Judy reminded him.

He looked at her.

She gave him the you know what I'm talking about look.

Andrea stood up and walked over to her grandfather.

Taking his hand in hers she said, "Granddaddy it's Wren. I hope you can hear me. I love you and want you to get well soon."

A tear trickled down her cheek.

Tony came to stand to next to her pulling her close to him.

In her moment of grief Andrea let him comfort her.

He smiled into her hair.

Awkwardly, it felt right to be in Tony's arms. Andrea didn't question why.

She stood holding Samuel's hand willing him back to good health.

Tony took advantage of her moment of weakness beginning the process of ingratiating himself to her.

Andrea didn't know how long she stood there but she felt eerily comforted by Tony's presence beside her.

"Wren." Andrew said.

She was startled out of her thoughts.

"Yes daddy." She answered.

"Twyla says we have to let daddy rest now, we have to leave." Andrew told her.

"Okay." Andrea said.

She leaned down to kiss her grandfather's cheek then hugged him.

Tony took her hand like he would a child, leading her out of the room.

Walking past Andrea's family, Tony led her out to her car.

Abby looked at them in consternation as they walked by.

Once in the car he asked, "Would you like to get something to eat?"

Realizing she was hungry Andrea said ""Yes, I'd like that."

Tony leaned over to kiss her.

Andrea didn't object. In her grief stricken state her mind wasn't functioning normally.

Given her grandfather's condition she was holding up remarkably well.

She didn't question Tony's relationship in her life. He was being a friend right now. She needed her friends.

Tony drove them to their favorite restaurant.

"Good evening Tony, Andie, it's been a while." Todd said.

"Hello Todd, I presume you've heard about Andrea's grandfather." Tony said.

"Yes, I'm sorry to hear about your grandfather Andie. If I can do anything please don't hesitate to ask." Todd replied.

"Thank you, Todd." Andrea said.

Todd nodded.

He grabbed two menus then led Tony and Andrea to an isolated table.

"Your server will be right with you." Todd said.

"Thank you." Tony said.

Todd nodded then walked away.

Tony took Andrea's hands in his.

Noticing her engagement ring he became angry but didn't show it.

"How are you holding up, Babe?" Tony asked.

Andrea had hated the endearment since Tony had begun using it.

"Tony, either call me Andrea or Andie but not Babe, it sounds like you're talking to a child." Andrea snapped.

Tony pulled her hands to his mouth kissing them.

"I'm sorry, Ba… Andie. Apparently your grandfather's illness has you more distressed than you're willing to admit." He said.

"It was difficult for me to see him like that, he's always been strong and self-sufficient." Andrea said.

"I'm here for you, whatever you need, I'm here." Tony told her.

"Thanks, Tony I appreciate that." She replied.

Their server arrived, took their drink order and left them to look over the menu.

Several minutes passed. Tony motioned for their server to take their order.

"Yes, sir what can I get for you"?" Mitch asked.

"I'll have the surf and turf and the lady will have the fish and chips, extra tartar sauce." Tony said.

"My pleasure." Mitch said.

He went to put in their order.

"You remembered to ask for extra tartar sauce." Andrea said surprised.

"We did date for four years. I'd like to think I learned something about you in that time." Tony grumbled.

"Tony." Andrea cajoled smiling.

She knew he couldn't resist when she coaxed him like that.

"Why can't I stay angry with you?" Tony asked rhetorically.

Andrea shrugged her shoulders.

"Have you been seeing anyone?" She asked.

"No one seriously. You're a tough act to follow." Tony admitted.

"Tony, you can't compare other women against me." Andrea said.

"When you've had the best the rest pale in comparison." Tony told her.

Andrea blushed.

"Anthony, you're embarrassing me." She said.

"At least I make you feel something." Tony said.

Andrea pulled her hands out of his, sitting back in her chair.

"What are you talking about? She asked.

"Obviously you didn't feel anything for me while we were dating… Suddenly you're engaged to Masterson. It all seems a little… odd." Tony said.

"I'll always have feelings for you, Tony." Andrea told him.

"Not enough to stay with me and take our relationship to the next level." Tony stated.

"We both knew our relationship had run its course, we couldn't go any further, Tony."

"We could have gotten engaged then when the time was appropriate then gotten married."

"And divorced when we both realized we'd made a mistake."

"Would it be a mistake, Andrea? Don't you love me?"

"Tony don't push it. We both know a marriage between us wouldn't have worked."

"Andrea."

Mitch appeared with their food, setting it down in front of them.

"Enjoy your supper. If I can get you anything else let me know." He said.

"A different supper companion." Andrea thought.

Aloud she said, "Extra napkins."

"Alright." Mitch said.

Tony reached over to take Andrea's hand in his.

She wasn't ready to forgive him quite that easily so moved her hand to her lap.

His anger didn't show on his face. He wouldn't let Masterson steal his woman.

Formulating a plan, he smiled sheepishly pulling his hand back.

Mitch brought the extra napkins, left them on the table then walked away.

Tony and Andrea ate silently.

Andrea stewed over Tony's assumption she would have agreed to marry him without love, on her side anyway.

Tony plotted his revenge against Quinton stealing his woman.

Silently agreeing they were finished with their meal, they stood to leave only stopping to pay their bill.

Awkwardly Tony took Andrea's hand as they walked to her car.

Surprisingly she didn't object. Wondering what was wrong with her, Andrea shook her head to clear the cobwebs that seemed to have lodged themselves there.

Tony opened the car door for her, assisting her in. When he leaned in to kiss her Andrea turned her head, forcing him to give her a chaste kiss on the cheek.

"Andrea." He chastised.

"Take me home, Tony." Andrea snapped.

He walked around to the driver's side, opened the door, stepped in and drove to her parents' house.

Silently Andrea fumed at the thought that Tony presumed they could begin where they left off.

She was engaged to another man. What was Tony thinking?

"Andrea, I'm sorry. What kind of man would I be if I didn't try to win you back?" Tony asked.

She hadn't heard him, she was lost in her thoughts.

Tony looked at her, she hadn't heard him. All the better.

Pulling into her parents' driveway, Tony set his mind to do whatever it took to make her his wife.

Andrea unsnapped her seatbelt, then opened the door to go into the house.

Tony didn't try to stop her, he followed her into the house.

"Where did you two go?" Andrew asked.

"We went to eat supper." Tony told him apologetically.

Andrew smiled unaware of his daughter's engagement, he was happy Andrea was seeing Tony again.

"No need to be apologetic. It's nice to see you two together again." Andrew said.

"Daddy." Andrea warned.

~ 121 ~

"Andie, is that an engagement ring I see?" Eric asked.

Andrea lifted up her left hand to show her ring to Eric.

"Yes, Quinton and I are engaged." She said without apology.

"When did you get engaged? Why didn't you tell us?" Judy asked.

"Quinton wanted to fly to Shelby to ask daddy's permission but he was busy with work." Andrea said embarrassed.

"Too busy to take the time to visit his future in-laws? That doesn't bode well for your future together, Wren." Andrew said.

"I'm sorry, daddy. I'll ask him to fly to Shelby the first chance he gets." Andrea said.

"Speaking of Quinton I need to check in with him. If you'll excuse me I'm going to call him." Kyle said.

"I'd like to talk to him when you're finished." Andrea said.

Kyle nodded as he went to use the phone extension in Andrew's office.

"Nana we're hungry." Kerry said.

"What would you like to eat?" Judy asked.

"Can we look in the kitchen?" Kayla asked.

"Of course." Judy said.

"I'll help." Andrea offered.

She followed her mother, niece and nephew into the kitchen.

"Look in the pantry children." Judy said.

"Mama, I'm confused about Tony." Andrea said.

"I know dear. I assumed that's why you came to help us look for something to eat." Judy told her.

Andrea looked puzzled.

"You've already eaten supper, you couldn't possibly be hungry." Judy said smiling.

Andrea smiled.

"Am I that obvious?" She asked.

"Only to me and possibly Abby." Judy replied.

"What am I supposed to do mama? I don't love Tony." Andrea said.

"You do love Quinton." Judy stated.

Andrea nodded.

"I know he has feelings for me but I'm not sure if it's love."

"Have you asked him?"

"Mama, I'm bold but not that bold. What if he says no?"

"You won't know unless you ask."

"Unfortunately my fear of rejection overrides my boldness."

Judy patted Andrea on the back then hugged her.

"Of all the traits you could have inherited from me you and Abby had to inherit my fear of rejection and expressing your love to the man you love and fear of commitment."

"You have a fear of commitment and rejection?"

"Lord no, not anymore. I've been married to your father too long. When I was a young lady I feared letting any man get close because my father abandoned us."

"Mama that doesn't make any sense. I don't recall daddy ever showing you affection."

"Your father shows affection in public with his teasing."

"I'm sorry, I missed something."

"For example, his endearment for Abby, Tabi because her name is Tabitha. He may be teasing but it's his own special nickname that no one else uses. You're Wren because your middle name is Renay."

"Oh, I see, daddy doesn't show it he says it."

Judy smiled.

"Yes."

"Nana, we found what we want to eat." Kayla and Kerry called from the pantry.

"Okay bring it out." Judy told them.

Kerry and Kayla each carried two boxes of Homestyle Bakes from the pantry.

"Mm those look good." Andrea said.

Kerry smiled.

"I want this one and this one." He said holding them out to Judy.

"I want this one and this one ." Kayla said mimicking her brother.

Andrea could see a fight beginning.

"Did you know there are several kinds to choose from? She asked.

Kayla and Kerry shook their heads.

Andrea took the two boxes Kerry held reading them. She then took the two boxes Kayla held reading them.

"There are three different kinds here. You both picked one that's different from the others and you both picked one that's the same as another." She told them.

Kerry and Kayla stood listening to her.

"We'll make the one that's the same." Judy said.

"Okay." Kayla and Kerry said in unison.

Andrea put the ones that were different in the pantry.

Going to help her mother she felt a heaviness in her heart.

After preparing the boxed meal Andrea wandered into her father's office where she found Kyle ending his conversation with Quinton.

"I have something I'd like to talk to you about when I return to Atlanta." Kyle said.

Andrea couldn't hear Quinton's response but by Kyle's reaction she assumed it was amusing.

"Yes, Little Brother it is good news. Your fiancée just walked in. I'm guessing if I don't give Andrea the phone she's going to take it from me." Kyle told him.

"Kyle." Andrea warned.

He walked to her, gave the cordless phone to her then kissed her cheek and walked out.

"Hello." Andrea said.

"Hello Little One how is your grandfather?" Quinton asked.

"Oh Quinton it's awful. He's hooked up to all sorts of machines, he's unconscious. I'm not altogether sure he knows anyone is there when we visit." Andrea wailed.

"Little One he's had a stroke. At his age it's going to take more time to recover. Don't give up hope, think positive. Granddaddy will pull through." Quinton soothed.

"I wish I had your optimism. He looks so helpless. I want to do something but I don't know what I can do." Andrea said.

"Be there for him, pray for him." Quinton said.

Andrea sighed. That's why she loved Quinton, he saw the bright side of situations.

"What have you been doing?" She asked.

"Working. I'm surprised Kyle has any time for a life the way I've been fielding problems since he left this afternoon." Quinton said.

"I'm sorry this is twice as hard on you." Andrea said apologetically.

"Andrea, don't apologize if I weren't comfortable with the situation I'd say so." Quinton said.

She knew he was serious, he rarely used her given name.

"I miss you." Andrea sighed.

Quinton chuckled.

"I miss you as well Little One. We'll be together soon. When your grandfather is recovered enough you'll come home, we'll get married and begin our life together." He told her.

"I long for the day I become your wife." Andrea confided.

Quinton wasn't surprised by the admission.

"Soon Little One, very soon." He told her.

Andrea looked at her watch.

"It's late, you have to work in the morning and I'm tired." She said.

"I'll say good night and eagerly await your next call." Quinton said.

"Good night, Quinton. I'll call you tomorrow." Andrea said.

"Sleep well Little One." He wished.

The line was disconnected.

"I love you, Quinton." Andrea said to the buzzing in her ear.

She put the phone on the cradle.

Tony walked into the office smiling.

"I have to go Andrea. Will you walk me to my car?" He said.

Unable to be rude to a guest Andrea said, "Of course."

Tony took her hand, leading her out of the office.

Andrea tried to pull her hand out of his, he refused to let her.

Walking into the living room Tony said, "I'm sorry I have to leave."

"Thank you for being here, Tony." Judy said.

He let go of Andrea's hand, walked to Judy and kissed her cheek.

"It's my honor, mama. I'll always be here for Andrea and the rest of you." Tony said.

Andrea groaned inwardly.

Tony walked back to her, took her hand again and walked outside.

"Tony I don't know what you're up to but I'm sure it's no good. Drop the act." Andrea snapped.

"Andrea I'm hurt. I'm being a friend, genuinely concerned about you." Tony said.

"You don't have an ulterior motive?" Andrea asked.

"No, what would make you think that?" He asked.

"Oh, I don't know. The fact you're being overly friendly." She said angrily.

"Andie, you're too sensitive. "I'm just being a friend, helping you through this difficult time." Tony told her.

"Uh huh. That's all it better be." Andrea warned.

They had reached Tony's car.

"Am I allowed to have a hug or is that suspect in your opinion?" Tony asked.

"Hugs are allowed." Andrea said.

Tony took Andrea in his arms hugging her..

The hug wasn't overly affectionate or long. Andrea was relieved.

Letting her go Tony kissed her cheek.

"Call if you need anything." He said.

"Thanks Tony." Andrea said.

"What are friends for?" Tony asked rhetorically.

He walked to the driver's side of the car, opened the door, stepped in settled into the driver's seat then drove away.

Andrea watched as his taillights faded into the darkness.

Walking back to the house she wondered again why her relationship with Tony hadn't worked out.

When she walked into the living room her family looked at her expectantly.

"Good night everyone." Andrea said.

"Wren." Andrew said sternly.

"Yes daddy." She said.

"Sit down, we need to talk." He told her.

"Yes sir." Andrea replied.

She went to sit next to her mother on the sofa.

"We know Quinton, he wouldn't avoid telling us about your engagement." Judy said gently.

Andrea's face drained of color.

"I'm sorry, mama I don't know what to say." Andrea said.

"Start with why you didn't call us to tell us you'd gotten engaged." Judy said.

"I'd just gotten out of a four year relationship, I didn't want you to think badly of me. You have to admit my relationship with Quinton would have come as a surprise." Andrea told her.

Andrew snorted.

"Andrew." Judy warned.

Andrea looked at her father. Nothing in his expression gave her a clue as to what he was thinking.

Mama can we talk about this tomorrow? I'm exhausted and unable to think clearly." she said.

"Of course, child. Sleep well." Judy dismissed.

Andrea leaned over kissed her mother's cheek, stood up then went to kiss her father good night.

She went to her room to get ready for bed.

Several minutes later there was a knock on the door.

"Come in." Andrea said.

Abby opened the door poking her head in.

"You may be able to fool mama and daddy but you can't fool me, Andie. What's going on? She asked.

"Nothing." Andrea said.

"Andrea, I'm not just your sister, I'm your twin. I feel what you feel." Abby reminded her.

"Oh, all right. Seeing Tony again has me confused." Andrea admitted.

"Confused how?"

"About my feelings for him."

"Do you love him?"

"I don't know."

"Andie."

"Abby, it's late and I'm tired."

"Okay, I'll let it go for now but we have to talk about it some time."

"I know, good night."

Abby hugged her sister then walked out.

Andrea settled into bed falling into a fitful sleep

CHAPTER SEVEN

Awaking the next morning she didn't feel rested.

Not wanting to deal with her family's questions she took her time getting ready for her day.

Taking herself to task for her cowardice she went down to greet her family.

"Good morning, everyone." She said cheerily.

"Good morning, Andrea. How did you sleep?" Judy asked.

"Not very well, mama." Andrea replied.

"I'm not surprised. Keeping secrets from your family isn't good for a healthful sleep." Andrew said.

"Daddy I'm sorry, I wasn't trying to keep anything from you. I wasn't sure how you'd react to my engagement so soon after my break up." Andrea said.

"Wren we're your family, we won't judge you. We'll support any decision you make." Andrew told her.

Andrea was taken aback at her father's attitude.

Her surprise must have shown on her face because her brother added his thoughts.

"Daddy has had to adjust to changing times, Andie. He realizes relationships are different today than they were when he was young." Eric told her.

Andrea smiled.

"We managed to pull you into the twenty-first century daddy." Andrea said happily.

"Reluctantly but he's here." Eric said chuckling.

"Son, shouldn't you be getting to work?" Andrew asked.

"Yes sir." Eric said smiling.

"Don't let the door hit you on the backside on the way out." Andrew said returning the smile.

Eric did something he hadn't done in years. He went over to hug and kiss his father.

"I love you daddy." He said.

Andrew clapped Eric on the shoulder. "I love you son. Get to work." He said gruffly.

Andrea looked at her mother.

Judy shook her head telling Andrea not to question the interaction.

Nodding her head, Andrea said, "Daddy, I have more news to tell you."

Andrew looked at her.

"I'm listening, Wren." He said.

"I've decided to go back to school to get my degree." Andrea told him.

Andrew looked relieved.

"I'm glad to hear that. What will you be studying?" He replied.

"Computers." Andrea answered.

"Does your choice have anything to do with your fiancée's career?" Eric questioned.

"I thought you were going to work." Andrea said pointedly.

"I was until you said you had more news." Eric said.

"Go to work brother dear, there's no more news to hear." Andrea told him.

Eric kissed and hugged his mother and sister then left for work.

"I'm going to the hospital after breakfast would you like to join me Wren?" Andrew said.

"Yes, daddy." Andrea said.

"Judy my dear will you be joining us?" Andrea asked.

"No, Andrew I thought I'd stay home and pretend I have better things to do." Judy said sarcastically.

Andrew stood up, walked to his wife and put his arms around her.

"Forgive me my dear. Daddy's illness has made me boorish." Andrew apologized.

"You're forgiven. I can't stay angry with you." Judy said.

Andrea liked seeing her parents' affection. She didn't remember a time when they weren't affectionate.

Would she ever have that or was she destined to be torn between two men?

Andrea shook her head to dispel the thought.

What was wrong with her? She loved Quinton, had loved him from almost the moment they met.

There was a knock at the door.

Andrea looked toward the door. Anthony stood there. She went to answer it.

"Tony, what are you doing here?" She asked.

"I came to take you to the hospital." Tony told her.

He kissed her cheek.

"Anthony." She reprimanded.

"Just a friendly kiss on the cheek." He explained.

"I'm going to the hospital with my parents." Andrea told him.

"I took the day off from work to spend with you." Tony said.

"You shouldn't have done that."

"It's one of the perks of being your own boss. You get to take time off when you want to."

"Doesn't that hurt business?"

"No, I have employees who can cover for me when I need the occasional day off."

Andrea wondered how often he needed the occasional day off.

She knew that was petty but something was nagging at her about Tony but she couldn't put her finger on it.

She stood aside to let him enter the kitchen.

"Good morning." Tony said.

"Good morning, young man." Andrew greeted.

"Good morning." Judy said guardedly.

"How is everyone this morning?" Tony asked.

"As well as can be expected." Andrea said.

"Is there anything I can do to help?" Tony questioned.

"No." Andrea said irritably.

Tony lifted her chin to make her look at him.

"Andie." He coaxed.

"Don't do that, Tony." Andrea begged.

"Do what?" Tony asked.

"Treat me like a child." Andrea said through clenched teeth.

"Andie, I'm being a friend. Friends help one another during difficult times." Tony told her.

"I don't need your kind of help." She said under her breath.

"Wren offer Tony some coffee." Andrew said.

"He isn't staying." Andrea said.

"I told you I have the day off, Andie. Why won't you accept my help?" Tony said.

"Your help comes with strings attached." Andrea stated.

"Am I that questionable?" Tony asked.

"Yes." Andrea said bluntly.

"How can I prove to you I don't have ulterior motives?" Tony questioned.

"Stop trying to ingratiate yourself to me and my family."

"Ingratiate myself? Is that what you think I'm doing?"

"Yes, I'd appreciate it if you'd stop."

"I won't stop being a friend, Andie."

"Suit yourself. Remember there's nothing to be gained from what you're doing."

"I didn't expect there to be."

Andrea snorted.

Going to the table she took her coffee cup off the top then went to pour herself more coffee.

"Would you like some coffee, Tony?" Judy offered.

"Yes, please." Tony accepted.

Judy took a cup out of the cupboard then poured coffee into it and took it to him.

She knew from the years Andrea dated him Tony drank his coffee black.

"We have to leave for the hospital soon." Andrew reminded them.

"Do you mind if I tag along?" Tony asked.

"Not at all, the more support the better." Andrew stated.

Andrew threw her father a "what are you thinking?" look.

Andrew shrugged.

Andrea looked at him as if to say "thanks a lot daddy" sarcastically.

He chuckled.

The kitchen door from the living room opened.

"Good morning." Abby said.

"Tabi, what are you doing here so early?" Andrew questioned.

"We came to work out a visitation schedule for granddaddy." Abby told him.

"We can work out a rotating schedule, that way someone is with granddaddy during the day." Andrea said.

"I'll leave the schedule up to you ladies, it's your area of expertise." Andrew said.

"We'll be in your office." Andrea told him.

She and Abby left to go to Andrew's office.

Once there and the door was closed Abby asked, "What is Tony doing here?"

Using air quotes Andrea said, "Being a friend."

"Seriously, that's his story?" Abby questioned.

"Yes, he claims he doesn't expect anything." Andrea told her.

"Yeah, right. What's he really want?" Abby said.

"I don't know yet but I'm sure he'll let me know soon enough." Andrea responded.

"You don't trust him do you?"

"Yes, Abby I do. Do I have stupid written across my forehead? Of course I don't trust him, he followed me to Atlanta for heaven's sake."

"What kind of sister would I be if I didn't watch out for you?"

"I know you're taking care of me but I'm a grown woman. Let me take care of Tony."

Abby gave her a look that said "You know I can't do that."

Andrea smiled.

Silently they began working on the rotating visitation schedule for their grandfather.

An hour later Andrea and Abby walked into the kitchen with their schedule.

"Daddy you need to invest in a computer." Andrea told him.

"What do I need with a blasted computer?" Andrew grumbled.

"It would make your life easier." Andrea told him.

"Seems to complicate life more if you ask me." Andrew shot back.

Andrea hugged her father.

"Here we thought we dragged you into the twenty-first century." She said laughing.

"Don't let him fool you. He has computers at The Pub. Eric discussed the prospect with him long ago, convincing your father it would save him time and money." Judy said.

"Daddy!" Andrea and Abby said excitedly.

Andrew laughed.

"My dear must you give away all my secrets." He joked.

Judy smiled.

"Only to preserve family harmony." She stated unable to stop smiling.

"We have the visitation schedule ready for your approval daddy." Andrea said.

She handed the paper to Andrew.

He looked it over.

Tony looked over his shoulder.

"I don't see my name on the schedule." He said.

Andrea let out a breath irritably.

"Why would we put you on the schedule?" She snapped.

"So I can help." Tony said matter of factly.

"Anthony." Andrea said through clenched teeth.

"Wren, Tony is being a friend." Andrew reminded her.

"Yes sir." Andrea conceded.

"May I see the schedule?" Tony asked.

Andrew handed him the paper.

Tony looked the schedule over.

"I can stop by the hospital to take a shift after work. Andie, if you go back to the hospital to relieve Kyle after the last shift we can have supper together which of course I'll bring with me." He suggested.

Andrea started to object then closed her mouth when Andrew gave her a subduing look.

She looked at her father as if to say, "Really?"

"Your suggestion will work out well, Tony. Daddy will have someone with him all day and we'll be kept updated on his condition." Andrew said.

"Are you ready to go to the hospital daddy?" Andrea asked.

"Yes Wren. Judy my dear are you ready?" Andrew said.

"Andrew I haven't finished cleaning the kitchen." Judy said.

"I'll clean the kitchen, Mama." Abby offered.

"Thank you, Abby. I'll get my things Andrew." Judy said walking out to get her purse and a sweater.

Andrea and Andrew followed her out. Tagging along behind was Tony.

Andrea sighed inaudibly regretting her father's decision to allow him to be part of her grandfather's support team.

When they were walking up to the nurse's entrance Tony took Andrea's hand in his as though it were the most natural thing in the world.

Andrea did her best to ignore his presence, instead focusing her attention on her grandfather's recovery.

Walking up the nurses' station on Samuel's floor. Andrew addressed the nearest nurse.

"How's my father?" He asked.

"Resting comfortably. We'll be starting physical and occupational therapy soon." Twyla said.

"We've made up a rotating schedule our family will be using to visit so daddy won't be alone during the day." Andrew told her.

"We're hoping it will help keep his spirits up and help him recover quicker." Andrea said.

"Any time the family is involved in the recovery process is a tremendous benefit to the patient." Twyla said.

"Daddy you and mama go in to see granddaddy first. Tony and I will go to the cafeteria for coffee." Andrea said.

Andrew nodded.

Andrea and Tony went to the cafeteria.

"How are you Andie?" Tony asked.

"I'm fine, Tony." Andrea answered shortly.

Tony smiled to himself.

"Is there anything I can do for you?" He asked.

"No, thank you." Andrea said absently.

Tony took her hands in his.

"Babe, I'm here for you. What can I do for you?" He said.

"Tell me granddaddy's going to recover." Andrea told him carelessly.

"Babe, granddaddy is going to pull through, he's tough as nails." Tony assured her.

Andrea wasn't aware Tony had gone back to calling her babe her grief was so deep.

She clasped his hands as if they were a lifeline.

Tony took advantage of her vulnerability.

He leaned across the table to kiss her.

Andrea didn't object, it felt natural to her.

~ 139 ~

The kiss wasn't like the ones Quinton gave her, just a short, unromantic touch of the lips.

Over the next few weeks Andrea and her family visited her grandfather in the hospital and helped him in his convalescence.

She kept Quinton updated on his recovery process, although her phone calls were short and awkward.

Quinton became suspicious so called Abby.

"Abby what's going on with Andrea?" Quinton questioned.

"She's worried about granddaddy." Abby said evasively.

"You can't tell me." Quinton stated.

"Of course." Abby told him.

"Andrea is with you." He guessed.

"That's right." Abby responded.

Quinton swore under his breath.

"Is it Caldoni?"

"Why, yes it is?"

"What the hell is he doing to her?"

"I don't know yet."

"You will keep me updated."

"Absolutely."

"I look forward to hearing from you."

"Count on it."

Quinton hung up.

He'd have to make the wedding arrangements on his own and possibly plan a trip to Shelby.

"Is everything all right Abby?" Andrea asked.

"Yes, just a friend inquiring about granddaddy." Abby lied easily.

Andrea smiled.

"It's nice to know our friends are there to support us." She said.

"Speaking of friends, where's Tony?" Eric asked.

"I don't know. He said something about making special plans." Andrea told him.

"Odd, he's been hanging around like a love sick puppy for the last few weeks. All of a sudden he's nowhere to be found." Eric commented.

"He hasn't been acting like a love sick puppy." Andrea snapped.

"Andie, he's always hanging around. He doesn't leave until you kick him out because you're tired." Eric said.

"He's being a friend." Andrea defended.

Eric opened his mouth to respond, Judy cleared her throat to get his attention.

Seeing the look on his mother's face, Eric gave up the urge to argue with his sister.

Andrea stood up.

"I'm going for a walk." She said.

Taking her cell phone from the stand she walked out.

As she walked she dialed a familiar number.

"Hello." Tony said.

"Hi." Andrea said.

"What's wrong?" Tony asked.

"Why does anything have to be wrong? Can't I just call a friend?" Andrea asked.

"Of course, what are you doing?" Tony said.

"Walking, the walls were starting to close in on me." Andrea told him.

'Would you like to go out for coffee?"

"I'd like something a little stronger."

"I'll meet you at The Pub in ten minutes."

"Okay see you then."

~ 141 ~

Andrea hung up then headed toward The Pub.

When she arrived Colleen greeted her.

"Hi, Andie how are you?" She asked.

"All right, Colleen. How are you?" Andrea asked.

"I'm great, pregnant again." Colleen answered.

"How nice for you." Andrea said.

"We're excited, hoping for a girl this time." Colleen told her.

Andrea almost broke down then.

"I'm waiting for Tony, I'll wait at the bar." She said.

Andrea walked to the bar.

"Diet Coke, please." She requested.

Several minutes passed before she felt Tony's hands on her shoulders.

He leaned over to kiss her cheek.

"Hi." He greeted smiling.

"Hello." Andrea said.

"What's wrong?" Tony asked concerned"

"I'm a little down." Andrea responded.

"May I suggest something?" Tony queried.

"Please, I'm open to suggestions." She said.

"We have a few drinks and talk."

"That's it? That's your suggestion?"

"You'd be surprised how just talking can help solve problems and make you feel better."

"I suppose we could try that."

"All right what's on your mind?"

"Granddaddy's recovery. He seems to be improving but rejects our help."

"That's a normal part of recovery. He believes he can do it on his own then gets angry when his body won't cooperate."

"It's very frustrating. I don't know if he's capable of doing the therapy or if he's refusing to out of obstinacy."

"Possibly a little of both."

Andrea and Tony talked late into the night.

She had drinks while Tony had soft drinks knowing he'd be driving her home.

When Tony parked along the curb in front of her parents' house Andrea was decidedly tipsy.

Andrea leaned over to Tony.

"Are you going to come in?" She asked in a loud whisper.

Tony chuckled.

"I don't think so. You need to get your sleep." He said.

"I wasn't suggesting we sleep." Andrea giggled.

"Andrea." Tony reprimanded.

Undeterred, Andrea said, 'You wanted to take our relationship to the next level."

"I changed my mind, Andie. Go into the house and go to bed." Tony commanded.

Andrea reacted as though he'd slapped her.

She fumbled for the door handle, pulled on it and when the door opened she stumbled out of the car up to the house.

Opening the door she found her father waiting for her.

"Hello, daddy." She said in a loud whisper.

"Andrea ." Andrew said sternly.

"Am I in trouble?" She asked slurring her words.

"Where have you been?" Andrew asked.

"Didn't Colleen call you?" Andrea said.

"She did. Why were you at The Pub?" Andrew questioned.

"Having drinks with a friend."

"Would that friend be Tony?"

'Yes sir."

"You must remember you're an engaged woman, Wren."

"I've broken my engagement, daddy."

Andrew's face showed his shock.

"Have you talked to Quinton?" He asked.

"No, I just decided tonight." Andrea said.

"May I ask why?" Andrew said.

"It's personal, daddy. If you'll excuse me I'd like to go to bed." She told him.

Andrew nodded his head in dismissal.

Andrea walked up to her room. Once there she closed the door, walked to her dresser and removed her engagement ring.

Tears started trickling down her cheeks.

Her grandfather's stroke, growing confusion over her feelings for Tony were all too much for her.

Andrea climbed in bed fully dressed crying herself to sleep.

She woke up the next morning her head throbbing trying to recall the previous night's events.

She remembered some things but others she was uncertain about.

Climbing out of bed she put her hands to her head groaning.

As she walked to the bathroom she undressed. Stepping into the shower Andrea adjusted the water temperature.

Noticing her engagement ring was missing she panicked.

What happened to it? Where could it be?

She vaguely remembered talking to her father when she returned home early this morning.

Did she really tell him she'd broken her engagement? Had she called Quinton?

"I have to talk to daddy." Andrea said to herself.

She quickly finished her shower and despite her hangover she forced herself to go talk to her father.

"Good morning, Wren." Andrew greeted.

Andrea put her hands to her head, closing her eyes.

"Not so loud, daddy. Can I talk to you?" She asked.

"Yes, come to my office." Andrew said.

Andrea followed her father to his office, closing the door behind them.

"What happened last night?" She asked.

"You don't remember?" Andrew questioned.

"It's all a little fuzzy. I do remember telling you I broke my engagement. I don't remember whether I talked to Quinton or not." Andrea said.

"To my knowledge you have not talked to your fiancée. My advice is that you not call Quinton." Andrew told her.

"Are you out of your mind, why would I call Quinton?" Andrea questioned.

"You were quite sure it's what you wanted this morning." Andrew said.

"Daddy I'd been drinking. I fully intend to honor my commitment to Quinton."

"Wren, do you love him?"

"Daddy…"

"It's a simple enough question, Wren."

"Yes daddy, I love him."

"You need to go to him."

"I can't I have obligations here."

"You have an obligation to Quinton."

"He understands, daddy. I talk to him every day."

"Wren, I only want you to be happy."

"I know daddy. I am happy. I'm going to the hospital."

Andrea walked over to her father, kissed his cheek then went to get her things to go to the hospital.

When she arrived on her grandfather's floor she could hear him speaking gruffly to the nurse.

"Damn it young woman, I can take a bath by myself." Samuel said slowly.

Andrea smiled walking more briskly to her grandfather's room.

"Granddaddy!" She reprimanded.

Samuel looked at her.

"Wren, I'm capable of giving myself a bath." He said gradually.

"Please humor your nurse, granddaddy. She has a job to do." Andrea said.

Samuel snorted.

"Mr. Phillips I promise I'll give you a bath as quickly as I can." Nicole said.

"I'll come back in fifteen minutes." Andrea said.

"Thank you, Miss Phillips." Nicole said.

Andrea went down to the cafeteria.

Alone she thought about what would have compelled her to tell her father that she was breaking her engagement.

Thinking she tried again to recall the previous night's events.

Her cell phone rang.

She looked at it.

Groaning, she pushed the connect button.

"Hello Tony." Andrea said.

"How's my favorite girl this morning?" He asked.

"Hung-over." Andrea said irritably.

Tony chuckled.

"I'm not surprised. You had quite a bit to drink last night." He said.

"Tony, what happened last night?" She asked.

"You don't remember." He stated.

"If I did I wouldn't be asking."

"We talked about your grandfather's stroke, how you've been feeling, you agreed to let me help you get through this difficult time in your life, nothing unusual."

"Did I say anything about breaking my engagement?"

"No, you were adamant about honoring your commitment to Masterson."

Andrea let out a sigh of relief.

"Andie, are you okay?"

"Yes, just tired. Tony I have to go I'll talk to you later."

"Okay, I'll always be here for you Andie."

"Thanks Tony."

Andrea hung up.

She finished her coffee then went up to her grandfather's room.

"How are you feeling granddaddy?" Andrea asked.

"I'd feel better it they'd let me go home to recuperate." Samuel grumbled.

"You need round the clock care, granddaddy. It's better for you to be here." Andrea told him.

"I'd rather be home. Where's your young man?" Samuel said.

Andrea thought her grandfather mistakenly thought Tony was her "young man."

In order not to upset him further she said, "He's working, he'll be by later."

~ 147 ~

Samuel smiled.

"Has he proposed? You should be thinking about settling down, Wren. I'd like to see my great grandchildren before I go to meet your grandmother." He said.

"Uh, yes he proposed. I haven't given him my answer." Andrea lied easily.

"Wren, I'm not getting any younger. This stroke was a wakeup call for all of us. You tell that young man yes." Samuel ordered.

"Uh, granddaddy…" Andrea began.

At the look on Samuel's face she couldn't tell him she and Tony weren't romantically involved.

"Yes sir." Andrea agreed.

Samuel smiled then settled back to watch TV.

Andrea sat silently contemplating the consequences of the promise she'd made to her grandfather.

What was she going to tell Tony?

"Oh, by the way I told my grandfather you proposed but I haven't agreed to marry you."

"Granddaddy thinks we're getting married."

Any scenario she mulled over in her head ended with Tony laughing at her.

Abby walked in to relieve her.

"Hi, granddaddy, how are you feeling?" She asked.

"Better now that I know Wren's future is secure." Samuel said.

Abby looked at Andrea.

"Excuse us granddaddy." Andrea said.

She led Abby out of the room into an empty waiting room.

"What's going on?" Abby asked.

"Granddaddy thinks Tony and I are getting married." Andrea answered.

"Where would he get that idea?" Abby asked.

"He was being difficult and asked about my young man. Naturally I assumed he was talking about Tony and told him Tony proposed but I haven't accepted his proposal." Andrea told her.

"Well at least you didn't accept the proposal." Abby said.

"I promised granddaddy I would." Andrea admitted.

"Andrea! What are you going to do when he discovers you're engaged to Quinton?"

"I haven't thought that far ahead."

"Now would be a good time to think about it."

"I know, I've made a mistake but I can't go back in there and tell granddaddy I lied, it would break his heart."

"No good ever comes from lying, Andie."

"I'm aware of that, Abby. Please don't say anything."

"I'll keep your secret for now but you have to tell granddaddy the truth."

"I will as soon as he's strong enough."

Andrea hugged Abby then walked out.

Not knowing where else to go she went to Tony's office.

"May I help you?" Brooke asked smiling.

"I'd like to see Mr. Caldoni." Andrea said.

"May I tell him who wishes to see him?" Brooke said.

"Andrea Phillips." She said.

"Of course, Miss Phillips. I should have recognized you from the picture Tony has on his desk." Brooke told her.

Andrea blushed from embarrassment.

Brooke picked up the phone, punching in Tony's extension.

When the line was picked up she said, "Miss Phillips is here to see you."

She hung up the phone.

"He'll be right with you." Brooke said.

"Thank you." Andrea said.

She went to sit in a chair in the waiting area.

Tony came sauntering cockily down the hall.

"Andie, I'm so glad you came by to see us." He said insincerely.

Andrea finally realized what it was about Tony that bothered her, his insincerity.

She gave Tony a tentative smile.

"Hello, Anthony." She said shyly.

"Anthony? What have I done to displease you my sweet?" Tony asked.

Andrea's face showed her anger.

Tony quickly took her from the waiting area to his office.

He closed the door.

"What are you doing?" Andrea spat.

"Calm down, Andie. I'm sorry some of my male employees have blatant disrespect for women." Tony explained.

Andrea's look told him she didn't believe him.

"Really, I don't have time to test your theory. I just came from visiting granddaddy." She said.

"He's not..." Tony said.

'No, he's fine. We do have a dilemma however." Andrea told him.

"Dilemma?" Tony repeated.

"Granddaddy, uh thinks you proposed to me." She said.

Tony smiled inwardly.

"Why would he think that?" He questioned.

"He was being difficult this morning, asked about you and I told him you'd proposed." Andrea stated.

"So we're engaged." Tony said straight-faced.

"No, I told him I haven't accepted your proposal but I intend to." Andrea said.

"How far are we going with this ruse?"

"We're only letting it go on as long as it takes granddaddy to recover."

Tony smiled.

"When are you going to accept my proposal?" He asked.

"I haven't thought that far ahead.' Andrea answered.

"Let me worry about it." Tony said.

He took her left hand in his.

Remembering she wasn't wearing her engagement ring, Andrea pulled her hand back.

"Tony, please we're only pretending while granddaddy recovers." She reminded him.

'Yes, of course." He said.

He'd noticed she wasn't wearing her engagement ring. This was his chance to take advantage of her fiancée's absence.

"Tony what are you thinking?" Andrea asked.

"Leave the details to me, you won't be disappointed." Tony promised.

"Tony…" Andrea said.

He put his finger to her lips to quiet her.

"It will be okay, Babe. I'll take care of everything. I have to get to work. I'll see you tonight." He said.

He kissed her, turned her toward the door and walked her out.

Andrea's days became seemingly endless and monotonous.

Every morning she woke up to have breakfast with her family then headed to the hospital to visit her grandfather.

In the evening she spent time with Tony pretending to be engaged to him for her grandfather's sake.

Tony had pretended to propose to her at her grandfather's bedside.

Seeing the look on her grandfather's face Andrea couldn't say no.

Her acceptance of Tony's marriage proposal seemed to motivate Samuel to recover without grumbling

.

CHAPTER EIGHT

During her grandfather's convalescence the days quickly turned into weeks, Andrea could see no way to gracefully bow out of the engagement.

Tony pressured her to break off her engagement to Quinton for her grandfather's sake of course.

"Andie, your grandfather has been steadily improving since we announced our engagement." Tony said.

"Tony, I'm not going to agree to marry you." Andrea said flatly.

"Do you want to disappoint your granddaddy?" He asked.

"Tony." Andrea begged.

He smiled to himself.

"Granddaddy will be expecting a wedding when he's released from the hospital." Tony told her.

"Tony, why are you doing this?" Andrea asked tearfully.

Tony took her hand in his.

"You know how I feel about you, Andrea. I only want to honor your grandfather's wishes." He stated.

Andrea looked into Tony's eyes. Seeing what she believed to be love and sincerity she resigned herself to her fate.

"Yes, Tony I'll marry you." She said.

"You won't regret this." Tony said.

He hugged her so hard the breath rushed out of her.

Andrea stood listlessly as he hugged her.

"For God's sake Andrea you just agreed to marry me show some excitement." Tony ordered.

"I'm sorry, Tony. This is all so sudden. Of course I'm excited." Andrea lied.

She gave him a false smile.

"That's better. My mother will be happy, she's been waiting to hear about our marriage." Tony said.

Andrea silently groaned.

Tony's mother wasn't only a busybody, she was also intrusive.

"I can't wait to tell her the good news." She said unenthusiastically.

He didn't hear the lack of enthusiasm in her voice.

Tony let go of her then.

"I have a surprise for you." He said.

"Oh." Andrea said hopeful.

"I've already started planning our wedding." He told her.

"You already... How did you know I'd... say yes?" Andrea questioned.

"You're grandfather's wishes are for us to be married. I know you'd want to honor him." Tony stated.

"Oh." Andrea sighed.

As Andrea's birthday grew near the more depressed she became.

Reluctantly she helped Tony finish planning their wedding. The day of her wedding grew nearer, she grew increasingly irritable.

"Andie, are you okay?" Abby asked.

"Yes, fine." Andrea answered absently.

"This is supposed to be the happiest day of your life, Andrea. You don't look very happy." Judy told her.

"I'm nervous, Mama." Andrea said.

"That's understandable. Are you sure this is what you want, to spend the rest of your life with Tony?" Judy asked.

"For the hundredth time, yes Mama marrying Tony is what I want to do." Andrea said irritably.

"Okay, if it's what you want we'll support you." Abby said winking at her mother.

Judy smiled.

"It is." Andrea said.

They finished helping Andrea get ready to walk down the aisle.

Andrea stood next to Tony as the Justice of the Peace prepared to marry them.

She hoped against hope someone, anyone would stand up and object.

No one seemed to think it odd she was standing next to Tony ready to marry him.

Every fiber of her being cried out "I don't love him, I love Quinton."

She'd scream that would get everyone's attention.

Opening her mouth she looked at Abby, seeing the look on her face she closed it when she shook her head.

What was wrong with everyone?

Andrea saw movement out of the corner of her eye, she turned to see what it was.

Kerry and Kayla were fidgeting in their seats, even they knew this was wrong.

Ethan began to fuss. Agnes stood up and began to walk to the back of the church.

"If anyone has just cause why this man and woman can't lawfully be joined in holy matrimony..." Justice Bryan said.

Quinton pushed the sanctuary doors open.

Samuel stood up.

"I object." He said.

"I second the objection." Quinton said.

Justice Bryan looked from Samuel to Quinton then back to Samuel.

"Mr. Phillips why do you object to this union?" He asked.

"This is not the young man I intended for my granddaughter to marry." Samuel said.

"Thank God." Andrea said to herself.

"Who is the young man you intended for your granddaughter to marry?" Justice Bryan questioned.

Samuel turned around to look at Quinton.

"The young man standing at the back of the sanctuary." Samuel stated.

Justice Bryan looked to the back of the church.

"What is your name sir?" He said.

"Quinton Masterson, your honor." He answered.

"What is your reason for disrupting this ceremony?" Justice Bryan queried.

"Miss Phillips agreed to marry me. If she doesn't honor her commitment to me I will have no choice to but to sue on the grounds of alienation of affection." Quinton stated.

Andrea gasped.

"Is this true, Miss Phillips?" Justice Bryan asked.

"Yes, your honor." Andrea said.

"Are you unable to honor your commitment to Mr. Masterson?: Justice Bryan said.

"No, your honor." Andrea answered.

"It seems you have a dilemma young lady. Two contracts of marriage. Have you bound yourself to either man?"

Quinton stepped forward.

"Our contract was consummated your honor and Miss Phillips may be carrying my child." He said.

Andrea sighed.

Through clenched teeth she said, "Quinton you had no right."

"I have every right if you're carrying my child." Quinton said.

The anger on Andrea's face didn't reach her eyes.

Justice Bryan snickered.

"Miss Phillips did you uh… consummate your contract with Mr. Caldoni?" He asked.

"No your honor." Andrea mumbled.

"As you have no binding contract with Mr. Caldoni you are released from your commitment to him. You and Mr. Masterson will have to work out your commitment to one another." Justice Bryan said.

"Wait a damn minute. You are not leaving me at the altar, Andrea. I came here to get married and I'm not leaving until I do." Tony said.

"She doesn't love you, Caldoni. Let her go while you still have your dignity." Quinton said.

Tony turned on Quinton, charging him.

Quinton stepped to the side.

Tony ended up running head long into one of the pews full of wedding guests.

Undaunted he stood up, straightened his clothes, dusted himself off and said, "You let this rabble rouser steal your virtue. You wouldn't sleep with me but the minute my back was turned you hopped into the sack with him." Tony sneered.

Andrea's face became red.

"He didn't steal anything, I gave it to him." She said sarcastically.

Tony started walking toward her.

Quinton stepped in his way.

"She will be my wife, Caldoni. Be a gentleman and let her go with dignity." He said.

Tony snorted.

"Like you were a gentleman seducing an innocent young girl." He said.

"She chose me, let her go leave with your dignity intact." Quinton said.

"She'll regret leaving me." Tony said.

"Stop talking about me as if I'm not in the room." Andrea said.

She gathered up her dress, walked up the aisle past Quinton and Tony and out the door.

Abby followed but not before stopping to talk to Quinton and Tony.

"She's not a prize to be won. Andrea is a human being with feelings." She snapped.

Walking out after her sister, she quickly caught up to her.

"Did you know that was going to happen?" Andrea asked angrily.

"Not quite that way but I knew Quinton was planning something." Abby answered.

"Why didn't you tell me, at least warn me?" Andrea snapped.

"He swore me to secrecy." Abby said apologetically.

"I'm your sister." Andrea stated.

"I did what I had to to protect you. We're not just sisters, Andie we're twins. We feel what the other is feeling you know that as well as I do." Abby told her.

"You could have at least given me a clue, a hint…"

"And ruin Quinton's grand entrance? Not a chance. It all worked out for the best."

"Yes but now I'm obligated to marry Quinton."

"Andrea, you can't fool me it's what you wanted all along. You love him."

"One-sided love doesn't make a marriage Abby."

Abby knew trying to convince Andrea that Quinton loved her would do no good. She saw only that Quinton wanted her but couldn't see the love that showed in his eyes when he looked at her.

"Someday we'll look back on this and laugh. For now let's get you out of that dress. I'm sure Quinton is chomping at the bit to go home to Atlanta."

"He's expecting me to go with him."

"Your wedding arrangements have already been made, we're just waiting for the bride."

"From the frying pan into the fire. Will I ever learn?"

Three weeks later Andrea found herself standing in front of a different church with the same wedding guests.

This time however the man standing next to her was Quinton. She could only have been happier if she knew the man she was marrying loved her.

Nothing could take the smile from her lips, she was the happiest woman in the world.

If they were fortunate they'd conceive a child on their honeymoon. Andrea hadn't refilled her prescription for birth control, which coincidentally had run out the day she was supposed to have married Tony.

Andrea's smile widened at the thought of Quinton walking into the church in Shelby and saving her from making the biggest mistake of her life.

"Andrea do you take this man to be your lawful wedded husband." The minister asked again.

Andrea snapped back to the present.

"I do." She said.

She looked lovingly at Quinton who had a Cheshire cat grin on his face.

Andrea knew what that meant, she wouldn't be getting a lot of sleep tonight. Her new husband would be making her his wife in every way possible.

The ceremony ended Quinton and Andrea stood in the reception line receiving well wishes from family and friends.

"What were you thinking during the ceremony?" Quinton asked.

"About how you saved me from making the biggest mistake of my life. And that we may possibly conceive a child on our honeymoon." Andrea answered.

Quinton smiled.

"You're not still angry that I told the church full of people that we'd become lovers?" He asked.

"I'm not one to hold a grudge." Andrea said.

"Do you want to start a family right away?" He questioned.

"I'd like to have a baby, do you object?" She asked.

Quinton smiled, putting his arm around her.

"Not at all. We'll have to practice a lot." He told her.

Andrea's face grew red.

Andrew walked up just then.

"What are you saying to embarrass my daughter, young man." He asked.

"We were talking about babies." Quinton said.

Andrew chuckled then kissed Andrea's cheek.

"Babies are a natural part of life, Wren." He told her.

"I know, daddy." Andrea stammered.

"Did I hear babies?" Judy asked.

"Yes, mama." Andrea answered.

"Are we to expect another grandchild soon?" Judy questioned.

"We were just discussing that." Quinton said.

"Quinton." Andrea warned.

Quinton looked at her, the look on her face told him to shut up or deal with the consequences.

He tried to look properly chastised but failed.

"Little Brother it looks like you've already gotten yourself into trouble." Kyle said.

"It seems I have." Quinton agreed.

"He'll be spending our honeymoon sleeping in the bathtub if he doesn't behave himself." Andrea threatened.

"I doubt that Mrs. Masterson." Quinton said confidently.

"Mr. and Mrs. Masterson time for pictures." Chris said.

With his arm around Andrea's waist Quinton lead her outside to the spot they'd chosen for pictures.

An hour went by as they posed for pictures with their wedding party, family and friends.

Climbing into the back of the limousine Andrea said, "I'm glad that's over with."

"Now you can relax and have fun." Quinton told her.

After they were seated he kissed her.

Andrea reveled in his kiss.

He cupped her breast through her dress.

"Quinton…" Andrea begged.

He continued to kiss and caress her as they rode to the reception hall.

When they arrived Andrea was warm with desire for him.

Quinton held her to him as her heated body cooled.

"Ready." He asked.

"No, but we can't keep our guests waiting." She replied.

Quinton opened the door, stepped out, extended his hand to Andrea and helped her out.

Together they walked into the reception hall to loud cheers of congratulations.

Quinton kissed Andrea sensuously which riled the rowdy crowd up even more.

"I'm going to enjoy every moment of making you my wife." He whispered.

Andrea blushed.

"Save it for the honeymoon, Masterson." Someone yelled.

Quinton and Andrea joined the party that had already begun.

Sitting at the bridal table, Andrea sipped the glass of champagne Quinton had poured her.

She didn't want to be tipsy her first night as his wife.

Although Andrea loved her family and friends she couldn't wait to get out of there to start her new life with Quinton.

She took another sip of her champagne.

Quinton noticed her hand shaking.

"Nervous, Little One." he asked.

"A little." She admitted.

"We'll spend some time mingling with our guests then we can leave. In the meantime try to relax." Quinton said.

"Okay." She said leaning over to kiss him.

Quinton led Andrea onto the dance floor for their first dance as husband and wife.

She melted against him as the band played 'You Are So Beautiful To Me' by Joe Cocker.

They became one as they danced.

Andrea wished she could tell Quinton she loved him but was afraid to.

She wasn't sure he loved her. Although Abby told her he did, he'd never said the words.

Andrea desperately needed to hear Quinton tell her he loved her but was afraid she never would.

Several hours passed as Quinton and Andrea celebrated their marriage with family and friends.

Seeing that Andrea was battling exhaustion and was anxious to leave, Quinton asked, "Ready to leave Mrs. Masterson?"

Andrea silently thanked God.

"Yes." She said aloud.

Quinton smiled.

Taking her hand, Quinton quietly led Andrea toward the door.

Kyle noticed their quiet departure. He looked at his wife, giving her the thumbs up.

Abby smiled.

When Quinton and Andrea arrived at his truck he trapped her between himself and the truck.

Bending his head Quinton kissed Andrea.

She kissed him back with a hunger she'd forgotten she possessed.

Their breathing labored, Quinton chuckled.

"We better go home before I make love to you." He said.

Andrea blushed in the darkness.

He took his keys out of his pocket, unlocking the doors.

He opened the passenger side door, a balloon drifted out.

Quinton pushed it back inside. It didn't budge.

"What the hell." He said.

~ 163 ~

Looking inside the truck he saw the cab had been filled with balloons.

Andrea saw them too.

"Kyle and Abby." She said giggling.

"Big Brother." Quinton chuckled.

"What are we going to do with them?" Andrea asked.

"Release them into the air." Quinton said.

"We can't do that." Andrea said.

"What do you suggest we do?" Quinton asked.

"Pop them." Andrea replied.

"Little One, there are at least fifty balloons in there."

"Where's your sense of adventure? For each balloon we pop we kiss."

"I'm listening."

"After all the balloons are popped we can go home and…"

"I like the way you think Mrs. Masterson."

Andrea laughed.

"We can use my brooch."

She took the pin from her neckline.

Quinton took it and stuck a balloon with it.

He kissed Andrea.

Another pop of a balloon, another kiss.

When they were halfway through both were longing to be alone to ease their hunger for one another.

Quinton made quick work of ridding the truck of the rest of the balloons. He made sure to get his proffered kiss after each pop of a balloon.

Finally all of the balloons were popped.

Quinton helped Andrea into the truck.

Her body was humming with excitement for him.

Arriving at their home Quinton turned to Andrea.

"Welcome home Mrs. Masterson." He said.

Andrea smiled.

She leaned over to kiss him.

Getting caught up in the kiss Andrea didn't notice that it had started to rain.

Quinton pulled away.

"It's raining, we should go inside." He said regretfully.

"Okay." Andrea agreed.

Quinton opened the door, stepped down from the cab and closed the door.

Walking to the passenger side there was a new spring in his step.

Opening Andrea's door he extended his hand to help her out.

Purposefully he slid her down his body, letting her feel his need for her.

Andrea gasped.

Standing in the rain Quinton kissed her bringing her to arousal.

"Quinton." Andrea begged.

Without a word he led her up to the house. Taking his keys out of his pocket, Quinton unlocked the door, opening it.

Andrea took a step to go inside.

"We're going to do this right, Little One." Quinton told her.

"What?" She asked.

Quinton swung her up in his arms carrying her into the house.

"Oh Quinton, you're a romantic." Andrea said her voice quavering.

He kissed her.

When the kiss ended Quinton lowered Andrea to the floor.

Leading her into the study he asked, "Would you like some champagne, Little One?"

"Quinton, I've had enough champagne." Andrea said anxiously.

"Chocolates?" He questioned.

"Quinton." She said.

Opening the door to the study Andrea saw that Quinton had created the perfect atmosphere for their honeymoon.

Tears sprang to her eyes as she looked at the room full of balloons, roses, champagne chilling in a bucket, chocolates sitting next to the champagne and the warm inviting fire.

At the center of the room was Quinton's bed, inviting Andrea to relax with her new husband.

"Happy Mrs. Masterson?" Quinton asked.

"Beyond words.' Andrea answered.

Quinton smiled then kissed her.

"Your overnight bag is down the hall. Would you like to change?" He asked.

"Yes, this dress is beautiful but it's not meant for long term wear." Andrea said smiling.

Quinton smiled back.

"Go change, I'll meet you back here in fifteen minutes." He said.

"Okay." Andrea agreed.

She left to change out of her dress and into the lacy, body hugging white chemise she'd bought for her honeymoon.

Arriving at the hallway bathroom she realized she was going to need help unzipping her dress.

"Quinton." She said.

He poked his head out of the study.

"Yes." He answered.

"I uh… need help unzipping my dress." Andrea said embarrassed.

Quinton smiled then began to walk toward her.

He'd already begun undressing. His shirt hung open exposing his strong chest and lean stomach.

When Quinton reached her he kissed her.

Andrea didn't want him to stop.

He pulled away.

She felt the loss of his warm, sensuous lips on hers.

"Your zipper." He said.

"What? Oh yes." She stammered.

Quinton slowly, seductively pulled the zipper down. He released the catch at the top of the dress.

Lowering his head he put his arms around Andrea and kissed the nape of her neck.

"Quinton." She cried out.

"Finish changing and come to the study, Little One." Quinton said huskily.

Andrea nodded.

Quinton went back to the study.

She unsteadily undressed, put on her chemise then went to join her husband.

Quinton stood gazing into the fire when she walked in.

He wore a pair of body hugging jeans, was shirtless and barefoot.

Andrea drew in a breath.

Quinton turned to look at her.

Her beauty took his breath away.

The chemise hugged her body like a second skin. It followed every curve of her body and pushed her breasts out inviting him to take them in his mouth.

"Would you like a glass of champagne?" Quinton asked.

"Yes, please." Andrea said gracefully.

Quinton went to the table where the champagne was already opened and poured them each a glass.

Andrea joined him at the table.

He handed her a glass.

"You are beautiful, Mrs. Masterson." Quinton told her playing with the fluffy garment she was wearing.

"Am I?" Andrea asked lowering her eyes.

He tipped her chin up forcing her to look at him.

"Yes you are. Never doubt your beauty, Little One." He said.

Andrea sipped her champagne.

"You are most gracious, my husband. May I say you are handsome?" She said putting her hand on his chest.

Quinton knew she loved and wanted him. She could tell him she wanted him by only a gesture but was afraid to express her love verbally.

Someday she'd admit it without being in the circle of his arms.

He smiled.

Taking her glass, he sat both glasses on the table.

"Come to bed, Little One." He ordered gently.

Andrea nodded blushing.

Walking hand in hand they went to the bed.

Quinton held her to him kissing her. He trailed kisses along her jaw to her neck where he gently suckled.

Andrea tilted her head to the side to give him better access.

He moved his mouth back up to her jaw, she turned her head to kiss him.

Boldly she took his lower lip between her teeth gently biting.

Quinton's hands flexed involuntarily on her back.

~ 168 ~

"Little One." He said.

A little bolder Andrea let her hands wander to the waist band of his jeans releasing the button.

Unzipping them she slid her hands inside.

Startled, Quinton picked her up carrying her to the middle of the bed.

"You want to have a test of wills, Mrs. Masterson? Let's see how you fare against this.' Quinton said huskily.

He swiftly undressed them both.

Using only his hands and mouth Quinton made love to her bringing her to the edge and back.

"Quinton, oh please." She begged.

Whispering in her ear he said, "Not yet, Little One I want you to want me."

Sliding his fingers inside her Quinton made her arch into him.

Andrea moaned, crying out for release. Her pulse pounded wildly.

"Oh, God please." Andrea asked again.

He took one aching breast into his mouth suckling, then he took the other aching breast into his warm mouth.

"Two can play this game." Andrea thought.

She gently took his manhood in her hand, gliding her hand up and down.

Quinton growled like a bear too long separated from its mate.

When he finally kneeled in front of her she welcomed him like a long lost lover, enveloping him with her warmth.

Quinton slowly made love to her.

Andrea tried to quicken the pace in her excited state.

"Slow, Little One we have all the time we need." He whispered huskily.

"Quinton, I want you." She cried.

He lost control at the longing in her words.

Their release was simultaneous, leaving them aching for more.

Andrea arched up to meet Quinton bringing pleasure to him.

"Andrea." He called when his release came.

Quinton felt Andrea's body shake from the tears she was shedding.

He felt pride at making her so happy.

Andrea pulled her mouth from his to catch her breath as their lovemaking came to an end.

Quinton was sure she'd heard herself say she loved him, he wasn't positive but he was sure.

He smiled.

"Lord, please let me be right." He thought.

Andrea suddenly shifted putting Quinton on his back.

At the surprised look on his face she laughed.

Quinton quickly rolled her on her back.

Misjudging the amount of bed they had left they rolled toward the floor.

He quickly put himself under her before she hit the floor.

Andrea hit his chest with a thud, knocking the wind out of her.

She put her hand on his chest, pushing herself up.

Quinton put his hand on her back pulling her against him. Kissing her he rolled over pinning Andrea beneath him.

Without regard to precautions they made love the night through.

CHAPTER NINE

On the day after her wedding Andrea awoke to an empty bed, her new husband nowhere to be seen or heard.

She strained to hear signs of Quinton anywhere in the house.

Knowing he hadn't abandoned her she started to climb out of bed.

Suddenly the door swung open startling her.

"Good morning, Mrs. Masterson. I trust you slept well." Quinton said clearly.

"Yes, very well." She said smiling.

Quinton walked to his wife holding two steaming mugs of coffee.

"Coffee, Little One?" He asked.

"Yes please." Andrea said.

Before he let her have her mug of coffee he leaned down to kiss her without spilling any coffee from the mugs.

Not that Andrea would have noticed or minded.

After the kiss she wouldn't have cared if she received the coffee or not.

At the look on her face Quinton chuckled.

"What's funny?" Andrea asked.

Quinton handed her a steaming mug.

Annoyed Andrea took the mug taking a sip.

Sitting on the bed next to her he asked, "Happy?"

"Yes, very." Andrea responded.

"As am I." Quinton told her honestly.

"I'm glad we decided to stay in Atlanta for our honeymoon." Andrea said.

"About that, I have a confession to make." Quinton said.

"What?" Andrea asked suspiciously.

"I sort of made travel plans for us."

"Quinton we agreed not to go on a honeymoon."

"I know but I saw how disappointed you were when your granddaddy couldn't be here for the wedding."

Tears welled up in Andrea's eyes.

"Quinton, what have you done?"

"I made arrangements for us to go to Shelby to see granddaddy."

Tears streamed down Andrea's face.

She put her coffee mug on the night stand.

Turning back to Quinton she put her arms around his neck.

"I love you...'re thoughtfulness." She said through her tears.

Quinton groaned to himself. He'd almost gotten her to say it. Almost gotten the woman he loved to say she loved him.

It was going to take time but she'd say it on her own, he just had to be patient.

"When are we leaving?" Andrea asked.

Quinton could see the excitement on her face, it showed in her emerald eyes.

"This afternoon." He said.

"What time is our flight?" She questioned.

"We're taking Kyle's plane." Quinton told her.

Andrea's love for Quinton could be seen in her eyes. They sparkled with all the love she had for him.

"Is there anything you haven't thought of?" She queried.

"A way for you to tell me you love me." He said silently.

Aloud he said, "As you know I'm very thorough Little One."

Andrea blushed.

She looked down at her hands.

"Yes, I know." She said.

Quinton put his coffee mug next to hers on the night stand.

Tipping her chin up forcing her to look at him he saw the desire in her eyes.

Bending toward her, Quinton kissed her.

Andrea responded hungrily.

She was wearing his shirt from last night. He slipped his hand inside cupping one aching breast.

Andrea moaned, arching into him.

Leaning toward her, Quinton forced Andrea to lay back.

While he kissed her, he fondled her breasts lovingly.

Andrea put her hands on his chest, caressing him as he kissed the line of her jaw.

"Quinton." She sighed.

He unbuttoned the shirt she was wearing to expose her beauty to him.

He took in a breath. He'd never tire of looking at this beautiful woman who was his wife.

"Beautiful." He stated.

Andrea put her hands on either side of his face bringing his mouth to hers, kissing him.

All thought left Quinton's mind as Andrea seduced him with her mouth.

Finding the button on his jeans she released it, slipping her hands inside.

Taking him in her hand, she caressed him to the point all he wanted to do was have his way with her.

"Little One." He warned.

"Am I bothering you my dear husband?" She asked playfully.

"Bothering me? You're beyond bothering me, my dear wife. You're playing with fire." He stated.

Andrea giggled.

"Something you want to do about it?" She asked.

Quinton didn't need a second invitation.

He swiftly undressed them both, making love to his wife gently and lovingly.

Andrea opened her eyes to find her husband watching her and smiling.

"Good afternoon." Quinton said.

"It's afternoon?" Andrea asked.

"It is. Time passes quickly when you're otherwise engaged." He told her.

She blushed.

"You have a way of distracting me." Andrea admitted.

Quinton chuckled.

"We're leaving soon. You have time for a shower and a cup of coffee." He said.

"Okay." Andrea said.

She looked for the shirt Quinton had so smoothly removed from her love starved body.

Reading her mind he said, "Little One, I've made love to you all night and again this morning, there's no sense in trying to cover yourself up."

"Quinton, I…" She started.

He put his finger to her lips to silence her.

"No, Little One." He said sternly.

Andrea looked into his eyes. They told her she would not win this battle.

She gracefully climbed out of bed and headed toward the stairs.

Twenty minutes later she came back into the bedroom wrapped in a towel, where Quinton waited.

She had wrapped the large towel around her ample breasts and seductive body.

Quinton almost gave into his desire for her. In thinking twice he reminded himself he'd planned their trip not just for her but so he could spend time alone with the only woman he'd ever love.

It wasn't a matter if she reciprocated that love, he knew she did. How was he going to get her to admit it?

"Oh, hell." Quinton said.

He couldn't control himself.

Quinton walked over to Andrea, slowly withdrew the towel from around her and pulled her into his arms.

"Quinton." She said.

He silenced her with a kiss. His mouth seduced her while his hands caressed her naked flesh.

"How can I resist you, Little One?" Quinton asked.

Andrea cried out as he nipped at the skin between her neck and shoulder.

"Oh, God Quinton… the bed." She said.

"Is downstairs." He reminded her.

"We should…" She tried to say.

"Damn the bed. I want you now." Quinton said.

He gently lowered her to the floor, shed his jeans and made love to Andrea for the second time that day.

Andrea started giggling.

Quinton looked at her.

"Are we going to make our flight today?" She asked.

He smiled.

"Yes, Mrs. Masterson. The questions is will be whether you'll be wearing clothes during the flight." Quinton said smiling.

As it turned out Andrea didn't wear clothing during much of the flight. Her husband was quite… amorous.

Quinton and Andrea were just finishing dressing when their flight landed.

He pulled her to him.

"Thank God Kyle loaned me his plane." He said nuzzling her neck.

Andrea giggled, snuggling next to him.

"You are a very… loving man, Quinton." She said smiling.

"You have no idea, but you're going to experience it as often as I'm able." He said gently slapping her on the bottom.

She giggled again.

"Mr. Masterson, we've landed., you're free to deplane at your convenience." The pilot said.

Quinton took Andrea's hand leading her to get their luggage.

After collecting their luggage they went to the truck Quinton had rented.

Helping Andrea into the truck, he took advantage of the position he had to make her aware of the desire that was never far from the surface.

Andrea clung to him as her body reacted to him.

"We better get to Kyle and Abby's house in Shelby before we get arrested." Quinton said.

Andrea groaned at the loss of his warmth next to her aching body.

Unfortunately Quinton found it necessary to obey the speed limit on each road leading to Shelby.

Each mile brought Andrea's irritability to the surface.

Her need for Quinton grew with each passing mile.

When Quinton pulled into the driveway Andrea's nerves were near the breaking point.

She sighed audibly.

"Little One?" Quinton questioned.

"I'm glad we're finally here." She said smiling tentatively.

"Andrea, what's wrong?" Quinton asked.

Knowing Quinton never used her given name, Andrea thought better of trying to brush aside his concerns.

"I'm having second thoughts about spending our honeymoon in Shelby." She told him honestly.

"Why?" He queried.

"We won't be alone." Andrea said embarrassed at her selfishness.

Quinton thought about her statement and her emotional state.

Taking her hands in his he said, "I'm sorry, I didn't take into consideration the dual emotional conflict you'd have."

"Quinton, don't fault yourself. It was very considerate of you to bring me to Shelby. The emotional conflict is entirely my own. I've lived with it my entire life. I should know how to deal with it by now." Andrea said.

"Does Abby have it too?"

"Yes, it seems we get it from our mother."

Quinton made a mental note. Andrea wanted to spend time with her family but at the same time she wanted to be alone with him.

He smiled.

Andrea was confused.

"Have I amused you?" She asked.

"No, I realized something." Quinton said.

"Oh." Andrea said.

"You are intriguing, Mrs. Masterson. Let's get inside. We have a busy day tomorrow." He told her.

Gathering their luggage Quinton and Andrea got ready to let themselves into the house Kyle and Abby lived in while they were in Shelby.

Quinton stopped Andrea at the door.

She looked at him.

"Tradition. I'm required to carry you over the threshold." He said smiling.

"Quinton you already…"

He kissed her.

They were lucky to make it past the door.

Upon entering the house they were surprised to see it had been decorated to invite them to linger in the living room.

Someone, their guess was Judy, left champagne chilling in a bucket, roses in vases, cold cuts, fruit and cheese on cellophane wrapped trays.

Tears sprang into Andrea's eyes.

"Quinton." She said

He pulled her into his arms. Holding her as the tears fell and her emotions were spent.

"This has been an emotional few days." Andrea said.

"Yes it has. I wouldn't expect you to react any way other than you have." He told her.

"You're so understanding. How'd I get so lucky?" Andrea asked.

"I'm the lucky one. Are you hungry?" Quinton said.

"Yes, a little."

"Let's try some of the food your mother left."

Quinton opened the bottle of champagne as Andrea found the glasses and arranged the trays around the fireplace.

Their makeshift picnic complete, Quinton and Andrea sat down to enjoy their light meal of snacks and champagne.

Quinton picked up a strawberry, dipped it in his champagne then offered it to his bride.

Andrea accepted it taking half into her mouth encouraging her groom to take the other half into his mouth.

Quinton smiled.

Obediently he took the other half of the strawberry into his mouth.

Andrea took a piece of cheese holding it between her teeth, urging Quinton to take the other half.

He was more than happy to share the light morsel with his wife.

Quinton took a piece of the rolled meats putting it into his mouth encouraging Andrea to take a bite.

When she finished chewing he encouraged her to take another bite.

Obediently she took the proffered bite. When she came to the end she lightly took his lower lip into her mouth suckling.

Quinton sucked in his breath. He enticed her to continue the game while he seduced her.

Silently they shared the food and drank the champagne as their desire for one another rose.

Quinton cupped Andrea's breast through her silk top.

Andrea arched into him.

"Quinton." She sighed.

He kissed her neck, caressing her aching breasts.

Andrea rolled her head to the side to allow him better access.

He kissed down her neck until he came into contact with the collar of her top.

Frustrated he quickly removed it.

Andrea boldly took his shirt off.

Quinton kissed her, then took her slacks off.

She reciprocated by removing his jeans.

Next came her matching bra and panties.

His briefs and socks.

Slowly they lay next to each other caressing, touching, seducing.

When Quinton entered her Andrea welcomed him lovingly.

"Quinton, I love you." She cried.

Quinton smiled.

Andrea lay within the circle of his arms her eyes slowly closing.

When she fell asleep, Quinton went to get a blanket to cover them.

Laying behind Andrea he drew her next to him holding her close.

"I love you." He whispered to a sleeping Andrea.

The following morning Andrea awoke to the smell of food cooking.

She smiled.

Sitting up she saw her robe laying at the foot of their makeshift bed.

Pulling it on, she stood up then went in search of her husband.

Putting her arms around his waist she hugged him.

"Good morning." Andrea said.

"Good morning, Little One. How did you sleep?" Quinton said.

"Well, how did you sleep.?" Andrea responded.

Quinton smiled.

Now that he knew what caused her inability to tell him she loved him he could plan for the future.

He turned off the burner he'd been using and turned toward Andrea.

Putting his arms around her he said, "I slept well. Sleeping with a beautiful woman in my arms is indicative of a good night's sleep."

Andrea snuggled closer to him.

"What did you make for breakfast?" She asked.

"Eggs, pancakes, bacon." He answered.

"Sounds good." Andrea said.

Quinton kissed the top of her head.

Together they sat their food on the table and ate breakfast.

During the meal Quinton and Andrea showed their love for each other by a touch, a look anyway other than verbally.

After breakfast heading to the shower Andrea hoped Quinton would take advantage of the small proximity to make love to her.

She was disappointed. The only seducing he did was to make her want him more by caressing her while he helped her shower.

Wrapping a towel around her Quinton could tell Andrea was disappointed.

Smiling to himself he went to get dressed.

Frustrated, Andrea had no choice but to get dressed.

After they finished dressing Quinton rushed Andrea out the door.

"Why are you rushing Quinton?" Andrea asked.

"Things to do, people to see." Quinton answered.

"We're on our honeymoon, how can we have things to do, people to see?" Andrea asked suspiciously.

"You'll see" Quinton said smiling.

He helped her into the truck, kissing her sensuously before closing the door.

Walking around to the driver's side, he had an infectious smile.

Climbing into the truck he leaned over to kiss Andrea again.

Andrea hungrily kissed him.

Quinton barely kept a control on his desire for her.

Pulling away from her, he clicked his seatbelt into place and set them on their way.

Arriving at Samuel's house Quinton parked in the driveway.

Andrea released her seatbelt getting ready to climb out of the truck.

Quinton put his hand on her arm.

"Granddaddy doesn't know we're coming, Little One." He told her.

"Why?" Andrea asked.

"I wanted it to be a surprise for him as well." Quinton answered.

Tears welled up in Andrea's eyes. She loved him more at that moment.

Wishing she could tell him of her love, she settled for kissing him.

Quinton didn't want the kiss to end but he promised his wife a visit to her grandfather.

Pulling away, he said, "I'm sorry Little One but we should go inside."

Andrea nodded smiling. She knew Quinton was feeling desire for her. She could feel it in the way he kissed her.

He slid out of his side of the truck, walking to her side to assist her out.

Walking hand in hand they walked up to Samuel's door.

Andrea knocked then opened the door.

Sticking her head in she said, "Granddaddy it's Wren."

Quinton stepped inside. "And Quinton." He said.

"I'm in the blasted kitchen." Samuel said.

Quinton and Andrea went to the kitchen.

"What are you doing here? You're supposed to be on your honeymoon." Samuel scolded.

"I thought you might like to see Wren since you couldn't be at the wedding." Quinton explained.

"Wren?" Samuel questioned.

"Where better to spend our honeymoon?" Andrea asked.

"I can think of a few other places. Hold up in a honeymoon suite for one." Samuel stated.

"Granddaddy!" Andrea said.

Quinton chuckled.

"Wren, you've got to admit spending time with your new husband is better than spending time with your old granddaddy." Samuel said.

"Granddaddy we're where we want to be." Andrea said.

Samuel raised an eyebrow at her then shrugged.

"Have you eaten?" He asked.

"Yes, just before we came." Andrea told him.

'Fresh coffee on the counter." Samuel told them.

Andrea kissed her grandfather's cheek then went to pour herself and Quinton a cup of coffee.

Quinton sat down at the table to talk to Samuel

"How are you feeling Granddaddy?" Andrea asked.

"Better than the blasted doctor thinks. He won't release me from assisted home care." Samuel grumbled.

"He's looking out for your best interests, Granddaddy." Andrea reminded him.

Samuel snorted.

Quinton and Andrea spent the morning with Samuel, deciding to leave when he started showing signs of fatigue and obstinacy.

They helped him into bed. Andrea kissed his weathered cheek.

"Sleep well, Granddaddy. I'm only a phone call away if you need me." Andrea said.

Samuel patted her hand.

"Go, enjoy your honeymoon Wren. Give me a great grandchild.' He ordered.

He settled down to nap.

Quinton and Andrea let themselves out.

"Would you like to get something to eat?" Quinton asked.

"Yes, that sounds good." Andrea said.

Once they were settled in the truck Quinton headed to the Pub.

When they walked in Wyman greeted them.

"Well, Miss Andrea we didn't expect to see you." He said.

"Hello, Wyman. This is my husband Quinton Masterson. Quinton, this is Wyman, daddy's most trusted bartender." Andrea said.

Wyman dried his hand on his apron then held it out to Quinton.

"Pleased to meet you sir." He said.

"Nice to meet you." Quinton said taking Wyman's hand.

"We were all wondering who would finally win Miss Andrea's heart." Wyman said bluntly.

"Wyman." Andrea reprimanded.

Quinton chuckled.

"Am I what you all expected?" He asked.

"Pretty much. Don't know you very well, but seeing you're Mr. Kyle's brother you had a better chance than most." Wyman stated.

"Glad to hear it." Quinton said smiling.

"Is my father here?" Andrea snapped.

"In his office." Wyman said undaunted.

Andrea began walking toward her father's office.

Quinton followed chuckling. He gave Wyman the thumbs up sign.

Wyman smiled.

When Andrea reached her father's office she knocked on the door.

Andrew looked up.

Surprised, he questioned, "Wren?"

"Hi daddy." Andrea said.

"What are you doing here? Why aren't you on your honeymoon?" Andrew asked.

"We are on our honeymoon. Quinton surprised me by bringing me to Shelby to see granddaddy since he couldn't be at the wedding." Andrea told him.

"You're very thoughtful Quinton." Andrew said.

"I try sir." Quinton answered.

"We came in for lunch." Andrea said.

"Tell Colleen it's on the house." Andrew said.

"Daddy no." Andrea stated.

"It's not open for discussion, Wren." Andrew told her.

"Will you join us?" Quinton asked.

Andrew started to refuse then looked at his daughter.

At the look on her face he said, "Yes, thank you son."

He stood up to join them in the dining room.

Walking to the best table Andrew motioned for champagne.

When they were seated at the table Quinton asked, "What do you recommend?"

'I'll let Wren make the decision. She's been coming here since she was born and has the whole menu memorized." Andrew said.

Quinton looked at Andrea a question in his eyes.

Andrea smiled.

"The burger and fries is filling, catfish and fries is all you can eat, that comes with Cole Slaw or cottage cheese, fish and chips…" She said.

"Little One what do you recommend?" Quinton repeated.

The nachos with extra sour cream." Andrea said smiling.

"Little One." Quinton warned.

Andrea giggled.

He reached over, pulled her to him and kissed her.

Her breathing became labored, her pulse was rapid, her heart rate was accelerated.

Colleen cleared her throat.

"Sorry to interrupt." She said.

Quinton was slow to pull himself away from his blushing bride.

"Hey, Colleen how are you?" Andrea asked.

"Not as well as you apparently." Colleen said smiling.

Andrea's face brightened again.

"Nice to see you again, Colleen." Quinton said.

"Nice to see you again, Quinton. What can I get you folks?" Colleen said.

"I'll have the nachos, extra sour cream, guacamole on the side." Andrea ordered.

"I'll have the all you can eat catfish and fries." Quinton ordered.

"Cole Slaw or cottage cheese?" Colleen asked.

"Cottage cheese, please." Quinton said.

"Boss, what will you have?" Colleen asked.

"My usual." Andrew said.

"Burger and fries it is." Colleen said.

Wyman brought the champagne Andrew had ordered.

"Oh, daddy thank you." Andrea said excitedly.

"It's non-alcoholic, Wren." Andrew told her.

"Daddy, it was thoughtful." Andrea told him.

Andrew waved off her compliment.

Colleen went to put in their order.

Wyman sat the champagne in the middle of the table along with the glasses.

"Thank you, Wyman." Andrew said.

Wyman nodded then walked back behind the bar.

"How long will granddaddy be on home assisted care?" Andrea asked.

"As long as he'll agree to let his care worker come into care for him." Andrew answered.

"So a week." Andrea laughed.

Andrew smiled.

"He tolerates her pretty well. She gets him out of his cantankerous moods, talks him into going for walks and talks to him about mama." He said.

~ 187 ~

Andrea was surprised. Her gruff old granddaddy never talked to anyone about his late wife.

"What did she do to get him to talk about nana?" She asked.

"Listened to him." Andrew stated.

"How many times have we asked him questions about nana? He always told us he didn't want to talk about her." Andrea said angrily.

"Little One, calm down." Quinton said.

"I will not calm down. My grandfather will talk to a complete stranger about my grandmother but not his own family?" Andrea snapped.

"Be grateful your grandparents were around while you were growing up." Quinton told her.

Embarrassed, Andrea lowered her eyes.

"I'm sorry, Quinton. I'd forgotten you didn't have contact with your grandparents growing up." She said.

Quinton put a hand on her thigh using the other to tip her head up to make her look at him.

"You have nothing to apologize for, Little One. I came to terms with my grandparents' indifference long ago." He said kneading her thigh.

When he did that her desire for him grew uncontrollably.

"Quinton please." She pleaded.

He smiled.

He'd been successful in directing her attention elsewhere.

Colleen brought their food.

"Here you are folks. If I can get you anything else let me know." She said happily.

She left their food then walked off to wait on the incoming lunch crowd.

"How long are you going to be home, Wren?" Andrew asked.

Quinton sat up straighter in his chair, his actions becoming measured.

Atlanta was Andrea's home now.

She looked to Quinton for the answer.

"A week." He answered shortly.

Andrea shrank back from his tone.

What had made him angry?

Andrew knew his son-in-law was angry that he'd called Shelby Andrea's home instead of Atlanta.

Without missing a beat he said, "Long enough to spend with your family before you settle down to married life and start a family of your own."

Quinton let out the breath he'd been holding.

Andrea looked at him oddly.

"Wren eat your lunch before it gets cold." Andrew said.

"Yes, daddy." Andrea said.

Quinton started eating his own lunch.

For the remainder of the meal he joined the conversation but didn't seem to be enjoying the company.

Andrea barely had time to say good-bye to her father before Quinton rushed her away after they finished eating.

Quinton drove them straight home, driving like the house was on fire.

He came to a sudden halt in the driveway, shoving the truck into park.

Making quick work of unbuckling his seatbelt he climbed out of the truck, went to Andrea's side, unbuckled her seatbelt and pulled her from the truck.

He began kissing her as though he were going to make love to her right there next to the truck.

~ 189 ~

"Quinton, oh God, please." Andrea begged.

Her pleading brought him back to his senses.

Taking her by the hand, Quinton led her into the house.

Continuing his seduction he undressed them both finally leading Andrea to their makeshift bed from the previous night.

She welcomed his warmth inside her aching body hoping he'd assuage her burning hunger.

Andrea lay within the circle of Quinton's arms. Her back was against his chest, she was drowsy, falling asleep.

Feeling him enter her from behind, Andrea cried out, "Quinton."

He slowly eased himself into her as she took him in.

Andrea pushed on his leg for leverage.

Quinton kissed her as he made love to her.

She enjoyed his lovemaking, it was exciting and he made her feel wanted.

Falling asleep, Andrea felt Quinton pull her against him.

"Atlanta is your home." He said huskily.

Andrea turned in his arms.

"Yes." She agreed smiling.

She wrapped her arms around him and went to sleep.

Quinton smiled.

CHAPTER TEN

Their time spent in Shelby went by quickly. They were back home before Andrea knew it.

Quinton had another week off from work for their honeymoon. He took advantage of every moment he had with his new wife.

Quinton and Andrea spent the remainder of their honeymoon making love, window shopping and adjusting to married life.

When Quinton's alarm went off his first day back to work Andrea climbed out of bed.

Going to the kitchen she started coffee so it would be ready by the time Quinton came downstairs after his shower.

She was sipping coffee when Quinton walked into the kitchen.

"Good morning, Little One." He said smiling.

Andrea smiled.

"Good morning, Quinton." She said.

"What plans do you have for the day?" He asked.

"Unpacking then possibly joining my husband for lunch." She said hopefully.

Quinton's smile grew wider.

"You won't get any objection from me." He said.

The look he gave her made Andrea blush.

"Would you like me to make breakfast?" Andrea asked.

"I usually grab coffee and a doughnut on the way to the office." Quinton told her.

"You have a wife now. I'd be happy to make you breakfast." Andrea said.

"I'd like that, thank you." Quinton said.

He reached down to caress her cheek.

Andrea went to the refrigerator to get ingredients for breakfast.

When she opened the refrigerator door she looked inside and found a few eggs, expired milk, beer, butter, jelly, several take out containers she guessed needed to be thrown out.

There were other food containers she had a sneaking suspicion needed to be thrown out as well.

"I'm going to have to add grocery shopping to my list of things to do today." Andrea said.

Quinton looked inside the refrigerator and grimaced.

Although he had a housekeeper who came in daily she had been neglecting her job duties lately.

"I'm sorry, Little One. I… we do have a housekeeper, obviously she's decided to neglect her job duties.' Quinton said.

'We don't need a housekeeper. I'm capable of keeping house." Andrea told him.

"Little One there isn't going to be a discussion. You're going to be busy with school come the winter semester and our newborn child if you've conceived our child." Quinton told her.

Andrea wanted to argue with him but knew he had a valid point.

Closing the refrigerator she said, "It looks like you'll be getting that doughnut this morning after all."

"I'll call Katie later to set down ground rules telling her she's to take orders from you now. I'll also call my bank and add you to my accounts." Quinton said.

"Gee thanks." Andrea mumbled.

"You're unhappy, why?" He questioned.

"I'm not unhappy, just… disappointed."

'Disappointed?"

"I have to depend on you for so many things. I'm used to depending on myself."

"Little One, we're married you're not depending on me. We support each other."

"How am I supporting you exactly."

"When I come home from work this evening you'll get the answer to that question, trust me."

Andrea looked into his eyes, then said "Alright. What plans do we have for Christmas?"

"We celebrated Christmas here last year so we'll celebrate in Shelby this year." Quinton said.

"Have you done any shopping?" Andrea asked.

"No, I haven't thought about it." Quinton confessed.

"Please don't tell me you have a personal shopper." Andrea said.

Quinton smiled.

"I didn't until two weeks ago." He said.

Andrea thought about his statement.

"Quinton Masterson! I am not your personal assistant." Andrea said heatedly.

Quinton laughed. Pulling Andrea into his arms he kissed her.

She half-heartedly tried to pull away.

Ignoring her half-hearted attempt to pull away from him, Quinton deepened the kiss.

Both were caught up in the moment taking delight in the kiss.

Quinton reluctantly pulled away.

"I'm going to be late for work." He said.

'We wouldn't want that would we?" Andrea asked.

"Little One, I don't want to leave. I'd much rather stay here with you." Quinton assured her.

Andrea gave him a shy smile.

"You have to work Quinton, I know that." Andrea said.

"Soon enough you'll be enrolled in the university." He promised.

Andrea's eyes lit up.

"Between now and then do you mind if I make some changes around here?" She questioned.

"Little One, this is our home, I expect you to treat it as such." Quinton said.

"Thanks." She said smiling.

"I have to go, I'll see you for lunch." He told her.

Quinton kissed her.

"I'll see you at lunch." Andrea said.

He left for work.

A few hours later the doorbell rang.

Andrea went to answer it.

When she opened it there was a car dealer standing on her front porch.

"May I help you?" She asked.

"Are you Andrea Masterson?" Jack asked.

"Yes." Andrea answered.

Jack held out his hand.

"I'm Jack Landry, Landry Auto Sales. I've been asked to deliver your new van." He said.

Andrea took his hand in hers shaking it.

"My new van?" She asked surprised.

"Yes, your husband ordered it for you. If you'll follow us down to the dealership we can finish the paperwork." Jack said.

"I'll have to get my purse and coat." Andrea told him.

"There's no hurry, Mrs. Masterson." Jack said smiling.

Andrea closed the door then went to get her purse and coat.

Going back to where Jack waited she opened the door.

"I'm ready." She said.

Jack handed her the keys to her new van.

Andrea gasped when she saw it. She walked over to look at it.

The van was a Dodge Grand Caravan Crew Forward with a stone white clear coat exterior and black/gray stone interior.

Andrea looked at the interior more closely. There was a DVD player in the second row, a compact disc player and built in car seats in the second row.

She walked around the van to look at the outside.

Coming to the license plate she giggled.

It read:

"Lil One."

"Quinton." She said happily.

"The van also has heated seats, Mrs. Masterson." Jack told her.

"Is there anything my husband didn't think of?" Andrea questioned.

Jack smiled.

"No, ma'am." He said.

"Shall we go, I'm anxious to drive my new van." Andrea said smiling.

Jack nodded, waited for Andrea to get settled in the van then lead her to the dealership.

When they pulled in Andrea saw her old vehicle.

Pulling up beside Jack she became curious.

After stepping out of the van she walked over to Jack.

"How did my old car get here?" Andrea asked.

"Mr. Masterson had it sent here. That's one of the reasons we needed you to come to the dealership. We're going to use it as a trade-in." Jack told her.

"What paperwork do I have to complete?" Andrea asked.

"Come inside it should only take half an hour or so." Jack told her.

"Okay, thanks." Andrea said.

Andrea followed Jack inside the dealership to complete the paperwork for her new van.

Half an hour later Andrea walked out of the car dealership the owner of a brand new Dodge Grand Caravan Crew Forward.

She couldn't believe Quinton bought her the van. She felt like the luckiest woman in the world and so full of love for her husband.

Getting into her van, Andrea buckled her seatbelt then headed to K.M. Enterprises, Atlanta Division.

When she arrived, Andrea suddenly became doubtful of her decision.

Knowing she wasn't being reasonable Andrea headed to Quinton's office.

The receptionist greeted her with surprise.

"Good morning, Mrs. Masterson." Sally said.

Andrea smiled.

"I'm sure you're a little confused. I'm Andrea Masterson, Abby's twin sister." She told her.

"Oh good, I was beginning to think you were a magician." Sally told her.

"Magician?" Andrea questioned.

"Mrs. Masterson just went into Kyle's office." Sally said.

Andrea nodded.

"Is Quinton busy? I'd like to see him." She said.

"I'm sure he'll clear his schedule for you." Sally told her.

She picked up the phone and put in Quinton's number.

"Yes, Sally." Quinton said.

"There's a beautiful young woman here to see you." Sally said smiling.

"Sally, I don't have time for games. Who the hell is it?" Quinton snapped.

Undaunted Sally said, "Your wife."

Quinton hung up.

His office door was nearly thrown open.

"Andrea are you okay?" He asked.

"I'm fine, just stopped by to see my husband.' Andrea said smiling.

"Come in." Quinton ordered.

Andrea walked into Quinton's office then closed the door.

Pulling her into his arms he asked, "To what do I owe the pleasure of your visit, Mrs. Masterson?"

Putting her arms around his neck Andrea said, "I just came from the car dealership."

Quinton pulled away slightly.

Andrea pulled him closer, kissing him.

She kissed his lips, his jaw. At his jaw she took little nips.

Quinton's hands reflexively squeezed her waist.

"Mrs. Masterson are you trying to seduce me?" He queried.

'I must be doing a poor job if you think I'm only trying." Andrea said unbuttoning his shirt.

Quinton's breath caught in his chest when she lowered her head and began kissing his chest.

"Is the door locked?" He asked breathing hard.

"I don't remember if I locked it." Andrea teased.

"Little One, is the damn door locked?" He demanded.

"You want to check?" She asked arousing him further by taking a nipple in her mouth.

He groaned.

"No." He managed to say.

Quinton made quick work of undressing them, getting them to the couch on one wall of his office and completing their union.

Her pulse pounded in her most intimate place. She reminded herself to breathe.

As their climax grew close Quinton kissed Andrea to prevent their lovemaking from being heard outside his office.

Quinton held Andrea in his arms.

Kissing her forehead he said, "I'm guessing you didn't plan this."

"Uh, no but I'm not complaining." Andrea told him.

"Why did you come in today?" Quinton asked.

"To tell you I love my new van and to have lunch with you." Andrea answered.

"It pleases me that you love the van. As for lunch we've both worked up a healthy appetite." Quinton said.

There was a rattling at the door.

"Kyle, I told you Quinton is in a meeting." Sally said.

"What meeting? Why wasn't I informed of this meeting?" Kyle asked.

"Not all of my meetings involve you, Kyle." Quinton said.

The doorknob turned.

"We're partners, Quint. What deal are you negotiating without me?" Kyle said.

"Kyle, if you open that door you're going to put us both in an embarrassing position." Quinton snapped.

"What the hell are you..." Kyle started.

"Go away, Kyle." Andrea said.

"Andie?" Kyle asked.

"Yes, Kyle. Now go away." Andrea spat.

"Come on, Kyle. Quinton obviously has plans for lunch." Abby told him.

Quinton and Andrea listened as Kyle and Abby walked away.

"That answered my question as to whether the door was locked or not." Quinton stated.

Andrea giggled.

"We'll have to be more careful in the future." She said.

"I like the way you think, Mrs. Masterson." Quinton said.

Andrea kissed him.

"Are we going to get lunch, I'm hungry." Andrea told him.

Gathering their clothes Quinton and Andrea dressed then went to lunch.

The weeks went by as Quinton and Andrea settled into married life.

Andrea set up house while Quinton went to work.

She couldn't wait for the winter semester of Georgia State University to begin.

Andrea prepared to enroll in Computer classes with Quinton's help.

In the meantime she redecorated the home she shared with Quinton to make it more a home than a bachelor's hang out.

One morning Andrea was making breakfast while Quinton was reading the morning paper.

Suddenly she went running out of the room toward the bathroom down the hall.

Closing the door behind her she partially emptied the contents of her stomach.

Quinton knocked on the door.

"Little One are you alright?" He asked.

In answer Andrea emptied her stomach again.

Quinton started to open the door.

"Don't come in here." Andrea snapped.

"I have to see if you're alright." Quinton said.

"I'm fine." Andrea said.

"Apparently you're not, otherwise you wouldn't be in there." Quinton pointed out.

"Go away." Andrea spat.

Quinton opened the door, walked over to her and pulled her hair away from her face.

"You're going to see Dr. Cooper." Quinton stated.

"I don't need to see a doctor." Andrea argued.

"Little One, there's no senses in being stubborn. You're obviously not feeling well." Quinton said.

"There's nothing a doctor can do." Andrea told him.

Quinton panicked.

"What?" He asked.

"I think I'm pregnant." Andrea told him.

"Have you had it confirmed?"

"Not yet."

"All the more reason to see Dr. Cooper."

"I'll go today. I don't think I can finish making your breakfast."

"Little One, I'm capable of making my own breakfast. When you're able come back to the kitchen, I'll make you some herbal tea."

"Okay, thank you."

"Anything to make sure you deliver a healthy child."

Stung by his thoughtless statement, Andrea didn't let him see how it hurt her.

Conceiving a child was the reason for their marriage after all.

How could she have let herself believe there was anything more to their relationship?

"I'll clean up then be right behind you." Andrea said.

"That's my girl." Quinton said.

He walked out closing the door behind him.

Andrea went about freshening up then went to join Quinton in the dining room.

He had a freshly brewed cup of herbal tea waiting for her.

"Thanks for the tea." Andrea said irritably.

Quinton didn't notice her irritability.

"Would you like to try some toast?" He asked.

"No, thank you." Andrea replied waspishly.

Attributing her irritability to her condition, Quinton said, "I've heard the first few months are the hardest."

"Thank you, that's very helpful." Andrea said.

She slowly sipped her tea hoping it would settle her stomach.

"Would you like me to go to see Dr. Cooper with you?" Quinton asked.

"No, I think I can make it there on my own." Andrea snapped.

"Little One, have I offended you?" Quinton questioned.

"Yes." She said silently.

"No, I'm just not feeling well." Andrea lied.

Quinton took her free hand in his.

"I know this is going to be difficult for you. I'll be here for you." Quinton told her.

"We are still going to Shelby for Christmas aren't we?" Andrea asked.

"Yes, Andrea what's bothering you?" Quinton asked.

She knew he didn't use her given name unless he was serious.

"Your cruel reminder that we married to have a baby." Andrea thought.

"I'm going to say my body is adjusting to the new hormones.." She said aloud.

Quinton arched an eyebrow at her.

Andrea pulled her hand out of his.

He felt coolness where her hand had been.

When he tried to take her hand again she shoved it into her pocket.

He leaned in to kiss her, she turned her head, leaving him to kiss her cheek.

"Damn it, Andrea what have I done?" Quinton barked.

Andrea shrank back from him.

"Go to work, Quinton." She said.

As soon as the words left her mouth she was rushing out of the room again.

Quinton followed close behind.

She shut the door behind her.

He opened it, following her in.

Andrea could no more object than she could stop the contents of her stomach from coming up.

She rested her head on her arm.

Quinton took a washcloth from the cupboard next to the sink. Running it under cool water he wrung it out the placed it on her neck.

Andrea jumped as the cool cloth came into contact with her warm skin.

"For God's sake go to work. I'm not a child." She snapped.

Torn between wanting to help his wife and doing as she asked Quinton was conflicted.

Hesitantly he said, "I'll see you tonight."

Andrea waved him off.

Quinton walked out, but not before giving Andrea a concerned look.

As soon as she heard the front door close Andrea forced herself to get up.

Going to the kitchen she called Abby.

"Masterson residence." Agnes answered.

"Hi, Agnes this is Andrea may I speak to Abby please?" She said.

"Yes, Mrs. Masterson." Agnes said.

Several minutes later Abby picked up the phone.

"Hi, Andie what's going on?" She asked.

"I'm not feeling well. Quinton wants me to see Dr. Cooper would you mind going with me?" Andrea said.

"No, of course not. What time?" Abby replied.

"In an hour and a half." Andrea answered.

"Okay, you want to pick me up?" Abby questioned.

"Yes."

"Okay, I'll see you then. I love you."

"I love you too."

Andrea hung up the phone.

She went to Quinton's rolodex to find Dr. Cooper's number, she crossed her fingers.

Why she didn't know. Probably out of habit for good luck.

This would be the baby she was longing for. It would also be the baby that she and Quinton had married for.

That last thought almost made her rush back to the bathroom. She took several deep breaths to calm her nerves.

Pulling herself together Andrea went to take a shower.

When she was done showering she wrapped her hair turban style, patted herself dry then put lotion on.

As she waited for the lotion to moisturize her body she put on her robe then went to make a cup of coffee hoping to keep it on her now empty stomach.

Going into office she rolled through Quinton's rolodex once more to find Dr. Cooper's number then punched the number into the cordless phone.

The phone rang twice before it was picked up.

"Dr. Cooper's office, Bree speaking." She said.

"I'd like to come in for a pregnancy test. Do I have to make an appointment?" Andrea inquired.

"No, just come in and we'll do a routine pregnancy test." Bree said.

"It is confidential isn't it? No one will know why I'm there?"

"Yes, your tests are kept in the strictest confidence." Bree assured her.

"Okay, thank you." Andrea said.

She hung up.

Getting dressed Andrea wondered if Quinton wanted a son or a daughter.

If she had to hazard a guess she'd say a son.

Gathering her purse and coat she went to wait for Abby.

Andrea walked out to the car when she pulled into the driveway.

"Hi." Andrea said cheerily.

"Hi, what's going on?" Abby asked bluntly.

"I'm not able to hold anything down and I may be running a fever." Andrea said only half lying.

"I hope you're not coming down with the flu." Abby said.

"I've rarely left the house to come into contact with anyone." Andrea told her.

"Quinton comes into contact with people all the time." Abby pointed out.

"I'm sure it will resolve itself in time."

"Let's hope so."

Andrea smiled to herself.

Abby drove to Dr. Cooper's office.

When they arrived Andrea checked in. Several minutes later she was handed some paperwork to fill out.

While she worked on that Bree made a copy of her driver's license and insurance card.

When she finished the paperwork Andrea took it back to Bree.

Andrea's knee involuntarily bounced as she waited to be called back.

"What's taking so long?" She asked.

"Did you make an appointment?" Abby asked.

"I called this morning." Andrea said.

"The nurse will call you back in a few minutes. Is there something bothering you?" Abby said.

"No, I'm just anxious to get this over with." Andrea responded.

"Andie, you can talk to me." Abby told her.

Andrea wanted to tell Abby why they were really there but couldn't. Quinton had to be the first one she confirmed her pregnancy to.

"I know. I'm just not feeling well. I'd like to know what's causing me to feel sick." Andrea hedged.

"Andrea." The nurse called.

Andrea stood up then walked to the nurse.

"Good morning." Nikki said.

"Good morning." Andrea responded.

The door closed behind Andrea.

"What brings you in this morning?" Nikki asked.

"I want to confirm that I'm pregnant. I don't want my sister to know yet." Andrea told her.

"Alright, Mrs. Masterson. You're Quinton's wife." Nikki said.

"Yes." Andrea replied.

"I'm sure we can accommodate you." Nikki told her.

Andrea smiled.

"Thank you." She said.

For the next hour Andrea had blood drawn, spoke to Dr. Cooper and generally made it look as though she were being examined for a communicable illness going around.

Walking back into the waiting room her expression gave nothing away.

"It's something going around." Andrea lied easily.

"What did Dr. Cooper advise?" Abby asked.

"Rest and plenty of fluids." Andrea said.

"What about nausea?" Abby questioned.

"Foods as tolerated." Andrea told her.

She hated lying to Abby but this was one of those time she couldn't confide in her.

As Abby drove back Andrea thought about how she'd tell Quinton they were expecting their first child.

Of course Dr. Cooper hadn't confirmed it yet, he was going to call her later.

Abby pulled into the driveway.

"If you need anything call." Abby said.

"I will." Andrea promised.

Andrea opened her door and stepped out of the van.

She was going to have a baby. The baby she'd so longed for, at long last she was going to be a mother.

There was a new spring in her step as she walked up to her front door, unlocked it and went in to wait for the call from Dr. Cooper.

CHAPTER ELEVEN

Quinton couldn't concentrate on the work in front of him. The news that he was going to be a father had him excited, nervous, anxious.

He wanted to walk into Kyle's office announce that Andrea was pregnant and he was going home to celebrate.

The only thing that stopped him was her mood when he'd left this morning.

Somehow his feelings of concern for her and their unborn child had made her angry.

He picked up the phone to call her. Replacing the receiver he wasn't sure what response he'd get.

Quinton laughed at himself. Shaking his head he tried to get back to work.

Half an hour later he hadn't accomplished anything.

Punching his desk, he put the paperwork aside.

"Problem, Little Brother?" Kyle asked.

"I was thinking about Andrea." Quinton confessed.

"I never would have guessed." Kyle said.

Quinton gave him a dark look.

"She wasn't feeling well when I left this morning." He said.

"What are you doing here? Go home, be with your wife." Kyle told him.

Quinton didn't have to be told twice.

He stood up, walked over to his door took his jacket off the hook on the back and put it on.

"See you tomorrow, Big Brother." He said.

Quinton winked at Sally on his way out.

She shook her head knowing there was no sense in trying to figure her boss out.

Quinton whistled a happy tune on the way to his truck.

Climbing in, he buckled his seatbelt then started on his way home.

As he was driving he paid particular attention to the road conditions, they looked to be clear and dry.

Driving along Quinton saw another vehicle headed down the road in the opposite direction.

He thought nothing of it until the vehicle which could now be identified as an older model truck crossed the center line and headed straight for him.

Quinton tried to avoid the collision but was hit head on.

"Lord, please take care of Andrea." He prayed before he lost consciousness.

The doorbell rang at Quinton and Andrea's house.

Andrea went to answer it.

She was in no mood for guests after her misunderstanding with Quinton this morning.

When she saw the officer standing on the porch she asked, "May I help you officer?"

"Is this the Masterson residence." Officer Morris asked.

"Yes." Andrea answered.

"May I come in, Mrs. Masterson?" Officer Morris said.

"What's this about officer?" Andrea questioned.

"I'm afraid there's been an accident involving your husband."

"An accident? Is he alright? Where is he?"

"I'm afraid all I can tell you is he's been taken to the hospital. I'll need you to come with me ma'am."

"I'll be right back."

Andrea shakily went to get her purse and coat then went back to where Officer Morris waited.

He led her to his waiting patrol car.

Andrea headed to her van.

"Mrs. Masterson?" He questioned.

"I'll need my van." Andrea said.

"Are you sure you're okay to drive." Officer Morris asked.

"I'm fine." She assured him.

He gave her a skeptical look then said "I'll feel much better if you ride with me."

"I'm capable of driving officer. I'll follow you." Andrea assured him again.

Officer Morris hesitated then stepped into his patrol car.

Andrea climbed into her van, buckled herself in and followed him to the hospital.

Upon arriving at the hospital she went to the reception desk in the emergency area.

"May I help you?" Wendy asked.

"My husband was in an accident and was brought here." Andrea said.

"His name." Wendy said.

"Quinton Masterson." Andrea replied.

Wendy typed some information into her computer then picked up her phone to call back to the emergency area.

"This is Wendy in reception, Mrs. Masterson is inquiring about her husband." She said.

Wendy listened to the instructions then hung up.

"Dr. Cooper is still assessing your husband, Mrs. Masterson. Please have a seat and he'll be with you as soon as he can." She said.

"My husband may be fighting for his life and you're telling me to sit tight." Andrea snapped.

"I'm sorry Mrs. Masterson, those are my instructions." Wendy told her calmly.

"Tell me Wendy, if it were your husband back there would you sit tight?" Andrea asked.

"I'm not married." Wendy said.

"That's not really the point now is it?" Andrea said through clenched teeth.

"Andie, the young lady is doing her job." Kyle said.

Andrea turned around so fast she nearly lost her balance.

"Kyle, what are you doing here?" Andrea questioned angrily.

"I'm listed as Quint's emergency contact." Kyle told her.

"Of course you are." Andrea said petulantly.

Kyle pulled Andrea to a private area.

"What's going on Andrea?" He asked.

She wanted to confide in someone but she couldn't.

"Kyle, my husband was involved in an accident, I can't get any information, excuse me if I'm a little irritable." Andrea said.

"Andie, he was on his way home. He couldn't concentrate on his work so I suggested he leave early." Kyle told her.

"Oh, that makes me feel so much better, Kyle. My husband was on his way home to be with me and was involved in an accident." Andrea said.

"Andrea that's not what I meant." Kyle said.

"Mrs. Masterson." Dr. Cooper said.

"Yes." Andrea replied.

"Follow me please." Dr. Cooper said.

Andrea and Kyle followed Dr. Cooper into the back of the emergency area.

When they came to Quinton's room Dr. Cooper said, "We have him stabilized. He's not responding to any stimuli at this time but we're hopeful."

"You make it sound like he's near death." Andrea said soberly.

"I'm sorry, Andrea. I don't believe in sugar coating the prognosis." Dr. Cooper said.

"When can I see him?" Andrea asked.

"I'll let you sit with him until we move him to a room. Remember he can hear you." Dr. Cooper told her.

He opened the door to Quinton's room.

Andrea gasped at the sight of Quinton.

He was pale, which was enhanced by the bruises on his face where he'd been hit by the airbag.

Quinton's left arm was in a splint. The emergency room personnel had cut off his shirt. Andrea could see where the airbag had hit him there too.

"Is he in pain?" She asked.

"We've given him something for the pain. We won't know how much discomfort he's in until he wakes up." Dr. Cooper told her.

"How long will he have to be in the hospital." Andrea questioned.

"That depends on how long it takes him to wake up. There's nothing physical keeping him from waking up." Dr. Cooper said.

"Psychological?" Kyle asked.

"Most likely." Dr. Cooper said.

Kyle looked at Andrea.

"Something you want to tell me, Andie?" He asked.

Andrea put her hands on her hips.

"Kyle Masterson if you say one word I'll put you in a bed next to your brother." Andrea threatened.

~ 213 ~

Kyle chuckled.

Quinton slowly opened his eyes.

He tried to put his hand up to his head but it was weighed down by the splint on his arm.

"Oh hell, what happened?" He asked.

Andrea, Kyle and Dr. Cooper turned to look at him.

"You were in an accident. Do you remember, Quinton?" Dr. Cooper said.

"I remember a damn fool in a truck heading toward me. I tried to avoid him but I couldn't get out of the way." Quinton told him.

"You were hit head on by driver who was high on alcohol and illegal drugs." Dr. Cooper said.

"Has anyone called my brother?" Quinton questioned.

Kyle stepped into his line of vision.

"I'm here, Quinton." He said.

He pulled a smiling Andrea next to him.

"Look who's here." Kyle said.

Surprise showed on Quinton's face.

"Hello, beautiful. Who are you?" Quinton queried.

Andrea's smile faded.

"Can I speak to you outside Kyle, Andrea?" Dr. Cooper asked.

When they reached the hall Dr. Cooper said "It appears as though Quinton has sustained more than bruises and a sprained arm in the accident."

"He has amnesia?" Andrea asked.

"Unfortunately, yes. We'll have to talk to him to see how far along the amnesia is." Dr. Cooper told her.

"Is it permanent?" Kyle asked.

"We won't know for certain until we assess him further." Dr. Cooper said.

"In the meantime my husband doesn't know who I am." Andrea said.

"Amnesia is unpredictable, Andrea. One can never tell when it will appear or for how long."

"You're telling me to sit tight." Andrea asked.

"I'm sorry, but yes." Dr. Cooper answered.

Tears welled up in Andrea's eyes.

Kyle put his arm around her.

"I'm sorry, Andie. I wish there was something I could do." He said.

"It's not your fault, Kyle. Did they at least get the driver of the other truck?" Andrea said.

"He was pronounced dead at the scene. Witnesses at the scene gave officers an eyewitness account of the accident. His girlfriend showed up on the scene telling her version of events." Dr. Cooper told her.

"He can't be prosecuted." Andrea snapped.

"As I said I'm sorry, Andrea. I must get back to Quinton." Dr. Cooper said.

He walked back into Quinton's room.

Andrea looked at Kyle.

He opened his arms and gathered her to him.

Andrea let the tears fall.

Life was playing a cruel joke on her.

She'd only been married six weeks, had planned a romantic evening with Quinton to tell him they were going to have a baby.

Now her world was turned upside down what was she going to do?

Pulling away from Kyle, she wiped her eyes to go into Quinton's room.

Walking into his room she looked at him.

He was still the man she loved even if he didn't remember who she was.

Kyle had followed her into the room..

Holding up his left hand, indicating the ring Quinton asked, "Big Brother would you like to explain this?"

"Uh what is the last thing you remember?" Kyle asked.

"Before the accident?" Quinton questioned.

"Yes." Kyle said.

"You called to tell me you were having Christmas at your house this year so everyone could meet your wife." Quinton answered.

Andrea sucked in a breath.

Quinton looked in her direction.

"Oh Lord Little Brother that was five years ago." Kyle told him.

"I've lost five years of my life." Quinton bellowed.

"It looks that way, but look on the bright side..." Kyle put his arm around Andrea. "This beautiful young woman is your wife."

"Gee thanks, Kyle." Andrea muttered.

"You're welcome." Kyle said.

Andrea rolled her eyes at him.

Quinton raised an eyebrow at him.

"I believe the young lady was being sarcastic, Kyle. Like you've just told me, 'I'm sorry you've lost your memory but here's a consolation prize." He said angrily.

Kyle looked at Andrea.

She looked back at him.

"I'm sorry, Andie." He said.

"I'm sorry, miss…" Quinton started.

"Andrea." She said.

"Andrea. Kyle that doesn't explain the last five years of my life." Quinton snapped.

~ 216 ~

"Quint, it's going to take time but your memory will return." Kyle assured him.

"No offense, Andrea." Quinton said looking at her. "I don't know when we met, where we went on our first date, how we fell in love…"

"As Kyle said it will take time. We should let Dr. Cooper finish his assessment. I'm going to get a cup of coffee." Andrea said abruptly.

She left Quinton's room heading to the cafeteria.

Kyle had no choice but to follow her.

"Andie, slow down." He muttered.

"My husband, the man I've pledged to spend my life with doesn't know who I am." Andrea snapped.

"I'm sorry, Andrea. What was I supposed to do force him to remember you?" Kyle asked.

"I don't know, Kyle. I'm going to be living with a stranger. How am I supposed to do that?" Andrea asked.

"One day at a time." Kyle stated.

Andrea snorted and kept walking.

Once she reached the cafeteria she poured herself a cup of coffee, added cream then went to sit at a table.

Kyle did the same, with the exception of adding cream to his coffee.

Andrea sat silently drinking her coffee as she stared across the room.

After several minutes of tense silence Kyle asked, "Is there something you want to say Andrea?"

"No." Andrea said irritably.

"Did you have something planned for today?" Kyle questioned.

"No." Andrea repeated.

"Your manner of dress suggests otherwise." Kyle stated.

"Shut up, Kyle." Andrea said.

Kyle smiled.

"I'm not above pouring my coffee over your head." Andrea said.

As she drank her hot coffee she let the warmth relax her.

Andrea thought how she could make Quinton's amnesia come out in a positive light.

She furrowed her brow.

He didn't know they married to have a baby, thought they had expressed their love for one another.

That last one could also be negative.

Quinton having amnesia was going to present some unique challenges.

How was she supposed to tell him she's pregnant? He'd just found he'd gotten married.

How could she tell him "Oh, by the way you're going to be a father too?"

She took a big drink of her coffee and began coughing, nearly spitting it at Kyle.

"Andie are you alright?" He asked.

Andrea coughed a few more times.

"I forgot the coffee was hot." She said.

"Gee, hot coffee, there's a new idea." Kyle said.

"I was lost in thought and wasn't thinking about the coffee." Andrea defended.

"I wouldn't have guessed." Kyle replied.

"Are you having fun? Getting a laugh at my expense?" Andrea snapped.

"Andie, what's going on? You're usually not so sensitive." Kyle said.

"Nothing. My husband was in an accident, he doesn't have a clue who I am and..." Andrea stammered.

"And what?"

Andrea wanted to confide in someone but she couldn't betray Quinton.

"I'm going to check on Quinton." She said standing.

Walking away she took her half full coffee cup with her.

Once she came to Quinton's room Andrea steeled herself to accept his rejection.

The reception he gave her was shocking.

"There you are. Where did you go?" Quinton asked.

"I, uh went to get some coffee." Andrea said.

"Will you please tell Dr. Cooper it's perfectly safe for me to go home?" Quinton pleaded.

Andrea looked to Dr. Cooper for guidance.

"I'm sorry, Andrea but we'll need to keep Quinton in the hospital for a few days, protocol." Dr. Cooper told her.

"Damn hospital protocol. I'm going home with my wife." Quinton said.

He started to get out of bed.

"Quinton, Dr. Cooper has rules he has to follow. You don't want him to lose his job do you?" Andrea soothed.

She pushed him back into the bed.

"Is there some reason you don't want me to go home?" Quinton questioned.

"Of course not, Darling. I want you to get the best care possible." Andrea said.

Quinton lifted his eyebrow at her.

"Really? You don't have an ulterior motive?" He asked harshly.

"Quinton, what are you accusing me of?" Andrea said angrily.

"Dr. Cooper can I have some time alone with my wife?" Quinton asked.

~ 219 ~

"Of course, I'll be right outside if either of you need anything." Dr. Cooper told them.

He walked out closing the door behind him.

Andrea turned to Quinton crossing her arms over her stomach.

"What's on your mind, Quinton?" She asked.

He gave her a dark look.

Andrea stood her ground.

Quinton smiled.

"Fiery temper?" He guessed.

"Only when you irritate me." She answered.

"Am I irritating you, My Pet?" Quinton asked.

"Nice presumption." Andrea said irritably.

"If I'm a good boy and stay in the hospital what's my reward?" He questioned.

"I don't strangle you." Andrea shot at him.

Quinton laughed.

"Fiery, interesting. I like that."

Andrea put her hands on her hips.

Quinton patted the side of the bed.

"I'm not a dog, I don't come on command." Andrea said through clenched teeth.

"Will you please come sit next to me?" Quinton asked.

Andrea thought about denying his request but realized that would be childish.

She went to sit next to him.

He took her hand in his.

Examining her engagement ring, he watched as the light played off the facets.

"Emerald. Almost as beautiful as your eyes. How long have we been married?" Quinton said.

"Six weeks." Andrea told him.

"How long did we date?" Quinton asked.

Tears threatened to well up in Andrea's eyes.

"Um, four and a half years approximately on and off." She answered.

"Approximately on and off?" Quinton questioned.

"Yes, we sort of played the do we or don't we game." Andrea said.

"We decided we do obviously."

Andrea smiled.

"With a little encouragement from our families."

"Our families?"

"Yes, they decided Kyle and Abby made such a good match they wanted us to get together."

Quinton could see the humor in their families' thinking.

"Do we?"

"What?"

"Make a good match?"

"I'm going to let you figure that one out on your own, Darling."

Quinton chuckled.

"Not going to help me anymore?" He asked.

"No, I can't force your memory to return." Andrea told him.

Quinton put his hand to Andrea's cheek.

"I'm sorry, My Pet. I know this must be hard on you as well." He said.

"You have no idea." Andrea muttered.

She turned away as the tears threatened again.

He put his finger under her chin forcing her to face him.

"What is it, Andrea? What is making you sad?" He questioned.

"Your… condition. I don't know what to do, how to help." She said sadly.

"We'll do it together." Quinton assured her.

Andrea gave him a wan smile.

There was a knock on the door.

"Come in." Andrea said.

"We're here to take Mr. Masterson to his room." Tyrone said.

Andrea stood up to let Tyrone and Jeffrey maneuver the bed out of the room.

Following them into the hall she stopped to talk to Dr. Cooper and Kyle.

"How long will Quinton be in the hospital?" Andrea asked.

"At least a couple of days to run tests and see what may have caused his amnesia." Dr. Cooper told her.

"Do I need to make special arrangements for when he goes home?" Andrea questioned.

"Do you have stairs in your home?" Dr. Cooper asked.

"Yes." Andrea answered.

"I don't want him climbing stairs for at least two weeks after he's discharged." Dr. Cooper said.

"I'll make arrangements for our bed to be moved into the study."

"I'll get a few friends to help me move it and anything else that needs to be moved." Kyle said.

"Thanks, Kyle." Andrea said.

Kyle nodded.

"He won't be allowed to shower alone." Dr. Cooper said.

"We have a shower on the main floor. I can wrap his arm in plastic." Andrea told him.

"I'll give you instructions when I discharge him. In the meantime go up to make sure he's resting comfortably." Dr. Cooper suggested.

"Thank you, Dr. Cooper." Andrea said.

Dr. Cooper nodded and walked away.

"How is Quinton?" Kyle asked.

"Okay, not happy that he has to stay in the hospital." Andrea told him.

"He always has been a bear when he was confined." Kyle told her.

"You heard Dr. Cooper, he won't be allowed to climb stairs or shower alone." Andrea said.

"You'll have to put away any object that can cause blunt force trauma." Kyle said.

"You think he'll become violent?" Andrea asked.

"No, it's to keep him safe from you. You're going to want to cause him serious bodily injury."

Andrea laughed.

After getting the room number Andrea and Kyle went up to Quinton's room.

Quinton gave Kyle a "what are you doing here?" look when he and Andrea walked in.

"Big Brother don't you have work to do?" Quinton asked pointedly.

Kyle got his brother's unmistakable "get lost" tone.

"Yes, of course. Andie call if you need anything. Little Brother behave yourself." Kyle said.

He kissed Andrea's cheek then walked out.

"Finally alone, come sit with me, My Pet." Quinton said.

"Quinton Masterson, you call me that one more time you won't have to worry about your memory returning." Andrea said heatedly.

"What would you like me to call you?" He asked smiling.

"Andrea is fine." She said.

~ 223 ~

"No, I like My Pet." He said.

Andrea groaned.

She spent the rest of what was left of the day at Quinton's bedside.

While he was in the hospital she spent her days at his bedside and her nights wandering an empty, lonely house.

Kyle and a few of his friends came over to move their bed down to the study. They also brought Quinton and Andrea's bureaus down.

Andrea walked into Quinton's room.

He was smiling.

"You're in a good mood." She said.

"I remembered something." Quinton said.

"Oh, what." Andrea asked.

"The first Christmas we spent together. You received underwear." Quinton told her.

Andrea blushed.

It wasn't the most flattering thing he could have remembered about her but it was something.

"Yes, Kyle and Abby gave them to me." She confirmed.

Quinton's smile grew wider.

Dr. Cooper walked into the room.

"Good morning." He said.

"Good morning." Quinton and Andrea said together.

"How are you feeling Quinton?" Dr. Cooper asked.

"Fine, ready to get out of here." Quinton said.

"I am going to discharge you but there are conditions." Dr. Cooper said.

"I'll follow any conditions you set down just get me out of here." Quinton told him.

"No climbing stairs, no showering without supervision, don't get your arm wet..." Dr. Cooper said.

"Yeah, yeah, yeah get me out of here." Quinton said irritably.

"Be patient, Darling." Andrea said happily.

"We'll see how patient you are when I get home." Quinton said.

"Quinton." Andrea warned.

"Alright then, here are your discharge papers. I've given you a prescription for a pain reliever. No driving for two weeks and you're not to return to work for two weeks. If you have any concerns don't hesitate to call my office. Call my office to make a follow-up appointment in two weeks." Dr. Cooper said.

He left so Quinton could get ready to go home.

At Quinton's request Andrea had brought him clothes from home on one of her previous visits.

She took them out of the cupboard by the door, then went to help Quinton get dressed.

Quinton took his clothes from her and tried to dress himself.

Andrea let him. She watched as he struggled with only one free hand.

"Oh for God's sake, I can't even dress myself." Quinton said angrily.

"There's no use in getting angry, Darling." Andrea told him.

She took his briefs, easily sliding them up his legs. Next she put on his socks and jeans.

"You're enjoying this aren't you?" Quinton asked irritably.

"Quinton, you're my husband. Why would I enjoy watching you struggle with the simple task of dressing yourself?" Andrea asked.

He pinned Andrea to the bed.

"There's one thing I can do without your help." He said triumphantly.

Andrea's body heated up and she became flushed.

Oh how she wanted him. She'd spent too many lonely nights in their big, empty bed.

Unconsciously she encouraged him to move closer.

Quinton accepted her encouragement and moved as close as he could get.

"Quinton." She breathed.

Using his free hand he started to pull her blouse over her head.

There was a knock at the door.

"Is everything alright in there?" The nurse asked.

Quinton looked into Andrea's eyes. He could see the desire in them.

"Fine, just having a little difficulty getting dressed." Quinton said.

"Undressed you mean." Andrea whispered giggling.

"Do you need assistance?" The nurse asked.

"No, we can manage." Quinton told her.

Quinton and Andrea listened as the nurse walked away.

"We better finish getting you dressed before we get arrested." Andrea said.

"Is that a problem?" Quinton asked.

"Is what a problem?" Andrea asked.

"Our… passion for one another." Quinton said.

"Let's just say there's been more than a few times it could have gotten us arrested." Andrea said smiling.

"Suddenly having amnesia doesn't seem so bad after all I get to learn all the things I know about you again." He said.

Andrea arched a brow at him.

"We're going to have a difficult time putting your shirt on." She said.

"We'll put my right arm in the sleeve and leave my left arm out." Quinton told her.

"You'll have to wrap your coat around you because it's cold." Andrea told him.

"Alright let's get going." Quinton agreed.

Andrea helped Quinton put his shirt on then his coat. He pulled it over his splinted left arm.

"I'll let the nurse know you're ready to leave." Andrea said.

She walked to the door then to the nurses' station.

"May I help you, Mrs. Masterson?" Lila asked.

"My husband is ready to leave." Andrea told her.

"I'll get a wheelchair." Lila said.

"He won't like that." Andrea said.

'Hospital policy." Lila replied.

Andrea nodded. She waited while Lila went to get the wheelchair.

When she came back Andrea followed her to Quinton's room.

"Your chariot, Mr. Masterson." Lila announced.

"I'm perfectly capable of walking." Quinton stated.

"Sorry, hospital policy." Lila told him.

Quinton looked at Andrea.

Her face was expressionless. He grudgingly sat in the wheelchair.

With a wave of his hand Quinton said, "Take me to my trusty iron steed driver."

Lila giggled.

Andrea burst out laughing.

Quinton looked at her smiling. "Have I amused you My Pet?" He asked.

~ 227 ~

Andrea looked at him but couldn't answer because she began laughing again.

Lila pushed the button to bring the elevator to their floor.

The elevator whooshed to a stop. When the door opened Lila wheeled Quinton inside with Andrea closely following.

She stood on Quinton's right side.

He slipped his hand into hers.

She knew he was hesitant to leave the hospital. He'd be going out into a world that was unfamiliar to him.

She squeezed his hand reassuringly letting him know they'd get through this together.

When they came to the main lobby of the hospital Lila took them to the main entrance.

"Wait here, I'll get the van." Andrea said.

"Van?" Quinton questioned.

"Yes, you bought it for me shortly after our honeymoon." Andrea told him.

Lila waited for Andrea to bring the van around.

Walking to her van Andrea wondered what Quinton expected to happen when they arrived home.

Climbing into the van she buckled herself in then started the van and drove to the main entrance of the hospital.

Parking, she undid her seatbelt, opened her door then went to the passenger's side to help Quinton get in.

"This is what I'm riding home in?" He asked.

"Well you can't very well go home in your truck. It was totaled in the accident." Andrea reminded him.

"Oh, right so instead of leaving the hospital with a bang I'm leaving it with a whimper.' Quinton said.

"Hey, be nice you'll hurt Gertie's feelings." Andrea said.

"Gertie?" Quinton said.

"Gertrude, that's what I named the van. Gertie for short." Andrea explained.

"You named your van?" Quinton asked.

"Sure, you named your truck." She told him.

"What did I name my truck?" He questioned

"Zeus." Andrea answered.

"King of the Gods." Quinton said smiling.

"That's why you named it Zeus."

"I was right, I'm going to enjoy getting to know you again."

Andrea smiled at him.

"Maybe this time you won't be reluctant to tell me you love me." She thought.

Andrea leaned in to kiss him.

He took advantage of her need of him.

"Excuse me, but I have to get back." Lila said hesitantly.

Andrea blushed pulling away reluctantly.

"I'm sorry. Thank you for all of your help." She said.

"You're welcome, Mrs. Masterson. Good luck, Mr. Masterson." Lila said.

"Thank you." Quinton said.

Andrea assured herself that Quinton clicked his seatbelt into place then went to the driver's side.

Buckling her own seatbelt she put the van in gear and maneuvered her way through the hospital parking lot to head home.

Pulling into the driveway Andrea heard Quinton take in a breath.

"What's wrong?" She asked.

~ 229 ~

"I don't think I've ever been so glad to be home." Quinton said.

"We won't know for sure until your memory returns. I have to warn you it's not the same. I've made changes." Andrea told him.

"The changes have to be an improvement over what I'm used to." Quinton replied.

"I'll let you be the judge." Andrea said.

She put the van in park then shut the van off.

She clicked the button on her seatbelt then opened her door.

Walking around to Quinton's side she opened the door and assisted him in getting out.

Slowly they made their way to the door.

Andrea unlocked the door then opened it.

Quinton whistled when they walked in.

"Darling?" Andrea said.

"When you said you made changes I didn't imagine this." He said.

"You don't like it." She said sadly.

"Are you always so negative, My Pet?" Quinton asked.

"No." Andrea said shortly.

Quinton stopped. He turned Andrea to look at him.

"You've done a wonderful job. The house looks like a home." He said.

Andrea smiled.

"Our bed has been moved into the study as well as our bureaus. Anything else we may need I can go upstairs to get." She told him.

"The only thing I want to do is lie down and hold you." Quinton told her.

"All right." Andrea agreed.

She lead Quinton into the study.

After making him comfortable on the bed she went to light a fire in the fireplace.

Quinton watched as she efficiently started the fire going.

He had a memory of them laying in each other's arms in front of the fireplace.

He sucked in his breath.

Andrea looked at him.

"Quinton?" She asked.

"I had a memory of us laying in front of the fireplace." He said.

"That's from our first date." Andrea told him.

"You haven't been with anyone else… ever." Quinton stated.

Andrea shook her head no.

Quinton sensed her reluctance to talk about her… experience.

"Come to bed, My Pet." He ordered.

"Let me lock the door." Andrea said.

She walked to the front door, locked it then went back to Quinton.

Pulling back the blankets, she lay down next to him.

Hovering close to the edge. She was surprised when Quinton pulled her to him.

"Amnesia or not, you're still my wife." He said sternly.

Quinton held her to him, he made no attempt to hide is desire for her.

"Quinton go to sleep" Andrea said.

"I've lost my memory, not my ability to get aroused, My Pet." Quinton said.

"You were just discharged from the hospital." She reminded him.

"Dr. Cooper didn't give explicit instructions about making love." Quinton told her.

"Quinton it's implied." Andrea forced out as he pressed against her.

"If he wanted me to abstain he would have given me instructions." He argued.

"You're impossible."

"Why? Because I have a valid point?

Quinton turned her to face him.

"Tell me you don't want me to make love to you."

Andrea lowered her eyes.

He forced to look at him.

The look of desire in her eyes told him what she wanted.

Quinton kissed her.

Andrea shyly kissed him back

Quinton deepened the kiss demanding her full participation.

She couldn't refuse him what he wanted nor deny herself.

As morning became afternoon Quinton and Andrea gave pleasure to one another without completing their union.

Sated, Andrea lay asleep in Quinton's arms.

Another memory came to him.

Andrea was dancing with Kyle on New Year's Eve.

He danced with someone who looked similar to Andrea.

He pushed his partner into Kyle's arms and pulled Andrea to him.

Andrea had been wrong. Their first date had been a double date with Kyle and his wife.

At least he was guessing the other woman was Kyle's wife.

Quinton wondered what he'd done in the years between his first meeting with Andrea and their second date.

He guessed a lot of it had been spent working and sowing his wild oats.

How many woman's hearts had he broken? Had he fathered any children?

Another memory came to him.

"My fathering your child would be humiliating?" He asked.

Quinton guessed parts of that memory were missing. At least he hoped they were.

Andrea was going to have to fill in some of the missing pieces of the puzzle for him.

He couldn't wait for her to wake up.

Making love with her had been one of the best experiences he could remember having.

He was guessing even though he had amnesia that would still be the case when his memory returned.

He smiled to himself, that was the memory he didn't think he could lose.

Quinton snuggled in next to Andrea drifting off to sleep.

CHAPTER TWELVE

Later they were awakened by pounding on their front door.

"Just a minute." Andrea yelled.

She found her clothes, hastily putting them on.

Going to the door she opened it to find Kyle standing on the other side of it.

"It's about time, I've been here for five minutes." He said.

"We were asleep." Andrea said.

"Did it occur to either one of you to call Abby or me to let us know Quint had been discharged from the hospital?" Kyle asked.

"No, we were anxious to get home." Quinton said from the study doorway wrapped in a comforter.

"Abby called the hospital to check on you. Imagine her surprise when she was told you'd been discharged." Kyle said.

"Abby is your wife?" Quinton asked.

'Yes, and Andrea's twin sister." Kyle said.

"She's going to have my head." Andrea mumbled.

"She's going to have more than your head." Kyle told her.

"Kyle, we're busy. I'll call you later." Quinton said.

"Abby wants you to come over for supper. She won't take no for an answer." Kyle said.

He walked out closing the door behind him.

"Come here, My Pet." Quinton ordered.

Andrea reluctantly walked to him.

He took her by the hand, leading her to the bed.

"We're going to be late for supper." Quinton stated.

He pulled Andrea to him kissing her.

She clung to him as he kissed the line of her jaw, then down her neck.

His mouth left a warm trail everywhere he kissed,

Andrea pushed the comforter off his shoulders then pushed it completely off him.

"Let me love you, My Pet." He said.

"I want to love you." Andrea said boldly.

Quinton sensed this was new for her.

He let her arouse him.

Andrea kissed his mouth lovingly, kissed his jaw line coming to his ear where she took little nips making Quinton groan with excitement.

Sensing his arousal growing, Andrea kissed down his jaw toward his chin.

She put her hands on his chest lowering her head to kiss him.

Together they lay on the bed touching, tasting, loving.

Quinton let Andrea take the initiative in their lovemaking.

Andrea glided her finger along the skin of his arms creating goose bumps.

She removed her own clothing.

Gliding her fingers across his legs she created goose bumps.

Sensing he was near the edge, Andrea pushed Quinton on his back.

Carefully she slid onto him, closing her eyes she arched her back.

"Andrea." He called.

Gently swaying her hips she brought him to full arousal.

Concerned only with his pleasure, she continued the movement until his climax was complete.

Andrea lay next to Quinton kissing him.

He was not happy that she'd sacrificed her own pleasure for him.

"Why?" He asked.

"I love you." She said silently.

"It's what I wanted." Andrea said aloud.

Quinton hugged her to him.

"I love you." He thought to himself.

The thought surprised him.

Why couldn't he tell her?

Another question that would elude him until his memory returned.

What if his memory didn't return?

He had to think positive. His memory would return.

"We have to go." Quinton said reluctantly.

"I know." Andrea said kissing him.

Quinton held her to him as though he'd never let her go.

She was arousing him again.

"My Pet if we don't get out of this bed we're not going to Kyle and Abby's for supper." Quinton said.

"What's your point?" Andrea asked innocently.

Quinton slapped her on the bottom.

"Hey, what was that for?" She asked giggling.

"A playful slap, My Pet." Quinton told her.

"I know, Quinton." She told him.

Andrea kissed him one last time then climbed out of bed to get dressed.

Quinton watched her as she gathered her clothing.

When she was dressed he climbed out of bed.

"I'm going to need helping getting dressed, My Pet." Quinton said.

"I know, Darling.' Andrea said.

She gathered his clothes then went to help him dress.

Afterward they headed out the door to go to Kyle and Abby's for supper.

"Hi Uncle Quinton and Aunt Andie." Kerry and Kayla greeted.

Quinton looked surprised.

Andrea laughed.

'Kerr Bear, Kay Rae you remember Uncle Quinton lost part of his memory." Andrea said.

"Yes, daddy told us." Kayla said.

"I'm Kerry Tyler, you call me K.T." Kerry announced.

"I'm Kayla Rae, you call me Kay Rae." Kayla told him.

Abby walked into the foyer.

"Kayla, Kerry go wash up for supper." She said. "Hi Quinton, I'm Abby."

Quinton did a double take.

Andrea and Abby did look alike.

As far as he could tell that's where the similarities ended.

Andrea had dark skin and blonde hair. Abby had light skin and dark hair.

Quinton turned to Andrea.

"You're a natural blonde?" He asked.

"Yes." Andrea said smiling.

He turned to Abby.

"You're a natural brunette?" He asked.

"Yes." Abby responded with the same smile as Andrea.

"How?" Quinton asked.

"We gave up trying to explain our differences a long time ago." Andrea said.

"I'm glad to know I'm not the only one confused." Quinton confessed.

Andrea and Abby laughed.

"We've confused many people." Abby told him.

Kyle walked into the foyer.

"Agnes says supper is ready." He said.

Everyone headed toward the dining room.

Quinton lagged behind.

Andrea noticed his hesitation.

"What's wrong, Darling?" She asked.

"Having amnesia is frustrating at times. People I know are introducing themselves to me." Quinton said irritably.

"It's only been a few days. Don't try so hard to recover your memory." Andrea said.

Quinton took Andrea by the hand, pulled her to him and kissed her.

A memory came flooding to his mind.

They stood in Kyle's living room kissing. Andrea was shaking with desire for him.

He deepened the kiss.

Andrea clung to him for support.

The memory was lost.

It lasted longer than the rest.

Quinton molded Andrea's body to his

Lifting his head he asked, "How do I leave you each morning?"

"With the promise you'll see me in the evening." Andrea said smiling.

"There was one day that promise could have been broken." Quinton said.

"It wasn't, Darling. Don't dwell on the accident. We have our whole lives ahead of us. Come on let's join everyone for supper." Andrea coaxed.

Quinton followed Andrea into the dining room.

Sitting at the table Quinton looked around at his family.

"Abby is short for Abigail?" Quinton asked.

"No, Tabitha." Abby told him.

Quinton looked at Andrea.

"Do you have a nickname?" He asked.

"My father and granddaddy call me, Wren, my middle name is Renay. Everyone else calls me Andie except you." Andrea told him.

"What do I call you?" Quinton questioned.

"Little One." Andrea responded blushing.

Quinton gave that some thought.

"I like "My Pet" better." He decided.

"Naturally." Andrea grumbled.

Quinton smiled.

"Shall we eat before supper gets cold?" Andrea asked.

Everyone helped themselves to the food.

Andrea helped make Kayla and Kerry's plates.

After supper Andrea helped Abby and Agnes clean up.

"How are things going?" Abby asked,

"As well as can be expected, I suppose. Quinton is frustrated at his loss of memory and thinks he can force it to return.' Andrea said.

"How are you dealing with the memory loss?" Abby questioned,

"The best I can for now." Andrea responded.

"It will take time for his memory to return, Andie. You have to be patient and have faith." Abby assured her.

Andrea gave her a doubtful look.

Abby smiled.

"I pray you're right." Andrea told her.

The dining room clean, Andrea and Abby joined the rest of the family in the living room.

Andrea sat on the floor between Quinton's legs and laid her head down. She wanted to be close to him.

Abby went to sit next to Kyle on the loveseat.

Andrea watched Kerry and Kayla play with their toys in a corner of the room.

She wished she could tell Quinton they were expecting their first child in less than eight months.

How would he react? He didn't know he'd suggested they marry to create a child. She loved him but didn't dare tell him, not now that he'd lost his memory of the last five years,

If she told him she was expecting what would he do? If she didn't tell him how angry would he be?

Quinton interrupted her inner musings.

"Are you ready to leave, My Pet?" He asked.

Andrea bristled when he called her "My Pet." She didn't like the pet name, but didn't know how to get him to stop using it.

"Yes, I'm tired." She said.

Kayla and Kerry gave Quinton and Andrea hugs and kisses before they left.

Quinton and Andrea said their good-byes to Kyle and Abby then left.

The ride home was quiet..

After he unlocked the door, Quinton indicated that Andrea should go ahead of him.

She ducked her head then went inside.

"Are you going to tell me what's bothering you?" Quinton asked.

"What makes you think something's bothering me?" Andrea retorted.

"I may have lost my memory but I haven't lost my ability to read people." Quinton told her.

"I'm just tired." Andrea hedged.

"You're going to stick with that story?" Quinton questioned.

"Yes." Andrea said stubbornly.

"Alright."

Quinton pulled her to him, kissing her.

Andrea tried to pull out of his embrace; he deepened the kiss making her want him.

Quinton trailed a line of kisses along her jaw to her ear where he nipped and bit.

"Oh, God Quinton." Andrea cried.

He held her to him rubbing her back in the most seductive way.

"Will we be lovers tonight, My Pet or are you an unwilling partner?" He asked.

Andrea's breathing was labored as he used his power of seduction on her,

"Lovers." She stated.

Quinton took her by the hand leading her to their makeshift bedroom in the study.

Leading her to the bed he unbuttoned her blouse, kissing her body as it was exposed to him,

In one swift movement he unclasped her lacy bra that molded her supple breasts.

Andrea cried out as he took one aching breast into his mouth and suckled.

Holding him to her she savored his mouth at her breast.

"Quinton." she managed through her want of him.

He moved his mouth to her other aching breast.

"Do you want me My Pet?" He asked huskily.

"Yes!" She cried.

Quinton slowly and seductively undressed them both while arousing her further.

~ 242 ~

Urging her up to the top of the bed he thrust into her.

Andrea dug her nails into the bed as he awakened her need for him.

"Quinton, love me." She cried tears of joy evident in her voice.

Quinton left no part of her untouched by his lovemaking.

Andrea fell into a sated sleep curled up next to him.

Quinton put his arm around her, pulling her close.

The next morning Quinton woke to an empty bed.

"Where the hell is Andrea?" He thought.

He rolled over to get out of bed then realized he wasn't wearing his sling. His arm hurt like hell.

Come hell or high water he was dressing himself this morning.

Quinton was just buckling his belt when the door to the study opened.

"Good morning, Darling. How did you sleep?" Andrea said smiling.

Quinton scowled at her.

"I woke up alone." He grumbled.

"I was making breakfast." She said.

Quinton gave her a sheepish smile.

Andrea walked to him, then kissed him.

She thought "Maybe I can tell him I'm pregnant."

His next statement stopped her cold.

"We haven't been using birth control. Is there any chance you could get pregnant?" He said.

"Do you not want children?" Andrea questioned.

"Did we discuss having children before getting married?" Quinton asked.

"Yes." Andrea said.

"And?" Quinton prodded.

"And what?" Andrea put the question back.

"What did we decide?"

"We decided to let nature take its course."

Andrea hoped he couldn't tell she was only telling him part of the truth.

"What has nature decided?" Quinton asked.

"It's too soon to tell." Andrea lied.

"You will tell me when we're expecting a child." Quinton said.

"Of course." Andrea said crossing her fingers childishly.

Quinton smiled.

"Let's eat, I'm starved." He said.

Andrea put the tray she was holding on the bed.

Together Quinton and Andrea ate the breakfast she'd made then settled into a comfortable housekeeping routine.

Andrea did make a trip to the bathroom that Quinton was unaware of.

The life growing inside of her wouldn't allow her to keep down the breakfast she'd eaten.

Dr. Cooper hadn't released Quinton to return to work yet so he'd be home with Andrea every day.

How she was going to hide the symptoms of her pregnancy she didn't know.

Every day Quinton and Andrea ate breakfast together, then Quinton went to his physical therapy appointments.

Andrea was grateful Dr. Cooper had scheduled physical therapy for Quinton that way she could have the mornings to herself to deal with her morning sickness.

One day after Quinton's physical therapy he took Andrea out to lunch then they went to look at trucks to replace the one he'd lost in the accident.

Finally Dr. Cooper released Quinton to go back to work.

"Are you sure you're going to be alright without me here?" Quinton asked.

"Quinton, I'm a grown woman I can take care of myself." Andrea said.

"I don't want you to feel like I'm abandoning you." Quinton said.

"How is going to work abandoning me?" Andrea asked.

"I just want to know that you need me." Quinton admitted.

"I do need you, just not around the house all the time." Andrea told him.

Quinton looked skeptical.

"That does not reassure me." He said.

"We discussed me going back to school. I won't be hanging around the house all the time." Andrea said,

"Going to school? For what?" Quinton questioned.

Andrea smiled.

"Computers, what else?" She said.

Quinton laughed.

"Keeping it in the family, I like that." He said.

"Now, go to work."

"Yes, Dear."

Quinton left whistling.

Andrea had gotten him to leave just in time. Their unborn child decided that she'd had enough breakfast today.

Andrea hastily headed toward the bathroom.

Without closing the door she lost the contents of her stomach.

She felt a tug on her hair where Quinton held it away from her face.

"I assume you don't have an eating disorder." He said angrily.

Andrea couldn't answer right away, their unborn child made that impossible.

Several minutes later a pale and shaking Andrea stood up, walked to the sink, washed her face, rinsed her mouth then turned to Quinton.

He let go of her hair.

"No, I don't have an eating disorder." Andrea admitted,

"You're pregnant." Quinton accused.

"Yes." Andrea said.

"Why did you lie to me?" He asked hurt.

"There was the accident, then your memory loss… I didn't want you to have something else to worry about." Andrea said.

"You didn't want me to worry. Did it occur to you that knowing you're pregnant would bring me joy?" Quinton asked.

"Um… no, I thought it might add to your stress."

"Keeping things from me will add to my stress. Is there anything else you'd like to tell me?"

"No, that's all the secrets I have. Why did you come back?"

"I forgot my keys. I saw you run down the hall and followed you"

"I'm sorry, Darling. I won't keep anything from you."

Quinton pulled her to him,

"See that you don't."

He kissed her.

"I'll see you tonight." Andrea said.

~ 246 ~

"Take care of yourself and our child." Quinton told her.

He kissed Andrea again then bent down to kiss her stomach.

Tears sprang to Andrea's eyes.

Quinton left happy.

Andrea was relieved that Quinton knew about the baby but embarrassed in which the way he'd learned she was pregnant.

Shaking her head, she took hold of herself. Scolding herself wasn't going to take back what she'd done.

Andrea went to take a shower so she could go to the local university to register for the winter semester.

Walking into the admitting office she was greeted by the receptionist

"May I help you?" She asked.

"I'd like to register for the winter semester." Andrea told her.

"Will you be applying for financial aid or student loans?" The receptionist asked.

"No, I'll be paying for classes myself." Andrea said.

"You'll have to fill out some paperwork."

The receptionist handed Andrea the paperwork.

"I'll take this home and bring it back." Andrea said.

"Alright. The winter semester starts after the new year." The receptionist told her.

"Thank you." Andrea said then walked out.

She went home to look over the paperwork and start filling it out.

When Quinton arrived home that evening she was ready to throw the paperwork in the trash.

"Hello, My Pet, how was your day?" He asked.

"Frustrating, I went to the university to register for the winter semester." Andrea said.

"Yes?" Quinton questioned.

"I'm not going back to school. All the paperwork discourages you from wanting to enroll." Andrea told him.

"I'll take a look at it after supper.' Quinton offered.

Andrea smiled.

"I made meat loaf, green bean casserole and mashed potatoes." She said.

"Sounds delicious." Quinton said.

"Let's eat, I'm hungry." Andrea said.

Quinton following her into the kitchen to help put the food on the table.

"We'll have to have a supper party to announce your pregnancy and intention of going back to school." Quinton said.

"I wanted to announce my pregnancy after I made it through the first trimester." Andrea said.

"My Pet you've already waited long enough. My parents are going to be thrilled."

"Alright." Andrea said.

They finished eating in a comfortable silence then cleaned up, stacked the dishes in the dishwasher and turned it on.

"Where's your paperwork for the university?" Quinton asked.

Andrea headed to the study.

Quinton followed her.

Together he and Andrea completed the paperwork for Andrea to enroll at the university.

"I'll of course pay the tuition." Quinton stated.

"You don't have…" Andrea tried to say.

"There will be no argument, My Pet, you are my wife." Quinton said stopping the argument.

"Yes, of course Darling." Andrea replied.

"Now let's start planning our supper party." Quinton said.

The rest of the evening he and Andrea planned the supper party they were going to have for their family.

Walking to bed Quinton took Andrea by the hand drawing her next to him.

When they came to the bed he kissed her.

Andrea kissed him back urging him to make love to her.

Their lovemaking wasn't conventional. Quinton used his hands and mouth to arouse her and bring her to climax.

"Oh my God Quinton." Andrea cried.

She gripped the bed as the waves of pleasure coursed through her body.

Finally she was able to reciprocate. Andrea teased him to the point of agony then finally she slid onto him completing his pleasure.

"Andrea!" He called huskily when his climax began.

Sated they fell asleep, their arms and legs entwined.

Andrea woke up to find Quinton had already left for work but he'd left her a note.

My Pet:

I'm taking half a day off to spend with you. We'll enroll you in your classes then spend the rest of the day as you wish. Think of something you'd like to do.

All my love,

Quinton

All my love? Did that mean he loved her?

Andrea grew excited. Would he tell her he loved her or wait until she declared her love first?

There was still the obstacle of his memory loss to get over.

"I can't forget he doesn't know we married to have a baby." Andrea said to herself.

How was he going to take that news? He'd be angry she was sure.

Deciding not to dwell on it, Andrea went to take a long, luxurious bath.

She didn't emerge until the water had turned cold and she was as wrinkled as a prune.

While she dried off Andrea picked out the clothes she wanted to wear. When she was dry she moisturized her skin with scented body lotion, applied other toiletries then finished getting ready.

When Quinton arrived a little after noon Andrea was ready.

"Hello Darling." She greeted him.

Quinton put his arm around her, then pulled her to him kissing her.

Andrea was lost in the kiss.

Quinton was carried away by her warmth to the kiss and the inviting scent she wore.

He wanted to abandon any plans they had for the day and make love to her.

Andrea pulled away.

"Darling, we have things to do." She reminded him.

"I know, I was working on that." He said.

Andrea blushed,

"I meant I have to get enrolled in the winter semester at the university." She said.

"I know. I was attempting to distract you." He countered smiling.

"It was working." She admitted.

"I'm pleased. Let's get out of here before I throw my good intentions out the window." He replied.

Quinton and Andrea left to get the paperwork so she could enroll in the winter semester at the university.

Afterward they left to go to the admitting office.

When Andrea handed in her paperwork the receptionist gave her a list of things she'd need and instructions on how to submit it.

Andrea thanked her then they left.

On the way to the van Quinton took Andrea's hand in his, kissing the back.

Andrea smiled at him.

"God, I love him please let his memory return." She prayed silently.

Arriving at the van Quinton maneuvered Andrea against the side then kissed her,

Her breath caught in her throat at his gentleness.

Raising his head, Quinton asked, "What did you plan for today?"

Andrea's mind wasn't working as quickly as his was.

"What?" She responded.

He repeated the question.

"Uh,... I forgot." Andrea admitted.

Quinton chuckled.

"Let's start with lunch." He suggested.

"Alright." Andrea agreed.

Quinton assisted her into the van then went around to the driver's side.

Soon they were on their way to get lunch.

Quinton pulled into a modestly priced restaurant, they went in to have lunch.

After being seated Quinton and Andrea looked over the menus.

"What would you like My Pet?" He asked.

"All you can eat spaghetti." Andrea answered.

"Does my child want pasta?" Quinton questioned.

"No, your wife does. Suddenly I have an overwhelming craving for it." Andrea replied.

"Cravings already. Shall I get pickles and ice cream on the way home?" Quinton asked amused.

Andrea wrinkled her nose in distaste.

"No, pasta seems to be the only craving I have right now."

"Any pasta in particular or will any pasta do?"

"Lasagna sounds good too. Oh and for dessert chocolate cake with cream cheese frosting."

Quinton smiled.

A picture of him dipping strawberries into a chocolate fondue pot and feeding them to Andrea came to mind.

Andrea bit into one half, he bit into the other.

Each ate their own half then when their lips met Quinton kissed Andrea.

The memory faded.

Damn! He wished the memory hadn't faded he wanted to know what happened next.

"What's wrong, Darling?" Andrea asked.

"I had another memory." Quinton told her.

"A bad one?" She questioned.

'No, I was feeding you strawberries dipped in chocolate." Quinton said.

Andrea smiled.

"Dessert from our second date." She said.

"Second date? This reminds me you told me that was our first date. I had a memory of another date we went on."

"Yes, I'd actually forgotten the first one we went on, a double date with Kyle and Abby."

"Continue."

"The reason was to make Abby think we didn't... um, dislike each other."

"Dislike each other?"

"Quinton, I don't want to talk about this."

Andrea waved the hostess over.

"Yes, ma'am?" Melanie asked.

"Our drink order hasn't been taken and our server hasn't come to talk to us yet." Andrea said.

"I apologize. I'll take care of that right away. What can I get you to drink? Melanie said.

"I'll have sweet tea. Quinton?" Andrea said.

"Coffee." Quinton ordered gruffly.

"Your server will bring those right over. Again, I apologize for the wait." Melanie told them.

"Thank you.' Andrea said.

Quinton took Andrea's hands in his.

"Andrea, what are you keeping from me?" He asked gently.

"I'm not keeping anything from you. There are some things you have to remember on your own." She said.

"Have I been cruel to you?" Quinton questioned.

"Do you honestly think I'm the type of woman who would marry a man who was cruel to her?" Andrea asked.

Quinton looked into her eyes, shook his head and said, "No."

"Can we change the subject?"

"Of course, My Pet. What would you like to talk about?"

"Work. How does it feel to be back at work?"

"Not much different than normal, there are some people I don't recognize, other than that it's fine."

"Are you working on anything special?"

"I'm trying to get a new account. Why are you interested in work, My Pet?"

"I'd like to be informed if I'm going to join K.M. Enterprises, Atlanta Division Darling."

"There's no if about it, My Pet. You will be joining the Atlanta Division."

"Hi, I'm Dottie your server. Here are your drinks." She interrupted.

"Thank you. I suggest you spend less time on your phone and more time working." Quinton said.

"Yes sir, I apologize for my lack of service. It won't happen again." Dottie assured him.

Quinton smiled.

Dottie stood straighter as if trying to impress him.

"My wife will have the all you can eat spaghetti and I'll have the steak and shrimp." Quinton said.

Dottie wrote down their order.

"How would you like your steak cooked?" She asked.

'Medium well." Quinton answered.

"Would either of you like to add the salad bar?" Dottie asked.

"I would." Andrea said harshly.

Dottie looked at her.

She saw that Andrea didn't appreciate a young woman flirting with her husband.

Quinton chuckle amused.

Andrea gave him a "Don't go there look."

He brought his amusement under control.

"Help yourself to the salad bar ma'am. I'll put in your order." Dottie said then walked away.

Andrea pulled her hands out of Quinton's.

She folded her arms across her stomach.

"I may have lost my memory but something tells me I'm in trouble." Quinton said.

"Whatever gave you that idea?" Andrea asked.

"Your withdrawal from me and your attitude." Quinton said.

Andrea raised an eyebrow at him.

"Really? How would you like it if I flirted with other men?" She questioned.

"I wasn't flirting." Quinton said.

"You weren't flirting. Our server completely ignored the fact that I'm sitting here and paid far too much attention to you." Andrea pointed out.

"Are you jealous, My Pet?" Quinton asked.

'Would it make any difference if I were?"

Quinton took her hands in his again.

"I don't want you to be jealous, My Pet." Quinton said aloud.

Silently he said, "I want you to love me."

Andrea looked skeptical.

"It's difficult enough with your memory loss, Quinton I don't want to have to worry about infidelity." Andrea told him.

"Infidelity? I would never be unfaithful, My Pet." He assured her.

"Can we talk about something else?" Andrea asked.

"Of course. What would you like to do today?" Quinton asked.

"Start setting up the nursery." Andrea said.

'First we have to move our bedroom back upstairs." Quinton reminded her.

"We can call Kyle when we get home to ask for his help."

"I can move the bedroom on my own."

'Quinton , Kyle had friends help him, don't be difficult."

Dottie bringing their food stopped any response he would have made.

Silently they ate lunch, paid then left.

CHAPTER THIRTEEN

Time seemed to go by slowly for the next few weeks.

Quinton and Andrea decorated for Christmas. Colored lights ran the length of the soffit on the house, on the banister, stairwell anywhere Andrea could find to hang lights she did.

An artificial Flocked Noble Pine Christmas tree decorated with red and green twinkling lights sat off to the side of the fireplace in the living room. It commanded attention in the room.

Quinton and Andrea made the house ready for Andrea's family's visit.

Their respective families would be spending Christmas in Atlanta this year. Andrea's family would be staying with her and Quinton.

His memories were more frequent and lasted longer.

Quinton shared the memories with Andrea, she sometimes helped fill in the missing pieces other times she told him he'd have to remember on his own.

Christmas Eve Quinton came home at noon.

Andrea heard him come in.

"Hi, Darling. You're home early, what's the occasion?" Andrea said.

'Does there have to be an occasion for me to want to come home to be with my beautiful wife?" Quinton asked.

Andrea blushed.

"No." She said smiling.

"What time is your family arriving?" Quinton questioned.

"Six o'clock." Andrea answered.

Quinton smiled, took her by the hand, leading her toward the stairs.

Andrea didn't object.

They spent a pleasant afternoon in each other's arms.

Quinton forced himself to untangle himself from Andrea.

She objected.

"Quinton no." She said.

'We have to be ready when your family arrives, My Pet." Quinton said.

"A little longer." She begged.

"We have tonight." He promised.

Andrea reluctantly climbed out of bed then headed to the bathroom for her second shower of the day.

Quinton happily followed.

Climbing into the shower with her he took the bath pouf pouring body wash on it.

Running it slowly over her body, Quinton made her quiver with longing.

"Quinton, please." She begged.

"Do you want me, My Pet?" He asked huskily.

"Yes." She said longing n her voice.

"We'll have to wait until tonight, My Pet." He told her.

"Oh, God Quinton, I can't" She begged again.

He used his hands to satisfy her hunger until they went to bed that night.

When she tried to reciprocate he said, "I can wait, My Pet."

Finishing their shower Quinton and Andrea went to finish getting ready for the party at Kyle and Abby's.

Walking into the house their families looked expectantly at them.

Andrea walked over to her parents, whom she hadn't seen since her honeymoon.

"Hello, daddy, mama." She said kissing them on the cheek.

"Wren, what's the secret you have to tell us?" Andrew asked.

Quinton walked up next to Andrea putting his arm around her.

"May I have everyone's attention please?" He asked.

Quinton and Andrea's families gave him their undivided attention.

"First, I'd like to wish everyone a Merry Christmas." Quinton started.

There was a chorus of Merry Christmas around the room.

"Second, I'm sure you're all wondering about the progress of my memory returning." Quinton said.

"Son, get on with your secret." Kindred said.

"In a moment, Father. My memory is slowly returning… Now for our secret. Andrea and I are expecting our first child in August." Quinton finished.

"Oh, Andrea I'm so happy for you. And you of course Quinton." Judy said.

"Thank you, Mama. I'm pleased." Andrea said smiling.

Everyone hugged Andrea and hugged and clapped Quinton on the back.

Kyle poured champagne for everyone. Andrea and Abby declined

Andrea because of her pregnancy and Abby because she was nursing her now five month old youngest son.

"How are you feeling, Andie?" Abby asked.

"Fine other than the morning sickness." Andrea answered.

"I know what you mean. It can be a bear." Abby sympathized.

"How are my two favorite nieces?" Millie asked putting her arms around them.

"We're your only nieces, Aunt Millie." Andrea said smiling.

"That's why you're my favorites." Millie told her.

"What are you up to Aunt Millie?" Andrea wondered aloud.

"Why must I be up to something?" Millie questioned.

"Really Aunt Millie? You don't think we know you better than that?" Andrea questioned.

"Have you told Quinton you love him yet, Andrea?"

"No, Aunt Millie, I haven't. Keep your voice down."

"Why not? Tabitha, why aren't you guiding your sister along this path?"

"Aunt Millie I don't know if Quinton loves me and with his memory loss I'm not sure if he does."

"Does or knows?"

"Knows."

"Tabitha, a little assistance please." Millie said.

'Don't drag me into the middle of this, Aunt Millie." Abby said.

"Don't you want your sister to be happy?" Millie questioned.

"I don't need anyone's help." Andrea stated.

"Obviously you do." Millie stated.

"Is everything alright, My Pet?" Quinton asked slipping his arms around Andrea.

'Yes, fine Darling. We were talking about the baby." Andrea lied easily.

"You're not a very good liar, you know." Quinton said.

"What?" Andrea said blushing.

"You weren't talking about the baby. You're much too tense." Quinton told her.

"I was asking her how she likes married life." Millie said.

"What was your answer?" Quinton said looking down at Andrea.

"I told her I love it of course." Andrea said.

"Very well. If that's the story you ladies want to stick with I'll play along." Quinton said.

He bent his head kissed Andrea seductively then patted her stomach gave them a salute and walked away smiling.

"I don't know how much longer I'm going to be able to keep from telling him I love him." Andrea mused.

"Why not tell him now, it's the perfect time.' Millie said.

"Aunt Millie I don't know if he loves me, besides there's his memory loss." Andrea said.

'You have to take a chance, Andrea." Millie said.

"Did you take a chance Aunt Millie?" Andrea asked.

"Yes, once." Millie replied.

"Once? Why didn't you try to find love again?" Andrea questioned.

"I didn't believe I'd ever find that love again. Don't make the mistake I did." Millie persuaded.

"I'll try Aunt Millie, that's the best I can do for now." Andrea promised.

"Supper is ready." Agnes announced.

Everyone went to the dining room catching up with each other's lives as they ate.

After supper the families went into the living room to have dessert.

Opening gifts would wait until tomorrow at Quinton and Andrea's.

Quinton could tell Andrea was ready to go home. She wasn't very good at hiding her weariness.

"We're going to say good night, Andrea's tired." He said.

"Quinton!" Andrea reprimanded.

"He's only speaking the truth Andrea. You're falling asleep in your chair." Judy said.

Andrea stood up.

"Good night everyone we'll see you at our house tomorrow." She said.

Quinton went to get their coats. He helped Andrea put hers on.

"Good night." He said.

"We'll be right behind you." Andrew said.

Quinton nodded then led Andrea out after she exchanged hugs and kisses with everyone.

He helped her into the van then went to the driver's side climbing in.

Before starting the van he turned in his seat.

"Is there anything you want to tell me, My Pet?: Quinton asked.

"I love you." Andrea said silently.

Aloud she said, " What makes you think I have something to tell you?"

"I have a feeling there's something you want to tell me." Quinton told her.

"I'm not comfortable with this conversation right now, Quinton." Andrea replied.

"Alright, My Pet but you can't put it off indefinitely." Quinton said.

"I just need a little time." Andrea told him.

Quinton turned back in his seat.

He started the van then drove them home.

When they pulled into the driveway Quinton put the van in park then turned off the engine.

Andrea had the feeling she should wait for Quinton to come to her side.

She was right. He opened her door, helped her out and closed the door.

Trapping her between himself and the van he kissed her sensuously.

Andrea responded passionately.

Quinton stopped abruptly.

"Quinton no." She pleaded.

"We have to go inside." He said.

Taking her hand, Quinton led Andrea inside.

Once inside the house he let his passion guide him.

Going upstairs he touched every part of Andrea with his lovemaking.

Her body responded as it had the first time they'd made love.

Making love they didn't hear Andrea's family arrive and settle in for the night.

The next morning Andrea was up early to start making Christmas dinner.

She found her mother and mother-in-law already hard at work just as she suspected.

"Good morning." Andrea greeted.

"Good morning." Judy and Roberta said in unison.

"How did you sleep Mama." Andrea asked.

"Well, of course I always seem to sleep well when I come to Atlanta." Judy said.

Andrea smiled.

"I'm happy you're relaxed while you're here." She said.

"How are you feeling this morning?" Roberta asked.

"Well, the morning sickness doesn't usually start until after breakfast." Andrea said.

"Try drinking ginger ale and eating saltines." Roberta suggested.

"Alright, I'll have to go pick up some ginger ale." Andrea said.

"Not necessary. I bought extra when I went to the store this morning." Robert told her.

Andrea walked over to hug her.

"Thank you, Mama that was thoughtful." She said.

Judy was busy working to get Christmas dinner ready.

Andrea noticed her agitation.

She walked over to her.

"What's wrong, Mama?" She asked quietly.

"Nothing.' Judy said shortly.

"Mama I know you better than that." Andrea told her.

"Alright, I know you and Abby call Roberta mama but to actually hear you say it upsets me a little." Judy admitted.

"I'm sorry Mama, I didn't mean to upset you." Andrea apologized.

"Don't apologize Andrea. I shouldn't be so vain, it isn't like me." Judy replied.

"You're right, it's not like you but sometimes you're allowed to be vain."

Judy patted Andrea's arm.

"Thank you, Andrea."

"You're welcome, Mama. I love you."

"I love you too."

"I'm going to eat some saltines and drink some ginger ale, if you two need any help please tell me." Andrea said.

"We will." Judy assured her.

Andrea poured herself a glass of ginger ale, took a package of crackers from the box in the cupboard then took them into the dining room to eat and drink.

Twenty minutes later she came back with an empty glass and a half eaten package of crackers.

"How do you feel?" Roberta asked.

"Good, I'll know if the ginger ale and crackers worked in about ten minutes." Andrea replied.

Roberta smiled.

Quinton came into the kitchen.

"Good morning." He said then leaned down to kiss Andrea.

He poured a cup of coffee then took Andrea by the hand leading her to the study.

"Is something wrong, Darling?" Andrea asked.

"You can stop the 'darling' act, my memory has returned." Quinton said harshly.

"When? How?" Andrea questioned.

"Last night, after we made love and you fell asleep." Quinton told her softly.

Andrea knew the softness in his voice was not a good sign.

"You're angry, why?" She queried.

"You agreed to marry me to have a baby?" Quinton asked.

"Quinton don't do this please." Andrea begged.

"Why Little One?" He questioned again.

Andrea knew she was defeated.

"I had no alternative. You refused to have a child otherwise." She told him.

"I told you my memory has returned. I know the conditions under which we married." Quinton growled.

"What do you want me to say, Quinton?" Andrea asked.

"That you love me." He begged silently.

Aloud he said, "I'm voiding any agreement we made."

Andrea's heart sank into her stomach and she turned pale, she was going to empty the contents of her stomach.

"You can't…"

"You will remain my wife regardless of what happens."

Andrea gave an audible sigh. She couldn't argue even if she had wanted to.

"I've already agreed to that, what else is there?" She said.

"My mother will never suspect we're not in love." Quinton stated.

"Oh God, he doesn't love me." Andrea thought.

"I would never hurt your mother." She snapped.

"As far as anyone else is concerned we fell in love." Quinton insisted.

Andrea nodded then walked out.

Walking into the kitchen she put a smile on her face.

"Is there anything I can do to help?" She asked.

"Cut the cranberry sauce." Judy said.

Andrea went to get the cranberry sauce out of the pantry. She opened the cans, placed it on plates, cut it, covered it then put it in the refrigerator to cool.

After she finished Andrea busied herself in the kitchen to avoid Quinton.

Finally dinner was announced.

Andrea tried to sit at the opposite end of the table from Quinton.

He pulled a chair out next to his indicating she would sit next to him.

Not wanting to make a scene, Andrea obediently sat in the chair Quinton offered.

His only acknowledgement was a slight nod of his head.

Andrea did her best not to let Quinton's annoyance prevent her from joining in the Christmas celebration. She was unsuccessful.

When everyone was through eating Andrea began cleaning up as her family and in-laws wandered into the living room.

Abby stayed behind to help clean up.

"Are you alright, Andie?" She asked.

"Yes, fine." Andrea said absently.

"Is there anything you want to talk about?" Abby questioned.

Andrea sighed.

"He doesn't love me." She replied.

"Quinton? Of course he does." Abby assured her.

"No, he's only putting on a front for everyone" Andrea told her.

"A front? What does that mean?"

"His memory has returned but he's being cold and distant."

"Andie, I'm sure you're imagining things."

"I don't think so. He wants me to make everyone believe we married for love, Abby. I don't want to discuss this anymore. What plans have you and Kyle made for New Year's Eve?"

"We're celebrating at home. Agnes is at her sister's for the holidays and we want a cozy, quiet evening at home."

'Cozy, quiet evening at home with twin five year olds and a five month old?"

Abby laughed.

"Okay, as cozy and quiet as it can be with twin five year olds and a five month old."

Andrea smiled.

"I have the feeling Quinton has something planned but he's not telling me what it is."

Andrea and Abby finished cleaning up in comfortable silence.

Andrea brewed a fresh pot of coffee waiting for it to finish then took it into the living room on a roll around table with tray.

"Fresh coffee." Andrea announced.

"Aunt Andie can we open our presents now?" Kerry asked.

"Would you like to help me pass them out Kerr Bear?" Andrea questioned.

In answer Kerry ran over to the tree and stood there waiting.

Andrea laughed then walked to where Kerry stood.

He handed her a present.

"This one is for Granddaddy Masterson." Andrea told him.

Kerry proudly carried the package to Kindred handing it to him.

"Thank you, K.T." Kindred said

Kerry smiled and hugged him.

"I want to help too." Kayla said.

"Alright, you pick the next present, Kay Rae." Andrea said.

Kayla walked over picked a present then handed it to Andrea.

"This one is for Uncle Quinton." She said.

Kayla took the package from Andrea walked to Quinton then handed it to him.

"Thank you, Kay Rae." Quinton said smiling.

Kayla smiled, hugged him then went back to Andrea.

Andrea continued to pick up presents, announce who they were for and took turns giving them to Kerry and Kayla to give them to the recipients.

Quinton pulled Andrea aside.

"I'll give you my gift later when we're alone." He told her.

Andrea nodded.

"I'll give you my gift later as well." She said.

Quinton put his arm around her urging her to join their families in the celebration of Christmas.

He limited his alcohol consumption because he wanted to be sober for the night ahead.

At last it was time to bid everyone good night.

Quinton's parents went back to their own home, Kyle and Abby packed up their children to make their journey home and Andrea's parents and brother settled in for the night.

Alone with Quinton Andrea was apprehensive.

He held her to him calming her fears.

"I wanted our first Christmas together to be special." He told her.

"Alright but this really isn't our first Christmas together." Andrea reminded him.

"It is as a couple. The past five years we just celebrated with our respective families. This year we're celebrating together." He said.

Andrea nodded.

"May I give you my gift first?" She asked.

'If you wish." He allowed.

Andrea walked over to her dresser, opened the top drawer and withdrew a long box.

~ 269 ~

Walking to Quinton she handed it to him.

He kissed her long and sensuously.

Andrea couldn't care less whether she received her gift or not.

Forcing himself to stop, Quinton pulled away.

Andrea pouted.

Quinton chuckled.

"First we exchange gifts, Little One." He said.

Andrea blushed.

Quinton opened the box Andrea had given him.

Inside was a man's bracelet with three birthstones on it.

The middle birthstone was a peridot that of their unborn child and on either side was a sapphire, Quinton's birthstone and an opal, Andrea's birthstone which were a quarter carat each.

Quinton smiled then kissed Andrea.

He walked to his dresser, opened the top drawer, withdrew a small velvet box.

Walking to Andrea he handed the box to her.

Slowly Andrea opened the box. Laying on a bed of satin was a half carat peridot and on either side was a quarter carat sapphire and a quarter carat opal ring.

"Oh, Quinton it's beautiful." Andrea exclaimed then kissed him.

Quinton accepted the kiss wholeheartedly, kissing her back.

His mouth wandered down her jaw to her neck where he suckled the soft, lightly scented skin.

"Quinton." Andrea pleaded.

Quinton pulled back.

"I'm sorry, Little One, I was carried away. We weren't finished exchanging gifts yet." He said.

Taking the box she'd given him and putting it on the nearest dresser he took the ring he'd given her and put on the third finger of her right hand putting the box on the dresser.

Andrea took his gift, opened the box, opened the clasp, indicated that Quinton needed to put his arm up.

He gave her his left arm.

Andrea clasped the bracelet in place and twirled it around his wrist for effect.

Quinton took her face in his hands and kissed her.

Andrea drew close to him wanting to be near him.

Her body ached to be satisfied by him.

Quinton urged her toward the bed.

Undressing her, he took his time making her ache all the more for him.

"Quinton, I want you." Andrea begged.

Pulling her to him, Quinton coaxed her to explore him.

"Love me, Andrea." Quinton urged.

She drew his sweater over his head, unbuttoned his jeans, drew them down, motioned for him to step out of them and tossed them aside with his sweater.

She hooked her arms around his neck kissing him.

Quinton pulled her against him to feel her naked body against him.

Lifting her, he laid her on the bed then followed her down.

Caressing each other they gave one another pleasure to the point they ached to be satisfied.

Moving between her legs, Quinton urged them apart to slide inside her to complete their union.

Andrea cried out with pleasure.

Making love Quinton and Andrea showed their love to one another.

Sated they fell asleep in each other's arms.

The week between Christmas and New Year's Eve went by quickly.

Andrea enjoyed spending time with her family during the day and the passion filled nights with Quinton.

New Year's Eve day arrived.

"The time sure has gone by quickly." Andrea said.

"It usually does when you're enjoying yourself." Judy said as she packed.

"I wish you all could stay longer." Andrea sighed.

"No, you don't Andrea, you're just being polite. You can't wait for us to leave so you can be alone with your husband." Judy replied smiling.

Andrea blushed.

"I'm sorry, Mama." She apologized.

"Don't apologize, Andrea. It's perfectly natural." Judy told her.

Andrea walked to her mother and hugged her.

"Thank you, Mama."

Quinton and Andrea reluctantly helped their families get ready for their trip home.

In the late afternoon Andrea took a hot bubble bath in anticipation of the evening ahead.

When she went downstairs in search of Quinton she found him in the study.

"Good evening, Mrs. Masterson." He drawled.

There was a fire roaring in the fireplace, a table set for two and lit candles on the table.

Tears welled up in Andrea's eyes.

"Oh, Quinton." She said happily.

He walked to her, took her by the hand, leading her to a chair at the table.

Pulling out a chair for her, he assisted Andrea into it.

Sitting in the chair Andrea looked lovingly into his eyes.

Quinton smiled, leaning down to kiss her.

Afterward he took Andrea's plate, filled it with food then handed it to her.

He picked up his plate, filled it with food then sat down across from her so he could gaze at her while they ate.

Their conversation flowed naturally as they ate.

As they ate Andrea relaxed, becoming more comfortable in Quinton's presence.

After their meal Quinton pushed away from the table, stood up then went to the CD player to turn it on.

The first song that came on was "Unchained Melody' by the Righteous Brothers.

Quinton walked to Andrea, extended his hand to her, she placed hers in his.

Standing she walked with him to the middle of the room.

Swaying to the music their bodies hummed with anticipated pleasure of the night to come.

When the song ended "Hopelessly Devoted to You" by Olivia Newton-John began to play.

Next came "Forever and Ever Amen" by Randy Travis..

Andrea realized Quinton had made a CD of love songs for her.

She laid her head on his chest snuggling close to him.

The rest of the evening was spent dancing and seducing one another.

In the early morning hours Quinton led Andrea up the stairs to their bedroom continuing his seduction.

"Happy New Year, Mrs. Masterson." He said huskily.

'Happy New Year, Quinton." She replied.

Quinton slowly and seductively removed their clothing to draw out Andrea's need for his lovemaking.

"Quinton please, I need you." Andrea pleaded.

He couldn't hold back any longer. Quinton thrust inside her completing their union.

"Touch me Andrea, I want to feel your hands on me." Quinton said to her shamelessly.

Andrea put her hands on his back pulling him to her.

She kissed his chest. Pushing him to his back, she took one hardened nipple into her mouth suckling gently.

"Andrea." He gasped.

Andrea took the other hardened nipple into her mouth repeating the process as his hands flexed on her backside letting her know how she was arousing him.

Suddenly she found herself on her back, Quinton urging her legs apart with him thrusting inside.

"Quinton!" She cried happily.

He left no part of her untouched by his lovemaking.

Andrea wrapped her legs around him urging him deeper inside her.

Their lovemaking continued through the early morning hours until almost daybreak.

Andrea fell asleep with Quinton's arms wrapped around her.

CHAPTER FOURTEEN

The next few weeks Andrea took in the paperwork she needed for her university enrollment.

At last she started classes.

Quinton called Katie back to work to take some of the pressure off of Andrea.

During the day Andrea was a studious college student and in the evening she was a devoted wife and mother-to-be.

Valentine's Day was nearing. Andrea didn't take much notice.

Quinton noticed she was so caught up in everyday things she didn't realize Valentine's Day was approaching.

Valentine's Day morning he didn't say a word to her about the holiday and she didn't notice he wasn't ready for work as usual.

Quinton kissed her good-bye as she was walking out the door.

He watched her drive away to her classes then set about getting ready for his Valentine's Day surprise.

Several times during the day he checked with Katie to be sure supper was coming along as he'd planned.

In midafternoon Andrea arrived home tired and crabby. She wanted a bath then a nap before Quinton came home.

"Good afternoon, Little One." He said walking out of the study.

"Quinton? What are you doing here?" Andrea asked wearily.

"Last time I checked I lived here." He said grinning.

Andrea was instantly suspicious.

"What are you up to?" She questioned.

"You've been so busy you forgot Valentine's Day." Quinton said with mock sternness.

Andrea blushed.

"Oh goodness. I'm sorry I never forget holidays." She apologized.

"As I said you've been busy. Go up and take a bubble bath. I'll meet you in our room when you're done." Quinton told her.

Andrea gave him a quick kiss then went upstairs.

She dropped her bag on the floor at the foot of their bed then went to take her bubble bath.

She stayed in the water until the bubbles were gone and it turned cold.

Stepping out of the bathtub she twisted her hair up into a terrycloth towel, put on her robe then walked into her bedroom.

Quinton stood there in a dark suit, white shirt and matching tie and barefoot.

Andrea caught her breath.

He was so handsome her eyes welled up with tears.

"Quinton?" She questioned.

He walked to her clasped her hand and led her out of the room down the stairs.

Going to the study Quinton slowly opened the door.

It was decorated with pink, red and white roses. The same color balloons filled the room. The table by the roaring fireplace was set for two with sparkling water chilling.

"Oh, Quinton what have you done?" Andrea asked her voice quivering.

"Showing you how much I love you." He said silently.

"Happy Valentine's Day, Andrea." He said aloud.

Andrea threw her arms around his neck kissing him with all the love she had in her.

Quinton felt the change in her, he could tell she was ready to declare her love. Now just to be patient.

He kissed her back, pulling away when she was aroused enough to beg him to make love to her.

"Quinton no." She begged.

"Supper, Little One." He reminded her.

"I'd forgotten." She said blushing.

Quinton smiled.

"I know." He said.

Leading her to the table he seated her then sat across from her.

They dished up each other's plates then began eating.

Andrea didn't care what she was eating all she wanted was to be there with Quinton.

After supper Quinton walked Andrea to a spot in front of the fireplace, moved the table and chairs, poured them each a glass of sparkling water then went to sit next to Andrea.

He took the towel from Andrea's head, unwound her hair and gently finger combed it out, smoothing it away from her face.

Andrea caressed the smooth line of his jaw.

They longed to be in the other's arms and before long they were.

Andrea unbuttoned Quinton's suit jacket then his shirt, pulling it free of the waistband.

He untied her robe, opening it in the front exposing her growing abdomen.

Quinton placed his hands where his son or daughter lay developing in Andrea's womb.

Bending down he kissed where his hands lay. Unable to stop he continued to kiss until Andrea lay helpless waiting for him to satisfy the ache inside her.

She didn't have to wait long. Quinton was longing to satisfy her want of him.

When he came to the point of her womanhood his tongue darted inside.

Andrea couldn't object, her climax began and there was nothing she could do to stop it.

"Oh my God Quinton." She cried digging her fingers into the floor.

Sliding inside her he brought more pleasure to her.

Andrea fought the battle of consciousness until she knew she brought pleasure to Quinton.

"Andrea!" He called.

She lost the battle to hold onto consciousness.

Several minutes later Andrea awoke to find herself completely naked and covered with a blanket, Quinton lying next to her smiling.

"Hi." She said smiling.

'Hi." Quinton replied smiling wider.

"I passed out." Andrea stated.

'Yes.' Quinton confirmed.

"Normal?" Andrea asked.

"Yes." Quinton assured him.

"Do we have any chocolate?"

"As a matter of fact Mrs. Masterson we do."

Andrea smiled again.

Oblivious to his nudity, Quinton stood up to get the chocolate he'd bought Andrea for Valentine's Day.

He walked to her, handing her the package.

"Happy Valentine's Day again." He said.

"Thank you, I'm sorry I forgot Valentine's Day." She said.

"You're all the Valentine I need." Quinton said.

He kissed her.

Andrea kissed him back.

They ate some of the chocolate and made love for the rest of the evening.

Eventually Quinton and Andrea made it to their bedroom.

The next morning they had less of a tendency to take each other for granted.

During the rest of the winter into spring everything in the Masterson household went smoothly.

At the beginning of summer Andrea suddenly began seeing what she thought were signs that Quinton might be having an affair.

He spent a little too much time with Katie or he complimented her too often.

Andrea became irritated.

Quinton brushed aside her attempts at seducing him telling her he was tired or had a lot of work to do.

Andrea's classes at the university had ended. She'd done well after being out of school for so long.

Quinton had taken her out to dinner to celebrate but had gone to work in the study when they'd arrived home.

She had been forced to go to bed alone, pretending she was asleep when he came to bed.

For weeks Andrea watched her husband flirt with another woman. Finally she couldn't stand it anymore.

One day in late July while Quinton was at work she began moving his belongings from the master bedroom to one of the guest bedrooms.

"What are you doing, Little One?" Quinton asked when he came home from work.

"What does it look like I'm doing? I'm moving your clothes out of the master bedroom into a guest room." Andrea snapped.

"I can see that but why are you moving my clothes?" Quinton questioned.

Andrea looked at him.

"You really have to ask why?" She asked.

"Since I can't read your mind, yes." He said.

"You said I would remain your wife regardless of what happens; you didn't say anything about sharing your bed." Andrea threw at him.

Quinton began to get angry.

"What have I done to be thrown out of my own bed?"

"Don't pretend you don't know. I've seen the way you look at Katie, how you talk to Katie, flirt with her. You've having an affair with her."

"An affair? What gave you that hair-brained idea?"

"Hair-brained? You flirt with Katie, you won't make love to me. I've done everything except throw myself at you and beg you to make love to me."

A pain shot through Andrea's abdomen.

She put her hand up to the spot where the pain was, crying out.

"Are you in labor?" Quinton asked.

"I think so." Andrea said through the pain.

"How long have you been in labor?" He questioned.

"Since this morning." She told him.

"We're going to the hospital." Quinton told her.

"I'm not going anywhere with you, you cheating rattle snake." Andrea managed through another contraction.

"Katie!" Quinton called.

Katie came rushing into the room.

"Yes sir." She said.

"Mrs. Masterson is in labor, please get her packed bag from the hall closet." Quinton said.

"Right away, Mr. Masterson." Katie obeyed.

The next contraction almost brought Andrea to her knees.

Quinton was done talking, he walked over to Andrea put his arm around her waist and proceeded to walk toward the door.

Her labor was so intense Andrea couldn't argue.

When Quinton lead Andrea down the stairs Katie was there with the bag.

"You're going to make a wonderful mother, Mrs. Masterson." Katie said.

Andrea glared at her.

Katie stepped back a few feet.

"Don't take offense, Katie. Mrs. Masterson isn't feeling quite herself.' Quinton said.

"I feel fine." Andrea said through clenched teeth.

"We have to get you to the hospital. I am not delivering this baby." Quinton told her.

Andrea didn't have the strength to argue.

Quinton walked her out to the van, helped her in, shut the door then walked around to the driver's side.

Soon they were on their way to the hospital.

Upon arriving Quinton went in to get a wheelchair.

Shortly thereafter he came out with one with a nurse following.

When Quinton opened her door Andrea nearly jumped out of the van. She was ready to have this baby.

Taking over the wheelchair Nurse May soothed Andrea's fears and anxieties while another nurse took Quinton aside.

"How long has she been in labor?" Dolly asked.

"All day." Quinton replied.

"How far apart are the contractions?" Dolly questioned.

"As near as I can tell about five minutes." Quinton answered.

For the next half hour the nurses bustled around preparing Andrea for the birth of her first child.

Quinton was by her side to comfort and encourage her.

Dr. Cooper arrived.

Andrea announced she was ready to push.

Dr. Cooper scrubbed up.

"Alright Miss Andrea are we ready to have this baby?" He asked.

"Yes." Andrea said through a contraction.

"Push Andrea." Dr. Cooper said.

Quinton was at her side encouraging her, holding her hand, talking her through each push.

After twenty minutes of pushing Quinton could see the head of their child.

'You're doing wonderful, Andrea. I can see the head.' Quinton said proudly.

Andrea lay back to catch her breath.

Looking into Quinton's eyes she knew he wasn't having an affair with Katie or anyone else. He would never betray her that way, he would never betray her at all.

She smiled.

Energy renewed, Andrea pushed for another fifteen minutes before Dr. Cooper told her not to push.

After several minutes he told her she could resume pushing.

Ten minutes later Andrea gave birth to her first child.

"It's a boy." Quinton announced proudly.

He kissed Andrea.

She kissed him back.

"Quinton Trey Masterson II." Andrea announced.

Quinton looked at her tears of joy in his eyes.

"Do you know how happy you've made me?" He asked.

Andrea smiled.

"I have a pretty good idea." She told him.

'Can we talk?" He asked hesitantly.

"About Katie?" Andrea asked.

Quinton nodded.

"I know you're not having an affair with her or anyone else. You'd never betray me." Andrea said.

"You're sure you know that, you're not going to come back later and accuse me again?" Quinton questioned.

"I'm sure." Andrea assured him.

"I'm sorry you felt unwanted by me and threatened by Katie. I've been preoccupied with work; there really is no excuse for my inattentiveness." Quinton apologized.

"It's alright, Quinton. I'll never again question your loyalty to me." Andrea said.

"Excuse me Mrs. Masterson, your son would like to meet his parents." Dolly said.

Andrea held her arms out to take her son from Dolly.

Both Quinton and Andrea looked their son over.

'He's perfect, just like his mother." Quinton declared.

'His mother isn't perfect, Darling." Andrea reminded him.

"You're as close to perfect as I'm going to get." Quinton said then kissed her.

After the kiss Quinton and Andrea called their respective families to tell them that Little Quinton had arrived.

It was late when Quinton could finally drag himself away from his family.

Little Quinton or Trey as they chose to call him was asleep in the nursery. Andrea was tired from delivering him.

Quinton thought she was on the verge of telling him she loved him several times but seemed reluctant to do so.

He left happily exhausted but with a heavy heart.

He'd only made it outside the emergency entrance of the hospital when his cell phone rang.

"Hello Little One, miss me already." He said.

"There's something I've been meaning to tell you.' Andrea said.

"Oh." Quinton replied.

Andrea took a deep breath and holding the phone steady she sang 'I Just Called To Say I Love You' by Stevie Wonder.

Quinton stood rooted in the spot he was standing until Andrea finished singing.

When she finished he quickly went to the elevator then pushed the button.

The elevator was taking too long. Quinton went to find the nearest stairs.

When he found them he sprinted up them two at a time.

Arriving at Andrea's door he took a moment to catch his breath.

Pushing the door open he smiled.

Andrea was looking expectantly at the door waiting for him.

Quinton walked over to sit on Andrea's bed, taking her hand in his he said, "That was the most beautiful thing I've ever heard in my life. Say it again."

"I love you." She said tears in her voice.

"I've waited five long years to hear those words from you. Do you know how much I love you?" Quinton asked.

Andrea could only shake her head.

"Since the moment we met I knew we were meant for each other. I couldn't go a day without thinking about you." Quinton admitted.

"Really?" Andrea asked.

Quinton nodded his head.

Andrea lowered her eyes.

"I have a confession to make." She said.

Quinton raised her chin forcing her to look at him.

"What confession?" He questioned.

"I couldn't stop thinking about you either." She admitted.

Quinton smiled.

"All that matters is we're together now. Nothing and no one can tear us apart." He said.

EPILOGUE

Twenty-seven months later

Andrea excused herself from the breakfast table. The last few mornings she hadn't felt like eating breakfast.

After having received her Bachelor's Degree from the local university she had gone to work with Quinton at K.M. Enterprises, Atlanta Division.

Going back to the dining room Andrea sat down.

"Are you alright, Little One?" Quinton asked.

"I'm not sure. The last few mornings I haven't felt like eating and I'm not feeling well." Andrea told him.

"Stay home today and call Dr. Cooper." Quinton suggested.

"Alright." Andrea said.

"Mrs. Masterson I'm afraid Trey doesn't want me this morning he keeps crying for you." Katie said.

"Thank you, Katie. I'll be home with him today. I have to make an appointment to see Dr. Cooper. Andrea told her.

"I hope you're feeling well." Katie replied.

"It's probably just a bug." Andrea said.

She went to check on her son.

When she arrived at the stairs she called, "Quinton."

Quinton quickly stood up from his chair and went to her.

"Andrea?" He questioned.

"Go to Trey." She said.

Quickly Andrea ran to the bathroom down the hall.

She made it just in time for her queasiness to tell her she had morning sickness.

Quinton knocked on the door.

"Little One, are you all right." He asked holding Trey in his arms.

Several minutes went by before Andrea answered.

She opened the door.

"I'm fine, take Trey into breakfast. I'll be in shortly." Andrea told him.

Quinton kissed her cheek then took Trey to get his breakfast.

Andrea went back upstairs to brush her teeth and rinse her mouth.

Twenty minutes later she was back downstairs.

"Feeling better." Quinton asked.

"For the moment yes." Andrea answered.

She went into the kitchen to pour more coffee into her cup.

Taking the coffee carafe into the dining room she poured more for Quinton.

Taking the carafe back to the coffeemaker she said, "Katie please add ginger ale and saltine crackers to the shopping list until further notice."

"Yes, Mrs. Masterson." Katie said.

Andrea went back into the dining room.

"I have to go to work. Let me know what Dr. Cooper says." Quinton said.

"I will. I'll probably stop into the office after my appointment." Andrea said.

"Alright, I love you." He replied.

Andrea smiled. She'd never tire of hearing Quinton say those three words.

'I love you too." She said.

Quinton kissed her sensuously then walked out smiling and whistling.

Soon after he left Andrea asked Katie to look after Trey so she could go into see Dr. Cooper.

When Andrea walked into Dr. Cooper's office she was greeted by Bree.

"Good morning Andrea, how are you?" Bree said.

"I'd like to take a pregnancy test." Andrea replied.

"I'll set that up right away." Bree said.

"Thank you." Andrea said then went to sit down.

Twenty minutes later the nurse came out to get her.

"Andrea." Nikki said.

Andrea stood up to follow her.

"How are you?" Nikki asked.

"Fine, just here to have a pregnancy test." Andrea said.

"Oh, how fun congratulations." Nikki said.

"I don't know if I'm pregnant yet, I only suspect." Andrea told her.

"Our bodies know before we do." Nikki told her.

Andrea nodded in acknowledgment.

Nikki took her weight, then put her in a room to take her vital signs.

"You won't need to see the doctor we can do a urine and blood test then you can be on your way." Nikki told her,

"Thanks." Andrea said.

After Andrea was done with her tests she paid her co-pay, gave Bree her cell phone number then left.

Walking out of the office she was nervous. She and Quinton hadn't planned on another child so soon but they would welcome any child they were blessed with.

Driving around Andrea was drawn to a baby clothing store. She parked her van and went inside.

Waiting for the call from Dr. Cooper's office was going to be torture.

Andrea looked around at the baby clothes, she was fascinated by all the new clothes there was for babies.

If she wanted her new son or daughter could set a new fashion trend.

She left the store after purchasing a frilly little dress that said 'I'm the princess' on it.

Unable to contain her excitement Andrea decided to go grocery shopping to pass the time.

She usually carried a list of household essentials with her and added whatever they needed or ran out of to get.

No sooner did she take the last bag into the house did her cell phone ring.

She looked at the caller ID, Dr. Cooper's office.

"Hello." Andrea said.

"Andrea, this is Nikki from Dr. Cooper's office." She said.

"Yes." Andrea replied.

"Congratulations, you are pregnant." Nikki told her.

"Thank you. I'll call back later to make an appointment." Andrea told her.

"Alright, again congratulations." Nikki said.

"Thank you." Andrea said.

Andrea went out to her van and drove to K.M. Enterprises, Atlanta Division.

Andrea walked into Quinton's office.

"Do you have a minute, Darling?" She asked.

"I have as long as you need." Quinton told her smiling.

Andrea closed the door.

"First I want to tell you Happy Anniversary." Andrea said smiling.

Quinton smiled.

"Happy Anniversary, Little One." He replied.

Andrea drew in a calming breath.

"I've just received a call from Dr. Cooper's office." She said.

"Yes?" Quinton questioned.

"Oh… um…" Andrea teased,

"Andrea." Quinton warned.

"I'm pregnant!" Andrea announced smiling.

Quinton gave out a delighted whooped and came out from behind his desk to hug her.

Twirling her around he couldn't contain his joy.

"I'm going to be a daddy again." He said happily.

"Darling please put me down." Andrea said.

Quinton looked at her face. She was pale. He put her down.

There was a knock on the door.

Quinton took Andrea with him to answer it.

He opened the door smiling.

"Andrea's pregnant." Quinton announced to everyone standing in the office.

There was a chorus of congratulations.

Quinton closed the door on Kyle and Abby's smiling faces, locked it then took his wife in his arms.

They made gentle, passionate love to one another for the rest of the morning and into the afternoon.